Tuesday's Child

by

Toni V. Sweeney

Small Town Georgia Tales, Book 2

Tuesday's Child

Cover Art by *Lisa Dawn MacDonald*

The Wild Rose Press, Inc.
PO Box 708
Adams Basin, NY 14410-0708
Visit us at www.thewildrosepress.com

Publishing History
First Edition, 2025
Trade Paperback ISBN 978-1-5092-5808-6
Digital ISBN 978-1-5092-5809-3

Small Town Georgia Tales, Book 2
Published in the United States of America

Dedication

For all the friends I left behind.
I wish I were with you now.

Monday's child is fair of face,
Tuesday's child is full of grace,
Wednesday's child is full of woe,
Thursday's child has far to go,
Friday's child is loving and giving,
Saturday's child works hard for a living,
But the child who is born on the Sabbath Day
Is bonny and blithe and good and gay.

~old fortune-telling nursery rhyme, 1838
Roud Folksong Index, #19526

Chapter 1

Never say Never, because if you do, sooner or later, those words will come back to bite you in the ass.

That was what I was thinking as I left the exit ramp from I-75.

The night my mother and I turned our backs on McAllister, Georgia, I swore I'd never come back.

Actually, my mother was the one doing the swearing. She was holding my hand at the time, but I remember her words, "I don't care if I ever see this damn town again," and if that was her attitude, it was good enough for me.

After all, I was just a child, but if she hated the place, then so did I.

Even now, I ask myself how much her attitude influenced me. If her perspective had been different, would mine have, also? We're so very influenced by our parents' ways of thinking when we're young.

For whatever reason, that was my preferred point of view until I received a certified letter two weeks before this trip, informing me my father had died and I was invited, though the wording made it clear it was more than an invitation, to be present at the reading of his will

At first, I stated quite plainly to my boss I had no intention of being there. Then, curiosity got the better of me. What would a man leave to a daughter he hadn't seen or heard from, or tried in any way to get in touch with.

1

for twenty years?

I was certain it'd be some laughable amount, like a dollar, or an equally insulting item, like "my second-best bed," or some other ridiculous and worthless piece of junk I'd have trouble disposing of before flying home again. Nevertheless, I was curious, so with my boss's encouragement and blessing, I went, though like the proverbial cat I was probably going to regret my curiosity when the smoke cleared.

There was another reason I went, something that had nagged at me for years.

My father had married again and I had a half-brother and sister I'd never seen, didn't even know their names, in fact. That same curiosity made me want to see just how alike we were.

I'd made reservations at McAllister Manor. There was a famous-name motor lodge on the outskirts just past the exit ramp, but I had a memory of the Manor from when I lived in McAllister. Not a clear memory, of course, just an impression of an elaborate, red-brick building with those revolving doors a five-year-old thought so amazing, and an overhang similar to a theater marquee, decorated with beautifully carved swags and festoons.

I'd never been inside but the exterior had always fascinated me, so whenever we were downtown, Mama and I would always walk by the old hotel so I could look at that ornate façade.

I wondered if the image in my mind's-eye was still accurate and hoped the place hadn't turned seedy and become rundown in the interim. If so, I'd settle up, posthaste, and hightail it back to the famous name. *Pronto.*

By now, I had arrived at the city limits. Before me loomed an old train station.

I'd forgotten about that.

The sign above the roof overhang read *McAllister, Georgia, Pop. 2,064*. Obviously not taken from the latest census.

Mother once told me McAllister was a small town with big city pretensions, and had the accessories to prove it...like a hospital serving a five-city area and a series of elite condos. The station, however, was one of the landmarks reminding everyone it wasn't a bustling metropolis...yet.

Perfectly preserved, it could only be described as *quaint,* like something out of a 1930s movie. It was a building about fifteen feet long with white-painted planking, the roof covered with red sandpaper shingles. I remember it housed a small waiting room, ticketmaster's cubbyhole, and a storage space for luggage. Four wooden steps at either end descended to the unpaved parking lot. To one side of the luggage room, a wheeled carrier hugged the wall, waiting to be loaded, because...*surprise!*...the station was still in operation.

All that was missing was the wooden tower with a tin pipe to be lowered to the engine, filling its reservoirs with water to be converted into steam. Maybe a post to hang the mailbag on, so it could be snatched and carried off as the train sped through.

A regular *Icon of Yesteryear. A Relic from the Past.*

I hated it. Every nostalgic, Old Southern splinter of it. Not for any of the current political reasons, but because it represented a life snatched away from me, and I still didn't understand why that had happened.

3

I had no trouble finding McAllister Manor. The GPS I insisted the rental car be fitted with when I picked it up from the company booth at the airport took me directly to the entrance.

There was a parking spot in front...*parallel parking*, one of the banes of my existence.

Who parallel parks anymore?

I managed to get the car into it with surprising ease. The fact the car was a compact probably helped. As I set the brake and switched off the ignition, I noted there was no meter next to the spot. In Orange County, California—my home—a good many parking places weren't metered but in a small town such as McAllister, it was a surprise.

After all, small community City Fathers needed all the monies they could get.

Right?

Then I simply sat there, staring at the Manor.

It hadn't changed a bit. If anything, it looked better than it had in my imagination.

The bricks were clean as if sandblasted. Weathered, of course, but the place had been built in the 1920s, so that was to be expected. The marquee's trim appeared freshly painted, a kind of off-white/creamy color contrasting nicely with the rich mahogany of the rest of the roof-like projection. I wondered if it was real wood or had been replaced somewhere along the line with a material more weather-resistant and longer lasting. No matter, the effect was the same.

So far, so good.

Sighing as if the appearance of the Manor were a sign whatever happened was going to go well, I opened the door and slid out, depressing the fob as the door swung shut. There was a sharp blast of the horn, more of a *toot!* actually, high-pitched in accordance with the car's size, as it automatically locked. Walking around to the trunk, I tapped another little pad on the keychain fob. In graceful slow motion, the trunk opened and I reached inside, pulling out my overnight case and the larger piece of soft luggage with its built-in rollers.

"Well, well…as I live and breathe…if it isn't li'l Gracie McAllister."

I stiffened. No one had called me *Gracie* in years. Not since I left McAllister. Who was doing it now, and how did he know who I was?

Setting down the bag, I straightened to see who had spoken.

A man…a very tall man, throwing a long shadow across my five-foot-two form. I immediately decided he was no one I remembered, but he was certainly acting as if he knew me, if the smile on his face was any indication.

"I'm *Grace* McAllister," I stressed the correct form of my name, coldly. "And you are…?"

He didn't answer, just continued standing there, the smile morphing into a tooth-brilliant grin. Nice teeth, too, white and very straight, probably some orthodontist had made a mint off this guy's parents.

Since he wasn't speaking, I did the same, giving him a quick up-and-down, starting with the tips of his slightly scuffed cowboy boots, trailing up the low-slung boot-leg jeans and black T-shirt, and aiming for the top of his curly hair…

…very curly, very red hair…

…hair a deep, dark, rusty red…

Oh my God! A slash of fear, overwhelmed by anger,

swept through me.

Dropping the overnighter, I took a step backward, raising my hands in an exaggerated karate defense gesture while realizing it was ridiculous in the extreme.

A mouse confronting an elephant.

"You can't bully me this time, Mayfield Donovan. I know self-defense!"

For a moment more he didn't say anything, though he didn't look shocked, insulted or afraid. If anything, he simply appeared amused.

"Don't worry, Gracie. I assure you I've outgrown my bullying tendencies." His voice was deep with a soft drawl, the way I'd always imagined a Southern romance hero should speak, television and movies notwithstanding. "I was afraid you wouldn't remember me."

"Don't call me *Gracie*," I snapped, knowing damned well he wasn't going to obey. Since when had he ever done anything anyone told him to? "It's *Grace*, and I remember you very well...*Mayfield*."

"Feisty as ever."

He didn't react to my use of *his* name, though he'd certainly done so when we were younger. Calling him *Mayfield* had been the only time I could get a rise out of him. *That* had been my superpower, now apparently rendered useless.

His eyes were an odd shade of brown, with hints of copper, almost matching that autumn bonfire hair. I remember I'd once teased him about them with violent results...for *me*...and my mother said as she soothed my tears, "May has his mother's eyes."

The corners of those eyes crinkled as he gave me a onceover matching the one I'd given him, with a total absence of malice and a great deal of appreciation. "You turned out nicely, Grace."

My eyebrows went up at that.

"Did you just get here?" He glanced at the car. "A rental? Carter would've sent someone to drive you."

Carter is my father's brother, my uncle. It felt odd even thinking that.

"Did you fly into Atlanta International, Falcon Field, or Malcolm McKinnon?" He named three airports all about the same distance from McAllister.

"Atlanta International," I answered, a little cautiously. "How did you…"

"Sugah, this is McAllister. Everyone in town's been looking forward to you getting here since the minute Benjamin Troup's lawyer sent you that letter."

I guess at this point I should explain…Benjamin Troup McAllister was my father's name. No one ever called him *Ben, Benji,* or *Bennie.* It was always *Benjamin Troup.*

Can you imagine hanging a moniker like that on a little kid?

Can you imagine always saying it when you spoke to him?

No wonder my mother left him. She probably got tired of dragging out that mouthful. I imagine it'd be difficult to have an argument with someone with that much name.

Now, you listen to me, Benjamin Troup McAllister…

Yep. That would get old fast.

Not seeming to notice my scowl or that I was suddenly thrust into a momentary memory, May was still talking.

"This all of your luggage?" He'd seen the bright

pink bag at my feet and the smaller case I'd so unceremoniously dropped. "I'm assuming you're going into the Manor? Here. I'll carry those for you."

He bent to pick up both bags.

"I can handle my own luggage, thank you." I didn't want Mayfield Donovan doing anything for me. I was still remembering the many times I'd been bullied and chased by a red-haired boy who towered over me.

Just like he was doing now as he straightened, a handle in each hand. *Damn, he's tall.* It made me feel small and helpless again, and the fact that I didn't exactly dislike the feeling this time around was disturbing.

Where's that coming from?

"I'm certain you can, but I'm being a *gentleman* and helping a *lady*." He stressed both words as if to point out he hadn't pulled my hair or knocked me down in the five minutes we'd been talking. Not yet, anyway. "And this is what gentlemen do."

Stepping back, he gestured with the overnighter toward the entrance. I stepped onto the curb and walked ahead of him to the revolving doors.

Without looking back.

There was a regular entrance to the side to take a luggage trolley through, and for those perhaps having a phobia about doors that spun like a carousel, but I ignored it. I walked into the open space and the door, fitted with a motion-detector, began to move. May entered the next opening and, in a few moments, we found ourselves inside.

I hopped out quickly to avoid being slapped in the rear as the doors kept moving. May came out as if he did this sort of thing every day. I'd hoped he might get stuck inside and solve the problem of how I was going to ditch him without being too rude. Considering his currently mild demeanor, I wasn't in a hurry to awaken any sleeping hostile tendencies.

Like the station house, the Manor's interior was a movie set dream. There were paintings in gilded frames with tiny spotlights focused on them and a glittering chandelier garlanded with crystal ropes and dangling drops, electric of course, but probably costing a goodly amount since even its bulbs were flame-shaped to further the illusion of being candle-lit. Potted plants were grouped attractively, with furniture from the same time period as the Manor itself. Guests chatting or reading newspapers sat on crimson velvet couches, or overstuffed armchairs, none threadbare or worn.

It was so much more than I had imagined. I was speechless, as if when I stepped out of the revolving door, I'd gone through a time warp.

May walked past me, heading for the desk where a young woman welcomed him with a smile. She wasn't wearing a Twenties-style dress, though if she had been, I wouldn't have been surprised. Standing by the desk's ornately carved barrier were two young men wearing bellhop uniforms, one blond and one mocha-skinned, and both smiling broadly.

Bellhop's uniforms? Black trousers with a stripe matching their short gold-trimmed jackets, and those silly little pillbox hats... *Woah.*

I goggled. I admit it.

"Hey, Mr. Donovan." The smile the young woman gave him said they weren't just passing acquaintances.

I quirked a brow.

"Hey, Tammy." May nodded at the two young men, then rewarded Tammy with the infamous May Donovan smile, another thing I remembered. Even as a child, he'd wound women around his finger with that expression, and convinced even my mother he could never be as mean as I swore he was.

He nodded to me as I pulled myself out of my enchantment of the Manor's interior and joined him at the desk whose ambience was spoiled by the flat-screen computer sitting on it.

"This is Grace McAllister. I think she has a reservation."

"She certainly does." Tammy gave me a bright smile tempered with evident curiosity.

My God, what has she heard and what is she thinking?

Keys rattled. I fumbled in my purse.

"Room 427." She handed over a keycard. I exchanged it for my credit card. She pushed it back to me. "Oh, no, ma'am."

I reacted to that with a grimace. No one had ever called me "ma'am" before. Surely there wasn't that much age difference between us.

"Mr. Simmons has already taken care of that."

I wasn't sure I wanted my father's lawyer "taking care" of anything for me. Not until I found out exactly what I'd inherited. I didn't want to be beholden to anyone or anything having to do with the McAllisters.

Nevertheless, I mumbled, "Oh. I see."

Really intelligent reply.

I put away my card and looked at May, who appeared to be waiting expectantly. Neither of the bellhops moved, probably because he hadn't set down the bags. Everyone seemed to be waiting for me to say something.

"Well." *Nice opening.* "Thank you, Mayfield."

I extended my hand, feeling another little twinge of triumph as this time he visibly winced as I used his proper name.

"I can take it from here."

"You can." His reply was still soft. "But you won't. I'll carry these up for you." He looked back at the girl. "Tammy, add a tip for Kyle and Chad to the bill, since I'm doing them out of it."

He winked. All three laughed.

Foiled, I stalked to the elevator.

"I'll be a little late tonight," I heard Tammy say. "Car's in the shop."

"No problem, sweetheart," came May's reply. "If you want, I can pick you up after work."

"Would you? That'd be great. It's a long walk to your house."

"Your shift ends at five, doesn't it?"

"That's right."

"I'll be here at five-fifteen, okay?" She must've nodded because I heard his footsteps behind me.

"Doing a little cradle robbing?" I didn't look at him as I pressed the *Up* button. "That girl's got to be…" I did some quick mental calculation. May was five years older than I and Tammy looked to be in her early twenties. "…ten years your junior."

"My *junior?*" He snorted.

The elevator doors opened. We got in and May set down one bag to press the button for the fourth floor. He waited until the doors shut and we were on our way upward before he spoke again.

"Tammy's *eleven* years my junior." He stressed that one word sarcastically. "She's nineteen, to be exact."

"That's even worse."

"And if you'll get your mind out of the gutter for a minute…" Briefly, those copper eyes held some of the emotion I'd seen in that cruel ten-year-old. "I'll explain that she's working to get her GED. She quit school, one of those teenage-pregnancy-had-to-get-married things, and I'm tutoring her."

"I'll bet." I smirked.

"When did you get so cynical?"

Did he have to ask?

I had an answer, but it appeared he was more interested in defending his reputation.

"She has problems with math. One might call her mathematically challenged," he went on.

I glanced at him. He was serious. *Will wonders never cease?* The Mayfield I'd known was a selfish little bastard. What had turned him into such a do-gooder?

The elevator stopped, the doors slid open, and that kept me from making any more comments. May waited for me to precede him out, then followed.

Such manners.

What miracle had happened to the boy who'd caught me by the ankles and pulled me bodily from the steps of the playground slide, throwing me to the ground so he could go first, and de-hiding my knees in the process?

"Let's see. 427…" He looked up and down the hall, making a decision. "This way, I think."

He found the door and stood patiently while I inserted the card and coordinated waiting for the green light, removing the card, and opening the door. A wave of refrigerated air rushed out.

"Don't expect me to invite you in, May, 'cause it ain't gonna happen." I moved to block the doorway.

"That's as it should be, Gracie." Not by so much as a flicker of an eyelash did he acknowledge I'd again insulted him. "You shouldn't invite strangers into your room, and, as much as I hate to admit it, I *am* a stranger. Right now, anyway."

He took a step closer. I stiffened but kept my hands by my sides, though they curled into fists.

"I'll just set these here and be on my way." He placed both bags just outside the door.

Huh? No threats, no trying to push past me?

He turned away, then stopped and looked back as if remembering something.

"Why don't you have dinner with me tonight? Then we can catch up and stop being strangers." That last sentence was punctuated by another smile.

"I'm going to be busy."

"I'm certain of that." He looked understanding.

What's going on?

May Donovan never understood anything where I was concerned, except if you punch someone hard enough it leaves a very big bruise.

"But you won't be spending every moment at Jefferson Simmons' office, and you have to eat. Let your first meal in McAllister be a *Welcome Home* dinner. On me."

"Okay."

Did I actually say that? I was agreeing to go out with the man who'd been the *bête noir* of my childhood existence? *What's wrong with me?*

"Great. Eight o'clock. I'll pick you up." He snapped out the arrangements as if they were memorized.

"Downstairs. In the lobby," I stipulated, then amended, shaking a forefinger as if to make a point. "But

13

no funny business."

"I wouldn't have it any other way."

Those copper eyes said otherwise, or was I reading something where there was nothing?

"'Bye now."

With that he was gone, back to the elevator, leaving me standing beside my luggage.

I didn't wait to see if he got into the elevator or was going to lurk around outside my door. I dragged the cases inside and pushed the door shut.

In keeping with the tone of the place, the room was spacious and elegant and furnished in an *Early Turn-of-the-Century to post-WWI-pre-Roaring Twenties* style, in that little pocket of time transitioning the two. The Manor must do a thriving business if all the rooms were like this one.

It had modern conveniences, telephone, cable and Internet, and air-conditioning. The phone was one of those elegant so-called French ones with a china base, looking as if it weighed a ton. The bed was brass with a puffy feather mattress, and the wall lights resembled gas lamps, while the bathroom...

I took a peek inside and was rewarded with the sight of a tub with attached shower pole and gilded claw-feet.

The tourists must be beating a path to this place.

Forcing May out of my mind, I got to work unpacking, opening the two cases and transferring clothing from bags to dresser drawers, determined to keep my thoughts on business and failing miserably.

Why do I keep thinking about him? He should be the last person I'd think about and he *had* been, until the moment I heard his voice. With a sigh, I gave up trying to push out of my mind the memory of the moment I'd raised my head to look at him.

Even now, I don't remember the first time I noticed Mayfield Donovan. He had always seemed to be there, and he was always bedeviling me, teasing to the point of cruelty.

Gracie Girl...Gracie-Wacie...then a sneaker-clad foot would shoot out and send me sprawling into the playground sandbox...*Tuesday's child is full of Grace...they sure didn't mean you, did they, Gracie?* I'd cried gallons of tears because of May Donovan and always wanted a chance for revenge.

And now, I'm going to dinner with him?

He's so much like his father. I remember hearing my mother confide to a friend during a phone call, after relating the latest injustice he'd perpetrated on me, something she brushed aside with, *"I'm certain he didn't really mean to knock you down, Grace."* Yeah, right.

I didn't argue, of course. You couldn't argue with people under the Mayfield spell. They just didn't see it.

So much like his father. I didn't remember William Donovan, but I remembered his reputation.

****

He'd been the town Bad Boy, smart and handsome. *Beautiful Bill*, they called him...quitting school as soon as legally possible...running around with a *fast* crowd but continuing to hang around the high school grounds as if lonesome for people his own age. He didn't appear to have a job but always had money, and there were whispers about drug deals and running numbers and other things I didn't understand. At nineteen, he surprised everyone by marrying and becoming a father at twenty. The day after his son's birth, he found himself a widower when his wife died of a ruptured uterine artery.

Too bad May was born a year after his parents married. Otherwise, he would've been a *real* bastard and I could've hurled that epithet at him with impunity.

My bad luck.

Using those unlimited funds, Bill hired a sitter for his son and went back to his aimless ways, still lurking wherever the kids who would've been his classmates gathered. He began to date again, and I still question the intelligence of parents who let their daughters go out with him. I guess, like his son, he had the ability to con both mothers and fathers, for not many objected.

Sometime along the way, he actually dated my mother for a while. She'd opted to go to secretarial school rather than college, wanting to get a *useful* education, though I always thought that sounded more like a parent speaking than an eighteen-year-old.

However, for six months, she and Bill Donovan were *an item.* Then they broke up, and he found and married someone else, Mama's best friend Angeline Ware, who became the mother of May's half-brother Billy.

Angeline didn't die in childbirth, and as far as I knew, she and Bill were still together.

****

Well. I paused in placing a blouse on a hanger. *I know more about May's father than I do about my own, and certainly more than I ever did about his son...*the man I'd agreed to have dinner with later tonight.

Suitcases emptied, I decided I'd better get on with the reason for my return to McAllister. There was a telephone directory next to the Bible in the drawer of the bedside table. Hadn't I read somewhere that Bibles were no longer placed in hotel rooms to keep from offending other religions? Guess the Manor's owners hadn't read that article.

I retrieved the directory, found Jefferson Simmons' address, grabbed my purse and went out.

At the front desk, I asked if I was supposed to turn in my key-card when leaving the premises.

"Goodness, no." Tammy was just as Southern-friendly as ever. "Just make sure you don't lose it."

I was tempted to ask her if May was really teaching her math, or if her studies with him involved something a little more athletic, like dancing the horizontal tango, but one look at that friendly, freckled face, and I managed to keep my acid to myself for a change. Since May defended himself and then shut up, not continuing to *protest too much* it made me think he was telling the truth, and I certainly wasn't going to insult this…child…just to get back at him.

Nodding, I said instead, "Can you tell me where 752 Magnolia Boulevard is?"

On top of everything else, McAllister has these cutesy names for their streets. They're all called after flowering trees. The main street is Cherry Street, which was where the Manor was located, then there's Tulip Tree Lane, Magnolia Boulevard, Wisteria Avenue…

You get the idea.

"Sure can." Tammy leaned against the counter, pointing to the doors. "Go out, turn right, walk a block and cross the street at the corner. It's two blocks down on the same side of the street. You can't miss it."

Nodding my thanks, I went out, repeating her words as I did so. At least I wouldn't need a GPS to find the lawyer's office.

Chapter 2

Escaping the revolving doors, I turned right as instructed and struck out down the street at a brisk walk. After a few moments, I wondered why I was hurrying. There were plenty of other people about and no one appeared in any particular rush to get anywhere.

Go with the flow, Gracie.

The flow in McAllister was definitely not at California Speed. I forced my steps to slow to an amble, glancing around and actually taking in some of the storefronts as I walked.

I found the building easily enough and stood looking up at it as if feeling justified in the mental image I'd had. Brick, *old* brick, spot-burned here and there so there were darker colorations within the deep red.

Jefferson Simmons' offices were located in the Seagram Building, its name engraved into the shield on the roof decoration. There were gargoyles, *actual stone gargoyles*, hovering on either side of the shield, peering down at me with those iris-less eyes most statuary possess. They were beaked, winged, and taloned, forelegs resting on the shield between them and the inscription *Seagram, 1876* chiseled into it. So Mr. Seagram, whoever he was, had flourished over a hundred and forty-something years before and had either owned the building or done something causing the people of McAllister to name it after him.

Enough dallying.

Nevertheless, I continued standing there, staring up at the two beasts as if they were the most fascinating creations in the world. Well, I certainly hadn't seen any other building guarded by gargoyles recently. Okay, so maybe I was delaying going inside. I wasn't really looking forward to meeting Jefferson Simmons because I had a feeling I already knew the answer he was going to give to the question I was going to ask.

Looking away from the gargoyles' leers, I took a step toward the double glass doors, reaching for a handle. They both swung inward at the moment I noticed the sign stating, *WARNING. Automatic doors,* and saw the treaded and metal-bordered mats on either side of the entrance.

I walked inside.

I was glad to see the building had been greatly modified and modernized since 1876. The marble floors might be original but the cherry paneling, potted plants, and chrome furniture were a shock after the Manor's time warp. There was an elevator, a directory, and a large counter with a suited gentleman behind it. He caught my eye, smiled, and waited to see if I was going to ask for help.

I smiled back and consulted the directory, found the floor I needed and pressed the *Up* button. There was a *ding*, the doors slid open and I stepped inside for a silent ride to the sixth floor. No music, thank goodness. Since the parts of town I'd seen so far appeared to still be about twenty years in the last century, it wouldn't have surprised me if that trend of forcing elevator-trapped patrons to listen to canned music still existed here. The elevator reached my destination. I got out, followed the arrows, and found myself before another glass door.

Simmons & Harris, Attorneys at Law
Family Law
Jefferson D. Simmons
Alexander H.S. Harris

Jefferson D. Simmons... I thought about that. His middle name had to be *Davis.* And his partner? *Alexander Hamilton Stephens Harris,* I'd bet.

I managed not to laugh out loud.

Where but in the Deep South would one find two men in business together, who were named after the president and vice president of the Confederacy? In today's censorious world? I did laugh then, the sound echoing down the quiet corridor.

I opened the door and went in. *Bring it on!*

The reception area was spacious, tastefully decorated with paintings and chairs in little groupings. The expected magazines, but no television attached to the wall by an extension brace as I'd seen in most California offices. There were doors on both sides, with plaques, one reading *J.D. Simmons,* the other *Alexander H.S. Harris.*

The receptionist was an older woman. More time warp. She was wearing a severe business suit looking like it had escaped from a 1942 movie, though the jacket was open to reveal a very ruffle-fronted blouse. She looked very stern.

With her gray suit and gray hair, she was a caricature of an old-maid schoolteacher. All she needed were a couple of pencils stuck through the messy bun on top of her head.

"Good afternoon, dear. May I help you?" She smiled, transforming into everyone's grandmother.

"I'd like to see Mr. Simmons…" I began.

She glanced at the desk calendar.

Knowing what she was about to ask, I hurried on, "I don't have an appointment, so I'd like to make one."

"I think we can arrange that." She smiled again, dimples appearing in the gently-wrinkled cheeks. "May I have your name?"

"Grace McAllister, I—"

"Oh, Grace… You're finally here." That exclamation stopped whatever I was going to say.

Huh? She knows me?

She went on, in a voice so Southern it made me smile involuntarily. I couldn't help it. Except for the residuals of my own, most of the Southern accents I'd heard in the past twenty years were on television or in the movies, and greatly exaggerated.

"Mr. Simmons was going to have me call the Manor if you didn't get in touch with him soon." She stood up, revealing the suit to be a pants suit, and hurried to the door on the right, knocking and then going in.

I waited, searching my mind for anyone resembling this lady, wondering if she was someone my mother had known. *Nothing. Total blank.* She looked to be older than Mama would've been by at least twenty years.

By now, she was back, holding the door open. "Please go in."

"Thank you." Nodding, I walked through, half expecting her to curtsey.

Inside, I found a Kentucky colonel, in a *haut couture* bespoke suit.

I have to stop this, was all I could think. With the exception of Mayfield, I'd characterized everyone I'd met as someone from a cartoon or a television show. Did that mean he was the one reality in my life now?

That was an unnerving thought.

"Grace." The Colonel...I mean, Mr. Simmons...came around the desk, holding out his hand. "So good to finally see you again." He didn't shake my hand, however, just clasped it between his own, patting it gently. "My God, how much you look like your mother."

That shook me a little. I didn't think I looked like her at all, especially since she'd been a blue-eyed blonde and I was red-headed and brown-eyed, though my hair was a great deal more gingery than Mayfield's. I thought I probably looked like my father, since Mama had once or twice strengthened this opinion by saying, "You're so much like your daddy."

It always bothered me when she said that because the gentle, tender tone of her voice belied the way she usually characterized him as *that son of a bitch Benjamin Troup.*

"Did you have a comfortable flight?" Mr. Simmons asked, releasing my hand and gesturing to a nearby couch. "Please, sit down, dear."

I did so, taking in his appearance and deciding he didn't look as much like the Colonel as my first impression thought.

Jefferson Simmons was tall and slender. I guess when younger, he might've been considered *wiry.* He was about the same age as his secretary, perhaps early sixties. His hair was snow-white and abundant, longer than I'd expect someone his age to wear it, curling over his collar, but definitely styled, and was the most beautiful stuff I'd ever seen. I wondered what color it had been when he was younger and had a feeling he'd been quite the ladies' man, and that hair was one of the features attracting women to him. He was still handsome, a cover model for *Senior Gentlemen's Quarterly*, wearing a very conservative navy pinstripe suit, a matching shirt, and a cream-colored tie, and was presently flashing me a smile exposing teeth looking to be his own.

Wow. For a moment, I found myself caught up in an aura I couldn't describe. *What's this guy doing in McAllister?*

I responded to his question. "I guess it was all right, as flights go. We got here in one piece."

"Not a fan of flying, huh?" His blue eyes twinkled as he leaned forward slightly, lowering his voice. "Can't say I blame you. That's why I do it as little as possible. So…" Instead of returning to his desk as I expected, he pulled up a chair and dropped into it. "What can I do for you?"

Tell me what I want to know so I can get out of here. I didn't say that out loud. Not just yet. Instead, I answered, "I just wanted to stop in, let you know I was here."

"I was hoping you would. I was getting a little anxious." He frowned slightly. "I really wish you'd have let Carter send a car for you. It would've saved your renting one."

"As I explained, Mr. Simmons…"

"Jeff, please."

"Jeff." I knew I'd never say that again. Mama had drummed it into my head to always…*always*…call older people by their titles and last names. "I don't want to be beholden to the McAllisters in any way."

I wondered if receiving an inheritance could be

construed as being in my estranged family's debt. Not unless there were strings attached, I decided.

"I can't say that's surprising. You and your mother didn't exactly leave here under the best of circumstances," he said. "I suppose it's natural for you to feel that way."

"I'm glad you understand." I wasn't going to go into my backstory. I'd promised myself I wouldn't bring up any more of the past than I had to and certainly wouldn't start throwing accusations around, since I still wasn't sure who to toss them at. I waited a couple of beats, then said, as if just thinking of it, "There *is* one thing I'd like to ask…"

"And what's that?" He looked as if there was nothing better in the world he'd like to do than answer.

"Is it possible for you to tell me right now what my father has left me?"

For just a moment, he looked startled, then sat there as if trying to formulate an answer. With a brief sigh, he said, "I'm afraid I can't do that."

"May I ask why not?"

"This is a bit complicated." He got up, walking away a few steps, then turning back. "You see, I didn't draw up Benjamin Troup's will."

"You didn't? Why did you write me then?" What's going on? Was this some kind of very bad practical joke? "Who did? Who do I need to see?"

"Let me explain."

"Please do." I'm afraid my voice got a little sharp.

"I don't blame you for being upset." He didn't appear insulted, however. "I admit I was, too, when I received the will."

He sat down again, this time behind the desk.

Making it a protective barrier between us?

"It was drawn up by a lawyer in Atlanta, and the day after the funeral, it arrived by special courier with a letter from Benjamin Troup, stating he didn't wish it opened until the day of the reading...and there *was* to be a reading." Jefferson smiled. "You see, Gracie, in spite of the way the movies portray it, wills generally aren't read to the family. There's no gathering in the library with the weeping widow and voracious relatives waiting to see what they're going to get as the lawyer intones the deceased's last wishes."

"No?" Another Hollywood fable washed down the drain. "Then what the hell am I doing here?" I mentally floundered a moment, wondering if I should apologize for my rudeness.

"You're here because your father wanted you to be." If he was shocked by my profanity, it didn't show. Maybe he'd thought the same thing before he sent that letter. "As I said, there was a letter from Benjamin Troup, stating I was to be executor of the estate, and he wanted the will *read*, instead of merely placed in probate and the heirs notified. There was also a list of people he wanted to be present. You are one of them."

He sighed again.

"I was not to open the will and read it before everyone was gathered. Under no circumstances."

"And you followed those instructions?"

"To the letter."

"Weren't you curious? To see what's in it? Maybe learn why he chose someone other than the family lawyer to write it?"

"Of course, I'm curious. And a little hurt, if you want the truth. It really put my nose out of joint for quite a few days."

I smiled at that Southernism. Couldn't help it.

"I've represented the McAllister family since my father died, three years after I graduated from law school. But I did what that letter said. I've learned from past experience Benjamin Troup McAllister isn't one to cross, and the fact that he's dead doesn't enter into it."

Now that definitely sent a chill down my spine. So the little hints Mama had thrown out here and there about dear old dad might just be true. That he was a dangerous son of a bitch.

"In that case…" I got to my feet.

He stood also.

"I guess I'll be on my way and I'll see you here tomorrow." I held out my hand. "Goodbye, Mr. Simmons. I'm sorry to have taken up your time today."

"You haven't, Grace." Again, he clasped my hand in both his. "I'm truly glad to see you, child. And to see what a lovely young lady you've grown into."

I beamed at his flattery. He released my hand and opened the door for me. As I went through, he asked, "Will you be going to the house this afternoon?"

"What house?" I looked back at him.

"Your old home."

"You mean, my father's house?"

"Well, I suppose technically it's not your home anymore, is it?"

Technically it never was, Jefferson. I shrugged. "There's really no need to, is there?"

"I thought perhaps…curiosity…to revisit the place where you spent your first five years." Did he look disappointed? "Ben and Sammi really want to meet you."

"Who are Ben and Sammi?" I gave him a blank look.

"Your half-brother and sister." He supplied the answer without asking the obvious. "They've been on pins and needles since they learned you were coming here." He smiled. "Sammi, especially, was looking forward to your visit. She told me if I spoke to you before tomorrow, to tell you she wants you to come to McAllister Place."

"I-I hadn't really thought about it."

I wouldn't exactly call my coming to McAllister a *visit* because I was going to leave as soon as I found out what was in the will. As for half-siblings, I admit I was curious as to how they looked. After all, it had been another of my reasons for coming, but actually *socializing* with them…?

I decided to be truthful with this man who was so congenial though privy to McAllister family secrets.

"Frankly, I didn't think they'd want to see me any more than they had to. Reminders of the past, their father's…uh…mistake of a first marriage, and all that."

"Now that's where you're wrong." He placed a gentle hand on my shoulder. "They want to meet you. Go to see them, Grace."

Nodding without actually giving a commitment, I left the office. He'd given me something to think about as I made my way back to the elevator and out of the building.

Was he correct in what he was saying? Would it be proper for me to barge into their lives, stirring up old memories? What about their mother? He hadn't mentioned how she felt about her children wanting to meet me. Would she appreciate the reminder of her husband's former marriage showing up like the Ghost of Christmas Past or something?

This was getting complicated.

I'd hoped I could get the information out of the lawyer and not even have to attend the reading. Now I learned it was a reading that was going to happen because my father specifically requested it and not because it *should* happen. That was odd in itself. Why ask for something if it wasn't the usual thing to do? What was in that will he wanted everyone gathered together to hear?

I had a feeling this wasn't going to bode well, especially for me.

In the meantime, I had the rest of the afternoon free and dinner with Mayfield Donovan to prepare for. I'd just remembered I didn't bring anything even remotely resembling something to wear when going on a date. Not that going out with May was going to be a date in the usual sense of the word, but I should at least look decent.

I slowed my pace. I was on a street lined with shops on both sides.

What's the hurry? Slow down and do some window-shopping. A faint memory popped into my mind. It was something Mama and I had done, on Sunday afternoons.

So I did it now, strolling leisurely back the way I'd come. I stopped before a little place called *Arlene's* as a cute little number in the window caught my eye. Burgundy red. Simple lines, a scooped neck, three tiers of ruffles starting at the high waistline. That ought to open May's eyes. Though why I'd want to do that I had no idea.

Maybe to make him sorry he'd bullied me so? To show him what he'd missed because I'd been snatched so quickly from his life? Whatever the reason, I walked in, found the dress on the rack, tried it on, and fifteen minutes later left with it in a box.

Mayfield Donovan, ready or not, here I come. Not exactly knowing what I was coming to. So far, none of this was turning out as I expected.

Back at the Manor, I took the dress out of the box and hung it in the wardrobe. Then I decided I'd better call my boss. When I left, he'd driven me to the airport, admonishing me to call him as soon as I got in, to make sure I arrived safely. I'd replied if I didn't, he'd hear about it on the news, but he still made me promise.

A great many people seemed concerned with my well-being these days.

Extracting my cell phone, I tapped the Quik-Dial button and #1, waiting while it rang. In a moment, a male voice informed me, "Clayton Law Offices."

That was Sean, my boss' paralegal.

"Hi. It's me. David free?"

"Hang on."

I was put on Hold for exactly five seconds. Then David Clayton's deep and hearty, "Grace? Hey kid! Didn't I tell you to call me *immediately*?" sounded in my ear.

"I know and I apologize, but things got a little complicated pretty fast."

"Not problems with the family?"

"Nothing like that. I saw Jefferson Simmons, who's a Southern Colonel look-alike, by the way, and a real sweetie…"

"Is he going to become your favorite lawyer now? Should I be jealous?"

"Yeah, right. Start turning green. He's sixty, if he's

a day."

"Ouch." David was forty and I often teased him about being an *old man*. He might be my boss but we were close enough that I could get away with it. "Well, you know those Southerners…lady-killers from cradle to grave, I hear. And if you're going to be an heiress, you just might want to latch onto a rich, older man, wrap him around your finger, and be his arm-candy."

I ignored that.

David knew I'd kept marriage at arm's-length, afraid I'd end up making whatever mistakes my mother had, though I didn't really know what those mistakes were. I didn't date much. The few times I had, if I felt the least attraction and was afraid I'd fall in love with the guy and mess things up, I usually found some reason to break up. Fast.

"I don't know about the heiress part. He won't tell me what's in the will."

"Didn't I say that?" He had, very specifically. "If he could, you wouldn't have flown three thousand miles, would you?"

"He says they don't actually read wills, anyway." I still hadn't recovered from that statement.

"If you'll remember…" He said it patiently. "*I* told you *that*, too. And you reminded me they always do…in the movies."

"I stand corrected. So sometimes the movies get it wrong."

"You think?"

"Let's just ignore that, shall we?"

"I still don't understand why you had to be there. I mean, if you were living in Georgia, I could believe he might want to tell you in person, but to ask you to fly across the country…"

"Because in this case, the will *is* being read. It seems my father left very specific instructions, and one of them is that they have a good, old-fashioned, movie set will-reading. And everyone involved has to be there."

"Ve-e-ery interesting."

"Look, I have to go." I glanced at the clock. It read four-thirty. "I need to rest a bit and…and I'm having dinner with someone," I finished in a rush.

"Not the lawyer? Grace, I was kidding."

"With someone I used to know."

"And who would that be? You were five when you left, so you couldn't have known him very well."

"I knew him well enough. If I didn't know better, I'd say you're jealous, and besides, how do you know it's a *he*? It might be someone who knew Mama, or—"

"There's something in your voice telling me it isn't an old friend of the family. God, Grace, don't hook up with some good ol' boy redneck, will you? I want my receptionist back."

"Don't worry."

"I will, and you know it. Go, rest, get ready for your date, and call me after the will's read so I'll know whether you're coming back or booking a flight to Monte Carlo to gamble away your inheritance."

With promises to do that, I disconnected the call, dropped the phone onto the bedside table, and headed into the bathroom. I was going to take a shower, have a nap, and get ready for my—*no matter what David says, it isn't a date*—dinner with May. Damn, that sounded like the title of an art film.

Chapter 3

There were little bottles of bath oil, bath salts, and bubble bath in a gold-wire basket. With all those enticements, I opted for a bath instead of a shower, selected the bubble bath, turned on the water and poured the contents of one bottle under the stream.

In a few moments, a thick layer of iridescent suds rose above the water's surface while I got my robe out of the closet. The Manor had supplied robes that were plush to the point of luxurious, but I always preferred taking my own comfy robe with me whenever I traveled.

I shed my clothes, pinned my hair atop my head to keep it dry, and in a few minutes, was immersed in frothy bubbles and warm water.

The bubbles had a lavender scent, and I scooped up a handful of suds, blowing them gently into the air…like someone in a soap commercial. They rose, floated, then drifted down to join the others, settling and bursting with tiny *pops.* From another basket, I pulled a washcloth, twisted and fluffed to look like a gigantic blossom, removed its ties and dipped it into the water. Raising a soapy leg, I rubbed from ankle to knee.

"Now *this* is luxury."

The bath didn't take long. Once finished, I lingered, propping a little inflated plastic pillow behind my head and leaning back in the bubbles while taking in my surroundings.

The bathroom followed the Twenties theme with its slight air of decadence in the tub's gilded claw feet and old-fashioned straight-handled gold faucets, and the toilet with the water cistern fastened to the wall several feet above the floor.

Wonder how much it cost to have that *installed?* I'd seen pictures of them but never one in real life. Didn't know they still made such contraptions.

Across from the tub was a large pedestal sink, its gold faucets matching those on the tub. The floor was tiled as was the wall, wainscoted with aqua and gold 4x4 ceramic squares to a height of four feet, and above that…*mirrors*, on the entire wall above the sink and the tub. In the wall over the sink, I could see myself in the tub, reflected in the wall above the tub, reflected in the one over the sink, and so on into infinity…a thousand Graces, hair pinned in an unruly topknot, bare shoulders above the layer of bubbles.

I wonder what David would think of these mirrors? Sighing, I leaned back, closing my eyes. I'd lie here a few minutes, luxuriate and relax.

I relaxed but continued thinking.

What would David think of this bathroom? His own home was decorated in ultra-modern, chrome and leather, stark white and black, accented with Chinese red. He'd probably take one look at this post-WWI era ambience and hoot, *Good God, I'm in an episode of a time travel movie. When does H.G. Wells show up?*

Dear David. Great boss, more like a big brother now. I'd worked for him for five years, and I'd been lucky to find him. First job, first boss, still there. Very lucky.

****

My mother's unexpected death caused me to drop out of college my sophomore year, and immediately face up to the fact that I was going to have to sell the little house she'd been buying since I couldn't afford the payments, and find myself another place to live, as well as a job so I could continue to live *anywhere*. The State of California is not an inexpensive place to reside, so I was very aware that not only was I going to have a difficult time but, with my lack of employment experience and training, it was also going to be tough finding a job at all, much less one paying enough for me to survive.

With the house already on the market, I scoured the want-ads daily, plus went through online employment websites, as well as registering with temp agencies. Anything to bring in some cash.

I had already decided I'd start off trying reception work. I was a good enough typist, having worked part-time in one of the offices on campus, and could keyboard with the best of them. I had a lot of Internet experience. I'd filled in during secretarial vacancies, so had fairly good phone presence. Yep, being a receptionist was my best bet...if I could get anyone to look past the no-experience-in-a-*real*-job fact.

On my resume, I'd inserted the stock phrase, "*I may not have much employment experience, but I'm willing to learn and am quick to grasp office procedures...*" So far, none of the ads I'd answered had even given me a reply.

Why should they? common sense asked. If there's someone knowing it already, why hire someone they're going to have to take time to train? I didn't even have Unemployment Compensation to fall back on, and though my faculty advisor thought I could qualify for scholarships and student loans, it would take too long for them to be processed to help me out right away. I needed something *now*, not eight months down the road.

I was fast going into a panic when I got the letter from *David Clayton, Attorney at Law.* I looked at the return address dumbly. *What?* Inside, unbelievably, was a request for me to call and make an appointment for an interview. I didn't even remember answering that ad…at least, I guess there had been an ad, *somewhere,* that I'd seen and desperately sent a letter to. I called the number, spoke to a young man who gave me a time, a date, and an address in Mission Viejo.

I was there half an hour early, nervous as could be.

The sign out front read *Stonehenge Plaza.* There was a logo of the famous upright stone pillars at Salisbury, the sun shining through them. Definitely unique. The building itself was two stories, with a rain forest in the center plaza, banana trees and ferns, boulders, and a waterfall and pond running through it. Beautiful, soothing, and typically Californian. I would've liked to sit on one of the stone benches, listening to the burble and gurgle of the water, but I had an appointment to keep, so I hurried on, promising myself I'd stop to investigate the little jungle after my interview.

I was pretty certain it wasn't going to take long. Probably no more than the time it would take Mr. Clayton to tell me that, *Sorry, I need someone with experience.* In that case, why ask me to come here at all? I felt defeated already, going in with a bad attitude.

The young man at the desk greeted me pleasantly enough.

"Grace McAllister. I have a two o'clock

appointment."

"Mr. Clayton's on a conference call just now." He glanced at the buttons on the phone next to the computer screen. One was blinking. He checked something off a sheet. My name, I supposed. "I'm Sean. I'll let him know you're here as soon as he's finished."

"Thank you." I looked around and selected a seat, feeling my discouragement grow as I took in my surroundings. Nice. Mr. Clayton looks to be doing very well. Sean returned to his keyboard, employing a very strenuous brand of hunt-and-peck.

"Damn." He scowled, hit another key several times, then started again. He hadn't typed many more words before the process was repeated. Obviously, he wasn't much of a typist. Was this why he was being replaced? I decided to ask.

"Tell me," I began, and he spun around in the chair, giving me his attention, looking relieved to stop what he was doing. "Why's Mr. Clayton advertising for a receptionist when he has one already? Are you quitting?"

"From the way I type, you'd think that, wouldn't you? Fifteen words a minute with twelve errors." He laughed. "I'm not the receptionist. I'm Mr. Clayton's paralegal, filling in until he can get a *real* receptionist, and I hope and pray he gets one soon."

He rolled his eyes heavenward.

"Not wild about the job, huh?" I was smiling at his somewhat dramatic distress.

"I've enough work of my own without holding down two jobs. His last receptionist got married and left the state. He's been advertising for three months now and so far...*nada.*" He gestured to a stack of papers in a wire box on the desk. "Letters of application...dozens of them…they call, I make appointments…they show up…" There was a sigh dangerously close to a snort. "Some of them don't even finish the interview, just walk out…"

"For heaven's sake, why?" I'd never heard of such a thing. Walking out of an interview? In this day of job shortages? I felt a sudden surge of fear. Was this David Clayton some kind of predator or something? Luring young women to his office to…do what?

"They don't want to work for *someone like him*…or rather, someone who handles the clients he does." His lip curled angrily. "And that's a quote from one little Miss Smart Ass. She actually came right out and said it. To his face." He looked as if she'd insulted him and not his boss. "I can't believe there are still so many prejudiced people in this state."

…the clients he handles… What did that mean? I thought back to the wording on the door. *Family Law.* That didn't sound so bad. Unless the "family" was the Mafia?

"Say…" He looked thoughtful. "You've got a bit of an accent. Southern?"

I nodded.

"Texas?"

"Georgia. I've been away from there a long time." I smiled. "Can't seem to lose it, though."

"You never do," he agreed. "I had friends in college who'd never been to the South but had parents born there. They had accents, too. I hope that doesn't mean you're prejudiced." He fixed me with a stern gaze.

"I-I don't think so. What do you mean? Exactly."

"You're not bigoted against Blacks…gays… Republicans?" That last seemed thrown in as an afterthought.

I laughed, started to ask, *Is Mr. Clayton black?* Not that it would matter. If he was a good boss, so what? If he was a bad boss, skin color didn't make any difference, either.

I didn't get a chance. Sean glanced at the phone. "He's free." He picked up the receiver and pushed a button. "Your appointment's here." Dropping it back onto the cradle, he said, "Go on in, Miss McAllister."

"Thank you." I stood and headed for the door. In a minute I'd get my question answered, anyway. At the door I stopped.

"Just knock," Sean said. "Then go on in."

To David Clayton's call, I walked into his office.

****

He wasn't black, not even brown, but he was definitely the most handsome man I'd ever seen. A blond Adonis. When they coined the words *eye candy, hunk,* and *stud-muffin*, they had David Clayton in mind. Late thirties. Blond hair the color of honey and pulled back in a ponytail, blue eyes, and his face…

Drool-worthy doesn't describe him. With his coloring, he should've had a name like Sven or Erik. If he'd been around when the Vikings were sailing the seas, they could've used him for their recruitment posters. I could see him, wearing a horned helmet, double-headed axe in hand, one finger pointing, *Uncle Leif Wants You!*

In other words, David Clayton was a knockout.

"Hi, I'm David Clayton."

"Grace McAllister," I responded.

There was a brief flicker of a reaction—was it to my accent?—quickly hidden. He came from behind the desk before I could shut the door, offering his hand and leading me to a sofa grouping to one side of the room in front of a bookcase arrangement filled with thick volumes. His palm was large and warm and strong but he didn't try to break my fingers. I'd had run-ins with guys who seemed to think they had to crush my little digits to prove something.

David Clayton simply pressed my hand gently, then released it and pushed shut the door.

Once I was seated, he dropped onto the couch beside me. I saw he held my letter. That made the little thrill I'd gotten upon seeing him fade as I remembered what a short, information-less piece it was.

"I got your application and—"

"David, Lee's on line one," Sean's voice cut in from an intercom on the desk. "Baby emergency."

"Excuse me." He looked a wee bit exasperated as he got up and went over to the desk, punching a button as he picked up the phone. "What is it, hon?"

For several minutes, he listened to what appeared to be a frantic tirade, nodding, and murmuring, "Unh-huh," several times, before saying, "Sweetheart, I know this is nerve-wracking but think how Davy feels."

More words, now so loud I could almost understand them.

"Lee...*Lee!*" The sounds stopped. He spoke quietly. "You've got the baby books we bought. Mother's handy. Call her. Don't be ashamed to ask for advice. After all, she raised three kids, so she knows a thing or two about babies." Quieter words now. "I know. It's okay. I'll see you tonight."

He dropped the phone back into its cradle, stood looking at it for a moment, then over at me and smiled. "Sorry. New baby. Panicsville whenever he cries."

"How old?" I smiled back. New daddy? Oh, well, that he might be single and my new boss was too much to ask for.

"Six months," came the answer. "He's been fussy for weeks. Teething's starting, I think. Now then…"

Phone call and baby problem dismissed, he sat down again, looking at the letter he still held. Then he looked back at me, transfixing me with that spotlight-blue gaze.

"You have absolutely no work experience?"

My heart sank. Nothing like getting right to the heart of the matter. No way I could lie about it either. "None official. No."

"How do you think you could fit in here?"

Something about that phrasing bothered me.

"I don't think it's a matter of *fitting in*," I answered. "But of *learning*. I'm a congenial sort of person and I don't have a problem with meeting people, so all I need to do is learn what I need to know."

He didn't answer, but seemed to be absorbing what I'd said.

Encouraged by the fact that he wasn't on his feet, showing me the way out, I went on, "I've got to start somewhere, and it did say in your ad 'no law experience necessary.'" I spread my hands. "Well, that's me, or is it I? I'll warn you…I always get those two bits of grammar confused."

I managed a smile.

"Anyway, I know how to answer a telephone correctly, and I can type a heck of a lot better than your current receptionist." I couldn't resist that little dig, thinking how Sean made a mistake almost every word.

He scowled at that. *Oops, did that go too far?* Then the smile was back. "He *is* pretty bad, isn't he? But Sean has the excuse he's not a receptionist."

"Sounds like someone else I know." I returned the smile. "I *could* be, with a little assistance."

"Have you ever typed any kind of legal forms?"

"Are they different from class registration or scholarship applications? I've typed plenty of those."

"That's right. You did mention you'd done part-time work in the English Department at Concordia College, didn't you?" He consulted the letter again. "That counts as experience, you know."

"My bad. I'll remember that." *For my next interview.* I didn't say that out loud.

"Typing torts, *et cetera,* is easy enough. I hand in the rough draft, you follow it and type the finished one. The templates for all forms are in the computer. You merely have to find the right one and start typing." He looked at the letter again. "You're not attending classes now? You *do* want a full-time job?"

"I've had to drop out, I'm afraid. Joining the out-of-work masses." In a few minutes, I was telling him the whole sad story, ending with, "I've put the house up for sale, and as soon as I get a job, or sell it, whichever comes first, I'll find an apartment."

"Well, that's a helluva mess, isn't it? I'm sorry you lost your mother, Grace."

He actually looked sincere.

"Won't say *Sorry for your loss*. I hate that phrase." Well-shaped lips drooped at the corners. "Sounds so phony." He swooped onto the next subject without batting an eye. "As the sign on the door says, I handle family law. Know what that means?"

"Not really," I admitted. "I'm guessing you don't defend murderers, gangbangers, and bank robbers?"

"Hardly." That made him laugh. "I draw up wills, handle divorces, adoptions, things like that."

That sounded safe enough. Nothing that would make me hop up and stomp out declaring I didn't want to work for *someone like him.*

"I handle all aspects of the law dealing with families, *any* kind of family," he went on. "That includes working with gays, specifically those who have partners they wish to provide for or want to adopt a child. Occasionally, that has overflowed into Civil Rights cases…a minority child being refused admission to a prep school though he qualifies and his parents can afford the tuition, or a same-sex couple not allowed to rent in a specific place with no reasonable excuse."

"Oh?" I hoped that one word didn't have the wrong inflection.

"What's your opinion on that, Miss McAllister?" Did I imagine it or did his body tense slightly?

"My personal opinion, you mean? Truthfully?"

He nodded. "I wouldn't want anything else."

I decided to speak my mind. After all, as far as I was concerned, this job was already lost, so what did I have to lose? Besides, I thought I'd sensed a smidge of hostility when he heard my accent.

"I hope you haven't decided that because I was born in the South, I'm biased against minorities, Mr. Clayton." I took a deep breath. "Because that's also a form of prejudice, you know."

Something flickered in his expression, one blond brow arching slightly. I wasn't certain if it was anger or surprise. *Not racking up points, Grace.* I shrugged, wondering if I was digging myself into a hole and saying too much.

"My mother taught me to accept everyone. *Everyone*." I emphasized that word. "I've always attempted to do that. *Live and let live.* As far as I'm concerned—"

The intercom interrupted my diatribe with, "David, Lee again."

Apparently, Mrs. Clayton was back. Baby Clayton's teething must have reached a crisis.

He was off the couch and at the phone before it could make a second sound, pushing a button twice. "Sean? Just tell Lee I can't talk right now." Sean said something. "I know, but it isn't really an emergency."

Not wanting to appear to be eavesdropping, for I could see this second call irritated him a little. Wondering how many others he'd gotten today, I got up, wandering over to look at the various photographs and diplomas filling the wall next to the bookcase. They were impressive.

"Explain I'm interviewing an applicant and can't be disturbed. I know, but do it anyway."

I studied two photos, one of Mr. Clayton and a younger man, arm draped over his shoulder, both laughing at the camera. Hair was mussed, faces smudged, they looked as if they'd been playing football. The other photograph was of a slightly older woman with beautifully frosted hair, and Clayton, balancing a laughing blond baby on his shoulder.

He dropped the receiver back onto the cradle and came to stand behind me. The picture with the two men was crooked. I reached out to straighten it as I looked at the one of the baby. "Is that your better half?"

I thought she looked a lot older than he.

"Yep, that's the ol' ball-and-chain." The words were

facetious but loving, and something else, oddly relieved. He tapped the baby's image. "And that's the subject of all the phone calls. David, junior."

"He looks just like you." I studied the blond curls and laughing toothless mouth. *And will be a lady-killer, too.*

"Guess he should." His fingers rubbed against the glass covering the picture, almost a caress. "We wanted a baby right from the start, but... There were only two routes open. Adoption or surrogacy."

So there was a problem with them having a child. Perhaps because of Mrs. Clayton's obvious age?

He laughed. "I'm afraid I'm a bit of a hypocrite."

"How do you mean?" I turned to look at him.

"I help gay couples adopt, but *I* wanted a child of *my* own. *Mine.* So I found someone willing to be my surrogate baby-mama and..." He shrugged.

I looked back at the baby again. Didn't really know what to say to that.

"Where were we?" He attempted to get back on track, struggling to find the lost thread of our previous conversation. "Oh, yes... Do you have any problem working with Blacks...or gays, Miss McAllister? Or do I already know your answer?"

Odd he didn't sound accusing or angry now, but anxious.

I answered hurriedly, "I've never had a problem with *any one*, Mr. Clayton. I've never let anyone's sexual orientation, or their color...uh, what's that word...*ethnicity?*...bother me. What I said was the truth. If there are any problems, I won't be the one making them."

I didn't know what else to say. I fell silent, waiting.

For what?

He bit his lip. Seemed to be mulling over everything I'd said. And then… "When can you start?"

"Wh-What?" Surely he didn't mean…

"I'm certain Sean'd like it to be right now, but I can wait until tomorrow, if you've any arrangements you need to make."

"You mean…" I didn't finish.

"You've got the job? Yes." He smiled. "If you want it, that is."

"If I want it? Mr. Clayton, I could hug you."

"Better not. My better half might get jealous. I'll just take that as a *yes*, shall I?" He led me to the door, informing me he'd see me in the morning at nine o'clock sharp, and then told Sean that tomorrow he was officially demoted back to his original position.

I walked out of the office in a daze, coming to a halt by the desk where Sean had stopped laboring over that same piece of correspondence. Swiveling in his chair, he said, "Thank God."

He wiped imaginary sweat off his forehead.

"You know. I had a feeling…" His voice trailed away, then he looked eager. "How about starting right now instead of tomorrow? *Please?* So I can get back to my own desk?"

"Sorry." I tried to suppress my smile but it was widening into a delighted grin. "Tomorrow."

"Better than nothing, I guess." He tried not to look disappointed and failed. He glanced back at the computer screen and sighed. "Darn it."

"Sean, may I ask you something?"

"You're about to become part of the family," he said, expansively. "Sure."

"Why in the world would anyone not want to work for Mr. Clayton? He's one of the nicest men I've ever met."

"For a lawyer, you mean?" His eyes twinkled to show he was kidding. He shrugged. "Well…you know…some people are still prejudiced in this day and age, if you can believe it."

"You're being sarcastic. Right?" I thought about that. "You mean, the minority business?"

"Yeah…the minority business," he repeated.

I shook my head. "So he has a lot of gays and Blacks as clients? So what?"

Sean didn't answer. I guess he thought my question was rhetorical.

"I don't see the problem. They're just people, for crying out loud."

"Did you tell David that?" Sean laughed and shook his head. I thought it was a gesture one might use with a child who'd said something slightly ingenious. That rankled a little since we appeared about the same age.

"Not in so many words, no," I admitted. "But I guess what I *did* say satisfied him."

"So you don't mind working with a gay person?" It was Clayton's question all over again. Was it my imagination or did he look anxious, too?

"Sean, I don't mind working with *anyone*," I answered, and frowned. "That seemed a pretty pointed question. You're obviously not Black. Are *you* gay?"

Was that the reason for his persistence?

"Nope." He turned my question back at me. "Are you?"

"No."

"Then that makes two of us in this office."

What? I glanced back at the door. "You mean…?"

He nodded. "You didn't know."

It wasn't an accusation, simply a flat statement.

All I said was, "I do *now*…" and felt like the most unobservant human on Earth. I shook my head. "My mother always said I sailed through life *without a clue* and this has definitely been one of those times."

"And…?"

"And…what?"

"Does it make a difference?"

"Not as far as I'm concerned."

Sean held out his hand. "Welcome aboard, Ms. McAllister."

"Grace," I said, and clasped his hand.

****

That was five years ago. I'm still Clayton Law Offices' receptionist, but I've gone from employee to friend to surrogate little sister. I've had dinners at their condo and babysat Davy when they wanted a night out. I've met David's mother, sympathized with Lee because his parents still refuse to acknowledge his association with David, as well as their grandchildren. Two years later, when there was another addition to their family, a little girl, fathered by Lee this time around, I helped plan the baby shower. It was David who'd consoled and patted my shoulder when I broke up with boyfriends, tentatively suggesting, *Perhaps you don't give any young man much of a chance?* He was also the one who talked me into going to Georgia when I received Jefferson Simmons' letter, and now, here I was…

…falling asleep in my bath water. I jerked awake as my chin dipped beneath what was left of the bubbles. Blinking, I spluttered water and sat up. "Guess I'd better get out of here before I drown."

Wouldn't that be a way to go? Falling asleep in the bath and sinking under. I wondered if that ever happened. Surely, the sudden change in temperature as well as the feel of water on the face would wake the sleeper. I stood up, reaching for a towel, again catching sight of myself in the opposite wall mirror.

I'm short, just skimming a couple of inches above five feet, and slim. Though I considered myself not having enough curves in all the right places, Lee assured me I looked great. I'd complained to him numerous times about wanting to lose weight or changing my hair color or any number of things I thought wrong with my appearance.

Believe me, Grace. If David were straight and I were a woman, you'd never set foot in this house and I'd be popping into the office a dozen times a day to keep an eye on both of you.

Perhaps I did look better than my mental self-image. What did it matter? Especially tonight. After all, I was merely having dinner, a Welcome Home dinner, with someone I'd known a long time ago. I wasn't out to seduce anyone, was I?

I knew the answer to that, but did Mayfield? I still wasn't sure of him or his reasons for taking me out.

Wrapping the towel around myself, I aimed for the bedroom. The clock said it was five-thirty.

Fifteen minutes before, while I was snoozing in cold water, May would have picked up Tammy for her math lesson.

If it wasn't true, and they were actually getting in some early evening delight, I wouldn't have to worry about any amorous overtures from the contradictory Mr.

Donohue, would I? Here's hoping he'd use it all on his pupil.

I quit worrying and decided to finish my nap.

Chapter 4

"You look good enough to eat," May said.

He was still in jeans and boots, though a different pair, and had changed to a white, open-collared, short-sleeved dress shirt, no tie. I felt vastly overdressed. Eyes twinkling, he went on as my lips thinned into a flat line. "But don't worry, I won't even nibble. Shall we?"

He offered me his arm and, with my hand nestled in the crook of his elbow, led me through the door to the left of the revolving one.

As soon as we were outside, I stopped. Parked at the curb was a crimson muscle car, a convertible such a bright red even the streetlamps couldn't dull its finish. It looked to be a fairly new model. That was definitely a surprise.

"What's the matter? Think I was going to be driving a 1933 pickup truck or something?" May asked.

"Of course not." I wasn't about to admit that was exactly the type of vehicle I'd envisioned. "It's just…it looks so *new*," I finished, lamely.

"Used," he corrected as he opened the door.

I slid in gracefully, sitting down, then lifting both legs and swinging them inside, a little trick I'd learned to show off my legs while not looking awkward. May barely gave them a glance.

"I traded the pickup in earlier this year. Kept losing parts when it hit a bump in the road."

He ran around to the driver's side and slid in. I shot him a glance. His expression didn't tell me whether he was kidding or not. He started the engine. It hummed, barely audible, even with the top down.

This car was *really* new.

I wondered exactly why he classified it as *used.* Did he buy it with a couple of miles already on the odometer or something?

"Seat belt on?" He looked my way. I was busy snapping it into place.

I nodded.

"Hang on."

He floored it. With a squeal of tires, the car peeled away from the curb and was skidding to a halt at the corner stoplight before I could take a breath, which I did, inhaling sharply.

"Sorry." May didn't sound the least bit apologetic. "Haven't yet figured out exactly how to drive this thing. Got too many bells and whistles." He nodded at the dashboard. "Still haven't found the radio."

Come on. Puh-leeze. I reached over, punched a button, and music blared out, floating into the air.

Beethoven's 4th Symphony? Classic Radio? You've got to be kidding me. I didn't say it, just leaned back as the light changed and the car shot forward at a legal speed this time.

"Yes, I do." He said it to the windshield.

"Do what?" I wondered if I'd regret asking that question.

"Like classical music." He was nodding his head in time to the music, I swear. "Also, some C&W, and old rock…old, in this case being the '70s and '80s."

"Really? I…" I stopped. I was about to add, *I do,*

too, then decided I didn't want Mayfield Donovan finding out he and I had anything in common. I was still so suspicious I wondered if I'd enjoy any of this evening. I'd probably end up with indigestion.

"What?" he asked, finally giving me a sideways glance.

"Nothing." I shook my head. "You'd better keep your eyes on the road."

"Hard to do with someone as pretty as you in the car, Gracie." He turned his attention forward again.

"Am I going to spend the rest of the night reminding you my name isn't Gracie?"

"Probably. I'm still having a little difficulty thinking of you as an adult…Gracie."

"Try."

"Yes, ma'am."

"Where are we going, anyway?"

By now, we'd made two turns and hadn't reached our destination, and I knew McAllister wasn't big enough to have many more turns. I was still leery enough of May's motives to wonder if he was going to strand me somewhere and make me walk back to the Manor in the dark. I was having trouble thinking of *him* as an adult, too.

"Somewhere we can have dinner and talk without a lot of noise and distraction."

That sounded fairly safe. Nevertheless, when we reached McAllister's city limits, which weren't all that far away, alarm bells went off.

"W-we're going out of town?"

"Nothing gets past you, does it?"

"Mayfield Donovan, if this is some kind of trick…" I decided to voice my fears. "You can stop this car right now and let me out."

"Gracie, honey…"

I stiffened at that. I'd never liked being called *honey*. Not by anyone.

"I'd never do a thing like that."

"Oh, yeah? What about the time you offered to give me a ride on your bike and left me at the turnoff to the house? I had to walk all the way back."

"Heck, Gracie, it was only a quarter mile, and you weren't on the highway. Bless your heart, you were on McAllister land the whole time."

That Southernism stopped me…for two seconds. True, but it had been a long way for four-year-old legs to walk.

"Just relax, will you? I swear the only ulterior motive I have is for some intelligent conversation. At least I hope it's going to be intelligent."

I wasn't about to get into an argument about my IQ or his, which I knew to be exceptionally high. Once, I'd heard Mama tell someone that. Pursing my lips into a half-pout, I stayed quiet.

In a few more minutes, he turned the convertible off the road onto a gravel driveway, and a few minutes later, stopped before a house set in a grove of pecan trees.

It was a two-story, country-style clapboard, with a wide porch running the length of the front. In the beam of the car's headlights, it looked freshly painted. From somewhere came a faint tinkling.

Wind chimes?

I saw them, hanging from a hook at a corner of the porch, metal butterflies, spinning and striking against each other.

May cut the lights and the engine and hopped out,

dashing around to open my door.

As he took my hand and helped me out, I asked, "Whose house is this?"

"Mine," came the surprising answer.

"You're taking me to dinner at your house?" As he nodded, I went on, laughing, "Who's cooking? You?"

"That's right." He took my arm, guiding me to the steps.

There were flowerbeds on each side, filled with a long mound of green thrift with tiny pink flowers, backed by what appeared to be bunches of Gerbera daisies, all well-tended, not a weed in sight.

I shook my head. Somehow, I couldn't see May crawling through flowerbeds in gardening gloves and straw hat, pulling weeds and digging out dandelions.

"What is it *now*?" He'd seen the movement.

"Are those pecan trees?" I nodded at the dark shapes on either side of the house.

"Very observant. Make good shade in the summer but the devil to rake when fall comes. Squirrels like the nuts, though." We were on the porch now and he fumbled with his keys, opening the front door.

I turned to look back over the yard, what I could see of it in the dark.

"You've crêpe myrtles, too?" I was certain that's what those shapes with the frilly flowers were on the other side of the driveway.

"Right again. Say, you're really the horticulturalist, aren't you? I've been thinking of cutting them down. They send up too many suckers from the roots. I spend most of the spring digging out the shoots."

"Don't." I turned and walked inside. "They're really pretty. What's that color called?"

"I'll think about it. Watermelon." He followed me inside. The screen slammed behind us and he shut the inside door.

"That's my favorite myrtle color."

This is the weirdest conversation I've ever had with you, May. It's just too damned normal. What can it mean?

"Then I'll say I planted them for you and leave them alone, even if they do drive me crazy with those rootlings." He flipped light switches as he spoke. "Let's put a little light on the subject."

I had to laugh at that. It was something Mama always said when she walked into a darkened room. That one phrase made me feel secure but, considering who it came from, I was confused again.

"Welcome to *Chez* Donovan." He waved a hand and I walked into a living room that was another surprise.

The furniture was white with gold insets, Italian Provincial, I think, upholstered in a soft, smoky-blue fabric complementing the pattern in the wallpaper and the drapes. Throw pillows of blue and white looked as if they'd never been touched by human hands, they were so crisp and clean.

The sofa was set before a fireplace, a real one, at the moment clean of ash and wood, with several chairs grouped around it. A long credenza-like table backed against the sofa, a silver tray with several wine decanters and glasses at one end. Across from it was a bay window and window seat, its woodwork also painted white, looking out onto the porch. Through it, I could see a swing I hadn't noticed while we were outside.

It looked like a page from some home decorating magazine, and again, completely un-Mayfield-like.

The air held the aroma of something cooking. Something delicious.

Involuntarily, I sniffed. "Is that dinner?"

"Right, and I need to check it. Have a seat. I'll be right back." Dashing across the living room, he tossed his keys onto the credenza and disappeared through an archway.

I heard a door open and shut as I walked around the sofa and dropped my purse onto the blue fabric. I wandered to the fireplace. Though it was midsummer, I wished there was a fire burning in it so I could stand there and gaze at the flames.

There was a painting hanging above the mantel, others on the walls. Two were forest scenes, another a beach. I reached up to brush my fingers over the canvas, feeling the thickness of the paint. Real paintings, not mass-produced copies, but originals.

They were beautiful. I wondered who…

A glance in the corner showed a scrawl in black. *May D.*

Another facet revealed, and something else. On the mantel, as well as the smooth surface of the credenza, was a fine layer of dust, smothering its pale gleam.

May was back.

"You did these?" I didn't give him time to say anything.

"I like to dabble when I have time."

"These are more than dabbles. They're beautiful. I didn't know you had it in you."

"Flattery will get you somewhere." He laughed.

I was beginning to get a little frustrated. Most of my insults were simply bouncing off. How was I ever going to pay him back when he wouldn't get angry?

"I suppose, as the host, this is the moment where I offer you a drink. What would you like?"

Aha! So that was it. Get me tipsy, then… What? I'd wake up nude in the arms of the Confederate statue in the town square?

"I'm not much of a drinker," I hedged. *True.*

"You can have a glass of wine, then. An *apéritif*, if you will." Darned if he didn't pronounce it correctly. "Some chardonnay, a quiet merlot…"

"All right, a little merlot, then." I'd hold it, pretend to sip.

The wine was supplied from one of the bottles on the credenza, in a tiny crystal glass. May poured himself some in a much larger one, tossed it down, then refilled it. I wondered if that meant he was a drinker or was just giving himself some Dutch courage for what he was planning, whatever that might be.

I told myself I'd better be on my toes. I wasn't worried that May would harm me in any way, but I was still pretty certain he was planning something ending in embarrassment for me.

"This room is lovely." I was determined to keep the conversation going. "Is the rest of the house as well-decorated?"

"That it is." He took a sip of his wine, looking around. "Surprises you, doesn't it?"

"As a matter of fact, it does," I admitted.

I'd envisioned him living in a shotgun house with a couple of early model beaters in the yard in various stages of disrepair and the interior furnished with 1950s chrome and plastic and orange crates.

"Not the kind of place for Beautiful Bill Donovan's boy at all. Right?"

Was that a bit of bitterness? It was gone so swiftly I couldn't tell. The twinkle in his eyes was still there, however.

"This place was done by someone with a fine fashion sense." I thought I skirted answering his question nicely.

"Thank my wife for that. She did the entire house."

"Wife?" I glanced at his left hand. No ring. No tan line, either.

"She's gone now." There was emotion on his face, but I still couldn't give it a name.

Had she died?

He lifted his glass. "And good riddance. Cheers."

He tapped the edge of the glass against mine. It gave off a clear ringing in the sudden quiet.

Whatever happened, it hadn't been a happy parting.

"Seeing the living room makes me want to see the rest of the house. Give me a tour?"

"Later." He was standing closer now. "There's something else I want to do first…"

There was a melodious *ding* from the kitchen.

"…and that's eat." He looked in that direction. "Everything should be just about ready."

Taking his glass with him, he disappeared into the kitchen again.

This time, I tagged along, snagging my purse off the sofa as I passed. Through the arch, I saw the shapes of a table and chairs, and to the right, a swinging door half-open next to a brick wall with a cutout giving a partial view of the kitchen. I pushed on the door and went through.

May was standing at the wall. I could see now that it was actually a room divider forming a chimney with a grill inset. He had tongs and fork in hand and was turning two enormous steaks over the flames of a gas fire.

"This I don't believe." I dug into my purse, extracting my cell phone, tapping the camera icon. "Smile."

"What are you doing?" He paused in turning one of the steaks, looking in my direction.

"Bad boy May Donovan toiling over a hot grill? I've got to capture this for posterity."

"Only if you e-mail me a copy."

"You've got it." I snapped the shot and dropped the phone back into the bag slung over my shoulder.

"All done." He nodded at two platters on the kitchen work island. "Get those, would you?"

"Making me work for my supper, eh?"

"Now that's where you're wrong. You're Tuesday's child, full of grace. Saturday's child is the one who works for a living." He patted his chest. "*Moi*."

I didn't have an answer to that. I hadn't thought of that old nursery rhyme in years, though I remember Mama singing it to me when I was small. *Monday's child is fair of face…Tuesday's child is full of grace…* and her whisper*, You're Tuesday's child, my baby…*

For some reason, that made me shiver.

"Don't tell me you're cold," May said as he slid a steak off the fork and onto one of the platters. "You can't be. Not in Georgia in June."

"Guess someone walked over my grave." I brushed off the feeling, though the chill it produced seemed to linger. I looked at the platters. "It appears you may be a passable cook, *Chef May*, but I'll withhold judgment until I see if I survive dinner."

"I guarantee no foxglove or monkshood was

included in the marinade, so let's get started." Tossing fork and tongs into the sink, he stuck his hands into quilted mitts and retrieved two bowls from the built-in oven, nodding for me to precede him through the swinging door.

An elbow against another switch made the dining room light up.

Places were already set.

I put a platter at each end of the table while May lined up the serving bowls he carried with the others on the sideboard, swapping his wine glass for an empty tea goblet. He pulled out a chair and seated me, whisking the napkin from the place setting onto his arm.

"Will *mademoiselle* have tea with her meal?"

He didn't attempt a French accent, thank goodness. With that Southern drawl, it would've been a disaster. Instead, he bowed, whipped the napkin open and onto my lap, and waited. I nodded, and he took a crystal pitcher from the sideboard, lifted my goblet, poured in just enough to cover the bottom, and handed it to me.

I accepted it. It was delicious. What they're now calling *sweet tea*, but something I'd known all my life as just plain *tea*. My Southern mother had never served tea without sugar and ice, so I never knew it any other way.

"Just right." I handed the glass back and he filled it and his own also. He returned the pitcher to its place and reached for my plate.

"May I serve you, *mademoiselle*?"

I hesitated, waiting for the double-*entendre*. When none came, I nodded, and he went to the sideboard, carefully lifting one spoonful from each bowl and depositing it on my plate. He returned it to me and while I watched, brought the salad to the table and tossed it, placing some in a little wooden bowl and putting that by my plate also.

"You do that with finesse," I commented.

"Worked as a waiter at one of Athens' finer restaurants while I was going to school." That done, he served himself and sat down. He raised his glass. "To a singular lack of indigestion on your part." After a sip of tea, he said, "At the risk of sounding vulgar, chow's on, dig in."

We both did. For a little while, neither of us spoke. I was enjoying the food and, after a few bites, said so.

"And you cooked all this yourself?"

"Actually, there was a little old lady working in the kitchen all afternoon. She slipped out the door as we came in."

I gave him a raised eyebrow. He'd said it so seriously…

"I'm lying. I confess I did it all. Everything except the steaks has been warming in the oven since before I picked up Tammy for her lesson this afternoon."

"Well, it's great."

More than great. The steak was perfect, the baked potato well done, the asparagus tender. I wondered if he'd remembered I was one of those rare children who liked asparagus or if that choice was simply a coincidence. The biscuits were fluffy and light…not like my own. When I actually made any, which was rarely, they were usually like stones more likely to sink to the bottom of the stomach and stay there. David once told me I could use them for slingshot ammunition.

The china and crystal were elegant and fit the rest of the decor beautifully and I complimented him on his selections.

"Thank my ex for that, too," he said, reaching for his tea to wash down a bite of potato. "A hundred fifty-five dollars a plate. Almost impoverished everyone on my side who bought us wedding gifts, though Veronica's folks had no trouble buying out the store. Nothing too good for their little girl...or her expensive tastes." This time, there was more than a little bitterness in his words. "No one asked about mine. In furniture or anything else."

"I take it you're not fond of Italian Provincial?"

"Do I look like Italian Provincial?" He shook his head. "If I'd had my way, the whole house would've been fitted with Colonial Maple."

"If you hate it so, why don't you get rid of it? Furnish it like *you* want?"

"Because I admit Veronica had a definite eye for color and style, and the place looks damned good." For just a moment, he didn't look up. "Seemed a shame to re-do it after all the work she did. Besides, it cost a lot."

"Veronica, that's her name?" I was back in Cartoonsville again, thinking of a certain high school hero and his rich girlfriend.

"*Ronni* to her friends. You notice I use her *real* name. I don't count myself as even remotely friendly. Not now." He took a deep breath and the story poured out.

It was as if May had been waiting for someone to listen, a sympathetic ear. I'll always wonder why he thought I possessed that ear.

He told me about meeting Veronica Smallwood when he was at the University of Georgia, *"God, I thought she was beautiful..."* then finding her again when he'd been teaching in Atlanta.

"She was registered with an agency there, doing

some modeling..." He took a swallow of tea and laughed. "I was so stupid in love I forgot about *handsome is as handsome does,* or in this case, *beautiful,* but I was reminded fast enough."

They'd dated, slept together, and May had shown a surprisingly old-fashioned streak by wanting to get married instead of just living together. Veronica agreed, and they had a church wedding with all the trimmings, an extravaganza with almost five hundred guests.

"Most of them from her side of the tracks."

There was a honeymoon in Bermuda and it was only when they returned that trouble appeared on the idyllic horizon. May was tired of the big city, wanted to return to McAllister to teach. He got a position at Wildwood Academy, a college prep school just outside town.

"A really progressive one. They actually allow the male teachers to have long hair and beards." He ran a hand through his own hair as if to illustrate. I didn't comment that it wasn't all that long.

He got ready to move back to McAllister. "Ronni didn't want to go. We had a big fight. The first, but not the last. Finally, we compromised, the one and only time. She'd keep working for the Jacobsen Agency and go to Atlanta for assignments, stay as long as necessary, then come back."

That went on for almost two years, Veronica commuting to Atlanta, staying the length of the shoot, then driving back, while May continued teaching. Then Fight Number Two began.

May wanted her to quit and become a housewife and a mother. She told him she was definitely not domestic and never planned to be. As for motherhood...

"We'd already discussed it and I thought it was

settled. Hell, we'd been married almost two years. Things were going well, or so I thought. Seemed to me it was a fine time to start thinking about making babies."

The fights got longer, as did the assignments. Something came up causing May to call the agency, needing to get in touch with Veronica. He learned she hadn't been with Jacobsen for six months but had signed with another agency. They gave him the name. He called, got a runaround that easily aroused his suspicions. He drove to Atlanta and found not only was his wife *working* for the agency, but she was sleeping with the owner.

"Divorce proceedings were finalized three months later." He wiped the napkin across his mouth, dropped it to the table and stood up. "Finished? Want to have coffee in the living room?"

I glanced at my plate. The steak was half-eaten, but everything else had disappeared.

"I'm afraid that steak was too big for me." I was apologetic.

Where had my usually overwhelming appetite gone?

"No problem." He was at the sideboard, pouring coffee into delicate cups. Oddly, they didn't look out of place in his hands. "I'll save it for lunch." He handed me a cup and smiled. "Doubt if you've got any germs that'll mow me down."

"Would you like me to help you clear the table?" Since this appeared nothing like the usual dinner date, I decided I'd ask.

"I'll do it later." He brushed aside my offer and led me back into the living room, where I sat on the sofa while he stood at the hearth.

"May I ask you something?" I'd been wondering

about it while he was talking. Things were going well, though most of it was a surprise, and I knew he still might get angry but I was curious.

"*Ask me no questions and I'll tell you no lies,*" he quoted. "What is it, Gracie?"

"All this…" I gestured around me. "As you've pointed out, cost a lot of money. Who paid for it? You mentioned Veronica's family…"

"*I* paid for it." He didn't sound so much angry as wanting to make that perfectly clear. "Contrary to popular belief, my beloved rich in-laws never spent a bit of their money on us after they paid for that award-winning wedding."

He set his cup on the mantel and dropped down beside me on the sofa.

"You see, Daddy decided to straighten up and fly right after Billy was born."

I stifled a smile. It sounded odd to hear a grown man call his father "Daddy."

"He got his GED, went to night school, and got a good job. Then he invested his money in a business he'd heard about that had just gone public. A certain computer software company."

"I see."

Former Bad Boy made it big and his sons profited.

"In spite of the fact most teachers are still paid lower salaries than other professions, I make good money, and I'd saved quite a bit before I got caught in the Veronica web. Still got a lot of it, so I don't have any need for anyone's money but my own." May was proud of that, I could tell, and I was glad he wasn't insulted by my question. He stopped, as if waiting for some smart reply from me.

I let the opportunity slide, putting a big period to the subject of Veronica Smallwood Donovan. "How about giving me that tour now?"

****

There was a basement, made into a den/playroom complete with billiard table and plasma television, and a bedroom May had converted into an office. There were more bookshelves and a recliner in front of the television, with a small table nearby on which an opened, but empty can of soda, a small crumb-filled saucer, and a couple of paperbacks rested, the only untidy note in the whole house. Combined with the untouched atmosphere, as well as the dust, upstairs, it wasn't difficult to see this was where May spent most of his time when home, and not in the display-window rooms of the house.

As we came back to the main floor, he glanced at the stairs leading upward, then guided me back into the living room, saying, "There are four bedrooms upstairs."

"I don't get to see those?" I spoke before I thought.

"Gracie girl, if I take you upstairs, it ain't gonna be to look at the rooms." That sounded more like the old Mayfield I'd kept alive in my memory. His grip on my arm tightened as he steered me away from the stairs and temptation.

"Four bedrooms?" I decided to ignore that remark as I sat down again. "A lot of space for just one person."

"I didn't expect to live here alone," he answered. Again, some bitterness seeped out. "We were going to have at least three kids, to fill those bedrooms. But…"

He shook his head. For just a minute, I saw real anger before he got it under control. When he laughed, there was no happiness in the sound.

"So, here I sit…in a house with empty rooms…no

wife, no kids…"

"Have you ever thought about selling it and…"

"No!"

I didn't get a chance to finish and his reply was so quick and brusque I knew I'd hit a nerve.

"This place belonged to my great-grandparents. My grandparents lived here, and so did Daddy when he and my mother were married, as well as when Billy was born. He gave it to me as a wedding present."

"I'm sorry, May. I didn't know."

"Being the stupid gentleman I am, I let Ronni file for divorce. She tried to take the house from me simply because she knew how much it meant." His mouth twisted slightly as he told me what his lawyer had said to the judge.

Four generations of Donovans have lived in that house, Your Honor. My client lived there as a child and it's now his only residence. Mrs. Donovan resides in Atlanta and she's gainfully employed and asking no alimony, so why should she force my client to sell the only home he's ever known and share the money with her?

"I can only thank God the judge was a levelheaded man." May turned to look at me.

I guess I must've appeared thunderstruck or something equally shocked, because he laughed and this time, while it wasn't completely happy, it was no longer bitter.

"God, listen to me, carrying on as if I'm the only one in the world who's had a problem. How about you, Gracie? Care to unload a little and make it even?"

"Nope. Sorry. I've lived a pretty calm and uneventful life since I shook the dust of McAllister from my boots."

"I'm glad." He caught my hands, pulling me to my feet. "You deserve it, Gracie. But right now..." He fell silent.

Here it was. The inevitable moment when we stared at each other.

I was aware once again of how tall May was, and something else I hadn't noticed before, or refused to notice...how very, very masculine. In that way making a woman aware of it without his ever saying or doing the least obvious thing. I'd only had one glass of wine, diluted by another of tea, so I couldn't fall back on that excuse, but I couldn't remember how many May might have had.

He leaned toward me.

He's going to kiss me. I braced myself, startled, as I realized I wanted him to. I thought of what he'd said about taking me upstairs...

"Guess I'd better get you home." He straightened and went into the dining room, retrieving my purse from where I'd hung it over the back of my chair.

Was that really what he'd intended? Was I actually disappointed?

Silently, I accepted the purse. Draping it over my shoulder, I allowed him to lead me to the door as he scooped his keys off the credenza.

We didn't say much on the drive back to town. All I could think was how I'd almost made a fool of myself. May obviously didn't have any designs on me. After all, he'd had plenty of chances to make passes or anything else while we were completely alone in his house, and he'd been a gentleman.

I was disappointed.

Damn it. I think I actually wanted him to try so I could shoot him down in flames. Or did I? I'd never know now. The moment was gone.

Perhaps it was for the best. It might've been a disaster anyway. Besides, I'd be leaving town day after tomorrow, and there was no sense in doing anything to leave a bad taste behind. Or starting something for which there'd be no finish. May had apparently buried the past, so I should as well.

At the Manor, he walked me to the revolving doors. "I won't go inside, but I'm going to stay right here and make sure you get in all right."

He did exactly that. Watched me go through the doors into the lobby before returning to the convertible. Then he sat there.

I headed to the elevator, stopping as a call came from the desk.

"Ms. McAllister?" Tammy's nightshift counterpart came toward me, a small card in his hand. "You had a phone call while you were out."

I took the little note. It was from Jefferson Simmons. *Place of reading changed. Abigail has requested it be held at McAllister Place at 9 a.m.*

The present Mrs. McAllister had decided to have the reading of the will at home. At the last minute. Okay.

I looked up to see May still standing there, raised a hand to wave, then punched the *Up* button. Behind me, I heard the car's engine. The elevator doors opened. When I walked in and turned around, May was gone.

Chapter 5

"Since everyone's present," Jefferson Simmons smiled at us as if we were at a church picnic instead of a will reading, "we may as well get started."

There was a loud sigh from somewhere. I couldn't tell which of the eager heirs it came from…Ben…Sammi…Abigail? I'd been introduced to each, but it was a brief and tentative thing. We'd all gone straight to the library and sat there, not speaking, to await the lawyer's arrival.

He'd been punctual, coming through the door as the clock in the foyer began striking nine. There were shakings of hands with Ben, a gentle pat on Abigail's shoulder, a hug for Sammi, and another for me. Then he sat at the huge mahogany desk dominating the room and made his announcement as he pulled a manila envelope out of his valise. He made a big show of placing it on the desk, holding it up and saying, "Please verify this hasn't been opened before now, as per Benjamin Troup's instructions," before breaking the seals.

I leaned my chin against my hand and let my gaze rove idly around the room.

This was a genuine library, just like they showed in the movies…books on four walls, the only break in the monotony of the shelves being the door entering from the foyer and two large windows on the outer walls.

There was a large, ornate light fixture overhead that

missed being called a chandelier by a mere fraction, and little tables with reading lamps placed strategically.

Most of the chairs had been drawn up to the desk. They were big and comfy and it made for a crowded arrangement. I tried to imagine myself as a child curling up with a storybook in one of those chairs.

It didn't work.

The volumes on the shelves were too thick. None of them looked as if they'd hold any interest for a kindergartner.

A large fireplace intruded on one inner wall, and above it was a portrait. When we came in, Sammi whispered to me, "That's Daddy," and all I could think was if any man looked less like he wanted to be called *Daddy*, it was the subject of that painting. She'd also said it was done a couple of years after Mama and I left, so perhaps that was why there was such an aura of anger and pent-up emotion in the painted face.

Don't get me wrong. Benjamin Troup McAllister was handsome, but he looked belligerent…forceful…a man who wanted things his way, and perhaps was cruel when he didn't get them. Maybe that's why he looked as he did, because something happened he couldn't prevent. His wife walked out, never to return.

The artist had captured what he thought he'd kept well hidden. The painting was a three-quarter, showing him sitting in a chair, possibly the high-backed one behind the desk. It looked like a throne, and he was the king occupying it…tall, blue-eyed, dark-haired, and furious that his queen had abandoned him.

"I, Benjamin Troup McAllister, Junior…" Mr. Simmons' words broke into my thoughts.

Funny, I'd never thought of my father as being

named after someone. Perhaps that's why everyone used his full name, to differentiate from his own father.

"...being of sound mind, do this day set forth in this last will and testament, the distribution of my monies and properties and also certain admonitions to be put into effect after my death."

God, that sounds ominous. I hoped he hadn't put in some weird stipulation like I had to live at McAllister Place for a year and a day to get whatever he'd left me.

As far as I was concerned, the will was set up to get the small stuff out of the way first. Mr. Simmons was going through a list of charities and other non-profit organizations to which thousands were being left, as well as smaller bequests, but still in the thousands, to various people who appeared to be employees.

All I could think was, *How much money did he have, anyway?*

Quite a bit, it appeared, if the amount already handed out, as well as the looks of the house, were any indication, but none had ever come to me in the way of child support, as far as I could remember.

"...to my beloved wife, Abigail Marsh McAllister, I give permission to continue to live in the domicile called McAllister Place..."

Now that's generous. Would she be kicked out with just the clothes on her back if he hadn't written that?

I glanced at Abigail.

She was a small woman, her face the kind another era would've described as *piquant* with a slightly tip-tilted nose. Blonde, blue-eyed, slender...with a shock, I realized she reminded me of my own mother. *Aha...* dear ol' Dad was a repeat offender, on his second time around marrying a woman who reminded him of the one who got away.

I hoped he hadn't made her pay for what Mama did.

Obviously he hadn't, because she was sitting there, tears trickling down her cheeks, hands clenched in her lap. Not the ostentatious sniffling into a linen hankie that's always portrayed on screen, but the silent sobs of a woman grieving.

I looked away, not wanting to be caught staring, and listened to Abigail be rewarded for her nineteen years of being my father's consort with a stipend of $50,000 a year for life "to spend in any way she pleases," the majority stockholders' share in several corporations, and a few other things sounding minor in comparison to the first two.

Another fact I'd just learned. My family owned quite a few businesses in Georgia, and a couple of franchises as well. I thought of the many things my mother had been unable to buy without first doing much budgeting and saving, and how she'd always refused to shop at certain stores, the ones I now learned were owned by my father.

Simmons paused a moment, gazing at Abigail as if to give her time to compose herself.

She raised her eyes to his. I thought she was going to speak. I had it already phrased in my mind she was going to tell him she'd give it all up to have Benjamin Troup back.

Instead, she nodded quietly. "Thank you, Jefferson. please continue."

Quiet, gracious, a real lady.

Clearing his throat, Mr. Simmons looked back at the papers in his hand. "To my son, Benjamin Troup the Third…"

I glanced at Ben. At least they'd been allowed to shorten *his* name. To keep from confusing him with his father, of course. He might even have been called Benji when he was small, I'll bet.

Ben was going to be a looker, too, once he'd completely grown up. Dark-haired and blue-eyed like his father, though his hair was tied back in a tangled ponytail and he sported a wispy millennium patch on his chin. He was going to be tall, though right now he was still gangly and lanky, being only eighteen. He was wearing a Georgia college sweatshirt, and jeans I'm certain his father would've cringed to see.

I hadn't really met Ben.

Earlier, as my car neared the front of the house, a butter-yellow sportscar zoomed past me, swerving in front of the little car and screeching to a stop, sending dirt flying. In the meantime, I was slamming on the brakes also, and kicking up my own dust to avoid a rear-end collision. I was glad I wasn't in a convertible.

As I sat there waiting for the dust to settle, a young man hopped out of the driver's side, slammed the door, and dashed up the front steps, taking them two at a time. Flinging open the screen and front door, he went inside, letting them slam shut behind him.

He didn't look around or say a word, not asking if I was all right, or acknowledging he'd almost caused a crash of the two cars.

That was our only introduction.

Ben perked up as he heard his name. He'd been sitting there fidgeting, obviously not wanting to be here, and just as obviously ready to leave. Perhaps that was the reason for his haste and rudeness before. I wouldn't be surprised if as soon as his portion was finished, he jumped up and ran out.

Abigail reached over and placed a hand over his, patting it. That made him look at her, return the pat, and let the impatient movements subside. For about two seconds.

"…I leave an allowance of $30,000 a year, and the admonition he spend it wisely, for there are to be no advances. The estate will also continue to pay the insurance on the sportscar he now drives, though the title is to stay in my wife's name with the stipulation that use of it be taken away permanently if he gets any citation for a traffic violation more serious than a parking ticket…"

Remembering our little encounter, I wondered if Ben was generally a reckless driver and this was his father's way of trying to keep his son safe. I wondered how recently the will had been made. Had he had some premonition he was going to die soon?

"… I also am providing enough funds to pay his tuition to college and law school, including matriculation fees, books, dormitory charges, and meals, plus he is to pledge to the fraternity of which I was a member…"

Ben's face darkened at that, lips compressing. So Ben Three wasn't really wild about an extended university stay? Becoming an attorney? Or the frat?

"…providing he maintains at least an A- average in all subjects. At the end of any semester in which he has any grade lower than that, funds will be terminated immediately."

Ben stiffened. He started to get up. Abigail's hand on his kept him in his chair. He sat there in frustrated silence, pinned by that deceptively small grip on his fingers while he was further told he was being given twenty-four percent of the remaining shares in all companies.

That did it. He was on his feet, wrenching his hand from Abigail's before Simmons could finish.

"That's bullshit. Twenty-four percent? Does that mean Sammi gets more than I do? What the fuck, Jeff? Hell, I'm his only son, and the oldest. I should be the one getting the larger share!"

"Benji…" Abigail reached up, catching at his arm. He shook her off.

"No, Mama. I'm sick of this. He ran my life while he was alive and now he's trying to run it from the grave. I don't want to go to college, I don't want to be in a fraternity, and I damn sure don't want to be a lawyer." He was around the chair, pausing at the door to look back. "I'm contesting it, Mr. Simmons. I'm getting my own attorney and fighting that damned thing."

With that he was gone. Footsteps clattered, doors slammed, a car engine roared into life, and wheels screamed. Silence prevailed, shocked and embarrassed.

Abigail said, quietly, "He's upset. Can anyone blame him? Please, Jefferson, hurry on and let's get the rest over with."

Sammi was next on the list.

Samantha. A sweet kid, from the brief conversation I'd had with her. Sixteen, a feminine version of her brother. Going to be tall and willowy, long dark hair falling in an untidy, ruffled shag, blue eyes probably mischievous when they weren't upset as they were right now. She'd greeted me with a hug.

I'm so glad to finally meet you. You can't imagine how I've wondered about you for so long.

"To my daughter, Samantha…" She sat up straighter

as the lawyer spoke her name, biting her lip and looking anxious.

Sammi was given an allowance just as Ben had. No mention of her car or driving ability. Funds for her education were also waiting for her. Unlike her brother, however, she was given permission to attend the college of her choice, her grades only had to be at the B level, and nothing was said of a sorority. As Ben guessed, she was given the majority of the remaining stock, to be handled for her until she became of legal age, again like Ben's shares.

She didn't say anything, just nodded.

I looked around. No one left except *moi*. Oh, Lord, after seeing how he treated the two children who'd lived with him, what was in that document for me?

"And last, but not least, there is the matter of Grace Stephanie McAllister."

The matter of...? I tensed, turning my attention to the man behind the desk. He'd stopped, was rapidly scanning the rest of the document and scowling.

He looked up, meeting my eyes. "I…Grace, I'm not certain I should read this aloud. Perhaps you could stop by my office? And we can…"

"Nothing doing," I said, realizing I sounded like Ben. "Do it here and now, Mr. Simmons, and let's get it over with."

"Very well." He didn't look too happy about that. "But first, let me say I had no idea what this will contained."

I nodded, letting him off the hook. He cleared his throat once again, more out of nervousness this time.

"…the matter of Grace Stephanie McAllister…" He hesitated an instant, then continued, "If you are present at this reading, as I imagine you will be, out of curiosity, if nothing else…"

You got that pegged right, Daddy.

"I leave you… nothing."

What? I visibly jerked. *Nothing? I came all this way for nothing?* Abigail's head came up. She looked shocked. Sammi stared from the lawyer to me.

"Though my name is on your birth certificate, you are not my daughter," Mr. Simmons plowed on, not looking anywhere except at the will now. "This fact was confessed to me by my first wife, Miriam Baker McAllister the night she left my home forever. Your mother was pregnant when I married her, though I was unaware of that fact at the time. I was led to believe your birth was a premature one. From the moment I learned this until now, I have not paid one cent toward your upbringing and don't intend for you to have a penny of my estate. Let this document be my official acknowledgement of Miriam's duplicity and her daughter's illegitimacy. I also wish you, Grace McAllister, to no longer use my name. Funds have been set aside for you to legally have it changed to your mother's maiden name. I suggest you do this immediately."

There was a slight pause before Simmons read the last words in a hasty mumble.

"So signed and sealed this day and in the presence of these witnesses, Benjamin Troup McAllister, Junior, August 2."

The silence after that last word trailed away was, to use a familiar cliché, thunderous.

My ears were ringing. I could feel my face getting hot, then cold, and my vision clouding. I wondered if I were about to faint. I didn't feel as if I could move. All I could do was sit there, thoughts whirling around and colliding against each other inside my head.

He wasn't my father...but she said I looked like him...she admitted it...pregnant before they married... Did that mean my mother slept around? Or had it been one of those accidents and my real father wouldn't marry her and Benjamin Troup was there and handy and willing? *Oh God... And now everyone knows...*

Not everyone, not the whole world, but people who now mattered. People I had hoped to build relationships with. My half-brother and sister...now *not* my half-brother and sister, complete strangers, not related by one gene, chromosome or drop of blood...

I was completely alone in the world.

"Grace?" A hand touched my shoulder.

I looked up, blinking. Abigail was standing there, Sammi hovering behind her.

Mr. Simmons was gone. I hadn't heard him leave but I couldn't blame him. To be the person springing that on anyone, even though he hadn't been aware beforehand... He was such a nice man, a gentleman. I'm certain he was as shaken as the rest of us, and just wanted to get out of sight as fast as possible.

"Grace, I'm so sorry. I assure you I had no idea."

"I-I guess no one did," I managed to get the words out. "Especially m-me."

Damn it, in about two minutes, I'm going to be bawling.

"Please." She caught my arm, pulling me to my feet and I let her.

I felt like a puppet, legs and arms a-tangle, someone else manipulating the strings, making me move. I wished

Ben were there. I had a feeling he'd have said exactly what everyone was feeling at his father's bombshell, in no uncertain terms and as many four-letter words as possible.

"You're upset. Come upstairs and lie down."

She was pushing me out of the library and toward the stairs as she spoke. I felt a smaller hand touch my other arm.

Sammi.

I didn't look around, remembering how the girl had hugged me, so delighted to finally meet her *big sister.* Now I was nothing to her.

"N-no." Gently, I extricated my arm from Abigail's grasp. "I'm going back to the Manor. I...think...I'd like to be alone just now."

"Will you be all right?"

Did she think I was going to drive my car off the road or into a bridge pylon or something?

I made my head nod. "I just need to think." I managed a half-hearted and completely false laugh. "After all, it's not every day a girl finds out she's a bastard, is it?"

She winced. I knew I shouldn't have said it, just as I knew if I didn't get away from her sympathy, and her horror at how cruel her husband could be, even deceased, I'd completely break down and sob out my distress in her obviously-waiting maternal arms.

I turned toward the door, pulling away from Sammi, also. Then I stopped.

"Th-thank you, Abigail." I remembered my manners. *Thank your hostess, even if you've just been slammed into the mud and kicked in the face.* "I-it was k-kind of you to..."

I didn't finish, just opened the door and ran down the steps to my car.

I didn't pay attention to the fact someone followed, just fumbled for my keys, and got in.

"Grace." As I slammed the door, Sammi caught up to me, hand on the open windowsill. "What will you do now?"

"I've a reservation on a flight out tomorrow. I'm going to take it." What was I supposed to do? "I'll go back to California and pick up where I left off."

It wouldn't be exactly where I left off, however, because I was now no longer Grace *McAllister*.

"Does that mean I'll never see you again?"

I didn't answer.

"Grace…" She tried again, took a deep breath, and blurted, "I don't give a damn who your daddy is. You're my sister, Grace, and I want you to stay long enough for me to get to know you. Please?"

"I-I…don't…know." I think that's what I said. "I have to think."

I started the car. She stepped back. I guided it out of the semicircular drive and back onto the highway. I looked back once. In the settling dust in the rearview mirror, Sammi still stood there.

****

Back at the Manor, I went straight to my room, grateful there were people checking in and neither Tammy nor the other clerk spoke to me. Locking the door behind me, I threw myself on the featherbed and sank into it, giving vent to the tears I'd wanted to shed.

I wondered how long it'd be before everyone in town knew. I was certain Jefferson Simmons wouldn't tell, but I wasn't so sure about his secretary. As for

Ben…

He'd struck me as the type to find someplace where there were as many of his peers as possible and blurt out the whole thing. He might not know about my non-inheritance yet, but I imagined he was probably already getting commiseration for his father's unreasonable requests, and when he returned home and learned of my humiliation, he'd just add them to the list.

No doubt by this time tomorrow everyone in McAllister would know about me, and about my mother, and I wouldn't be able to walk down the street without the whispers and stares. Sammi's wishes to the contrary, and I really did hate to disappoint her, the faster I went back home, the better.

Eventually, I was all cried out. Raising my head from the tear-soaked pillow, I stumbled into the bathroom. Snatching a couple of tissues from the box on the vanity, I wiped my eyes, blew my nose, and stared at my reflection in the mirror. Red-laced brown eyes, a scarlet nose, and a trembling mouth stared back at me, as well as a couple of truths.

Why hadn't I seen it before? Because it wasn't thrown in my face, that's why.

A tiny hope inside insisted this was all a mistake. That Benjamin Troup was just having his last chance at revenge. I knew that wasn't so and the mirror now proved it. My mother had been blonde and I'd always thought I got my red hair from my father. Hadn't she said I looked like him?

Benjamin Troup was dark-haired, and blue-eyed. Mama had been blue-eyed, too… *I have brown eyes.* Two blue-eyed people can't produce a brown-eyed child. Hadn't I learned that in Freshman Biology 11?

Abigail was blonde and blue-eyed but neither Ben nor Sammi looked like her. They both looked like their father, his darker genetic heritage strong enough to overcome hers. If I were truly his, I'd be blue-eyed and most likely brunette, too, and I'd have a strong nose and that broad McAlister face, just as they did.

Nothing to do but accept it and soldier on. I washed my face, combed my hair, and freshened my makeup, promising myself I wasn't going to start crying again and wash it away a second time. Then…

I'm going downstairs to the bar, and buy myself a drink…or two…or three.

The coward's way out, but so what? Call me a coward. At that precise moment, being a coward was better than being a bastard. At least now I knew why Mama never attempted to get child support.

Yes, I was going to the bar and dull the shock with strong drink. Then I'd get into the elevator and come back to my room and fall asleep and forget today completely.

Deciding that, I got my purse and headed for the bar in the Manor's restaurant.

That was where May found me, two hours later.

Chapter 6

"Celebrating, are we?"

The question, asked in that jovial tone, made me glare at the speaker. It was May, looking so bright and happy, I wanted to deck him. I remembered the thought I'd had about him upon my arrival.

Son of a bitch. You know who your father is. I shouldn't hold that against him, but sudden rage buried my previous decision to let bygones be bygones.

"Not especially," I managed to grate out, not daring to speak louder. If I did, I just might say something I'd regret.

Though I intended to get drunk, I hadn't accomplished that, so far. Not being much of a drinker to start with, I'd ordered my usual alcoholic fare, a Tom Collins, and proceeded to guzzle it and order a second, then a third and a fourth. The bartender hadn't blinked an eye at someone drinking at that time of morning, but either he deliberately made them weak or a Collins wasn't that strong to start with, for so far, I barely had a buzz.

I went back to my drinking.

"So? How'd it go?" May tried again. "Am I talking to an heiress now, or what?"

"More of a *what*."

This time I didn't look at him, just pulled the little plastic sword out of my drink and attacked the slice of orange skewered on it, biting it off the tiny blade with my teeth. I chewed, swallowed, and dropped sword and rind to join the others on the table. Abruptly, I felt all the energy flow out of me, as if I'd been punctured. With it went my unreasonable anger at May.

"Isn't it a little early in the day for that?" He nodded toward the empty frosted glasses that hadn't been taken away yet.

"As far as I'm concerned, it isn't early enough," I answered.

I picked up the fourth glass and tilted it, slurping out the last of the gin and lemon juice. I held up the glass.

"You know, they used to call this gin and sparkling lemonade. They should leave out the lemonade and put in more gin. Hey!" I looked toward the bar, waving the glass and gesturing.

The bartender nodded and reached for an empty Collins glass.

"Wait up on that, son," May ordered. "Gracie, what the hell happened?" He pulled out the other chair, falling into it. Taking the glass from me, he set it down, then caught both my hands in his, leaning toward me. To anyone seeing us, we probably looked like lovers huddled together, whispering sweet nothings.

My nothings were anything but sweet.

"Oh, May…" It came out in a gush of tears and anger. He just sat there, listening.

He didn't speak at all until I'd finished and was crying as silently as Abigail had. Reaching into a pocket, he produced a handkerchief, offering it.

"I knew Benjamin Troup was a son of a bitch," he said as I blotted and honked. "But I didn't realize he'd stoop that low. Gracie, I'm sorry."

"Not as sorry as I am." I snorted once more into the handkerchief, then folded it carefully. "Do you want this back?"

"Keep it until you're sure you don't need it." He spoke absently.

Did he expect me to cry some more? A river, maybe? That wouldn't work. People only cried rivers over other people they loved.

The bartender brought my fresh drink.

"It's weak," he said in answer to May's scowl, setting it down and removing the other glasses to a tray without commenting on my current emotional state. I picked it up and took a long swig.

"Do you really need that?"

I was dismayed by the concern and disapproval in his voice.

"Maybe not, but I want it. I want to forget today completely. When I wake up in the morning, I want to know this specific date in time never existed." I raised the glass higher, gulping.

"Keep that up and Wednesday won't be the only thing missing." He caught my hand, forcing the glass to the table. The next instant he was up and reaching for me. "Come on."

"Wh-where are we going?" He lifted me from my chair and set me on my feet.

As I jerked around to look at him, I felt dizzy. My head seemed to spin. I blinked and caught at the back of the chair to steady myself.

"Away from here." Arm around my waist, he steered me to the door. "If you're going to drink yourself pie-eyed, at least go somewhere not so public."

"…can't drive…" I protested.

"Don't worry, I'll be there to make sure you get home safely."

"In that case..." I leaned against him and caught his free hand. My legs felt very lax and wobbly. "I may need just a teensy bit of help getting to wherever we're going."

I was certain Tammy was watching from the desk as he marched me across the lobby and out the door. I didn't even question why he hadn't just taken me upstairs and dumped me onto my bed.

We went through the side door. I doubt he could've managed maneuvering both himself and me through the revolving one. The muscle car waited patiently in the same parking space as it had the previous night. He had me inside and strapped in before I realized it.

When he got in, he sat there staring at me. I kept my gaze on the hood of the car, watching how the overhead streetlight changed its color to a deeper, duller hue. Dark red. Like dried blood. *Like May's hair.* Why hadn't I noticed that the night before?

"Are we going somewhere I can get another drink?" I thought to ask.

"I think right now what you need is lots of people and loud music and a chance to talk," he decided.

He started the engine and pulled the car away from the curb.

****

The place was called Shedd's. I guess it would've been categorized as a dive, a pre-fab on the southern outskirts of McAllister, with a bar, a dance floor and band, and two pool tables. It was noisy all right, and filled with people, meeting May's requirements perfectly, but we weren't doing much talking. Currently I was the only one saying anything. I thought of what

May had said about drinking in public. In spite of the crowd, Shedd's was about as un-public as you could get. No one even gave us a glance.

In the plate glass window, a neon sign flickered, making garish pink and blue streaks across the table where we sat. For a while, I stared at that one word as it blinked backwards at us. It was hypnotic and I finally had to turn away as I felt myself wanting to nod off every time I paused in my endless harangue.

Maybe May had decided it was better to sit with me and be quiet while I continued to hash and re-hash what had happened at McAllister Place, beating that particular dead horse into smithereens. Whatever the reason, he hadn't said much since we got here, except for an occasional expletive.

"I don' unnerstand," I said for the umpteenth time, my words slurring. "Why do it? 'Spesh'ly like *that*?" I lifted my drink.

Yes, I'd insisted on ordering another one. Ordering something was required at Shedd's, though May attempted to order me some sparkling water.

"Think about it." He caught my arm before I could get the glass to my mouth. He'd been doing that for some time, his way of keeping me from drinking any more than I had to since I'd insisted on an alcoholic drink. Nevertheless, I'd still managed to put away quite a bit. There was an open bottle of beer on the table before him, but I doubted if he'd taken even three swallows from it.

May was determined one of us was going to stay sober.

"If he'd let it be known when he divorced your mother, he'd have been a laughingstock...the great Benjamin Troup...cuckold."

It was such an archaic word it made me lower the glass to stare at him. I stifled a snicker. Right then I was thinking of much more descriptive ones.

"This way, even though he's not around to savor the moment, he gets his revenge by humiliating you, and by extension, labeling your mother a whore."

I winced slightly at his frankness.

"And coming out as a saint." His voice went up into a mocking falsetto. *"That poor man, knowing all these years that child wasn't his and not telling anyone. How noble."*

"M' ex-father's def-nit'ly *not* a nice man." I brushed a hand across my forehead. The noise was becoming too loud and the room too hot and too dark. I peered at May through the dim light. *Was his image actually wavering?*

Setting down the glass, I leaned my cheek against my hand and closed my eyes. I was *so* tired.

"That's an understatement," May muttered.

Behind us, someone pushed away from the bar and staggered toward the door. As he passed our table, he stopped.

"Well…hel-lo, former sister." The voice was drunk but familiar.

"Ben?" I opened my eyes and swung around, nearly overbalancing. I grabbed at the table to keep from sliding out of my chair.

"Hey, Grace." He stumbled over to the table. "Hey, Mr. Donovan."

"Ben." There was disapproval in May's voice.

"You two know each other?"

Idiot, this is McAllister. It was a stupid thing to ask, but the way May said Ben's name held something more than just a nodding acquaintance.

"Mr. Donovan's m' 'visor at Wil'wood."

"And Ben's one of my best students," May added and fixed the boy with what had to be his *stern teacher* stare. "Unless he spoils it all by getting picked up for drunk driving. Since when did you become twenty-one?"

"Since I gotta fake ID." Ben flipped out his wallet, snapping it open and waving it in front of May, who pulled it out of his hand.

"Damn it, Ben." He pointed to the third chair at the table. "Sit down. This is why Shedd's gets closed every other week."

I noticed he didn't give the wallet back but set it on the table next to his bottle.

"Sorry 'bout what happ'ned, Grace." Ben weaved around to look at me.

"Sammi told you, I 'spose?"

"Called me an' cried it all int' m' ear." He nodded. "Looks like dear ol' Dad screwed us both. You're no longer a McAllister an' I won't be goin' t' Juilliard."

Juilliard? My eyebrows went up.

"Ben's a very gifted pianist," Ben explained. "I was helping him apply. But now…"

"Not goin' t' be a lawyer, don' care what fam'ly tradition dictates," Ben declared. "An' if that means I'm onl' good for baggin' groceries at the local grocery store when I graduate, I'll do that 'fore I give in to what *he* wanted."

High-sounding words. I wondered how long it would take for Ben to cave after he met the Real World.

He looked at me again. "What're you goin' t' do now, Grace?"

"Go back home, I guess." I'd have thought that was obvious.

Ben fell silent. In exact copy of my own posture, he leaned his chin into his palm, his head tilted toward mine, eyelids drooping. We probably made a great picture.

Two Drunken People.

"With your grades, you should be able to get some scholarships and financial aid," May said.

"Ri'." Ben didn't sound as if he were listening. In fact, he sounded semi-conscious.

I wondered how many drinks he'd had. How long it would take for the police to be raiding the place? That's all I needed. To get arrested. Was I going to be calling David to bail me out? To fly across country and defend me in court? He wasn't a criminal lawyer. Did that mean he couldn't take a criminal case?

"I mean it. Look, go home," May ordered. "Sleep it off. When school's in session, we'll see just what kind of help you're eligible for. This is one time Benjamin Troup isn't going to get his way."

"'kay." Ben pushed back his chair.

"But you're not driving." May held out his hand, wiggling his fingers.

Surprisingly, Ben didn't argue. With a grunt, he surrendered his keys. He didn't look as if he cared one way or the other.

May pulled his cell from his pocket. "What's McAllister Place's number?"

As Ben slurred it to him, he punched the keys. Someone answered immediately.

"Miz Abigail? Mayfield Donovan. I've got Ben here and he needs a ride." He listened a moment. "That's right. Shedd's. If you want to do that, you've my blessing. This is no place for kids, just us decadent adults. Just wait until we leave." He laughed as he said it. "He'll be waiting at the curb."

Stuffing the phone back into his pocket, he got up, scooped the wallet off the table, and walked around Ben. The next thing we knew, he was hauling him to his feet. "Come on, kid. Your mother's on her way."

"Really know how t' 'barrass a guy, doncha?" Ben came out of his stupor long enough to give him a baleful glance.

"Better embarrassment than a DUI charge or another funeral in the McAllister family so soon."

Ben didn't answer, just allowed May to half-carry him toward the door. I watched them disappear through it, then closed my eyes again. It seemed only seconds before May was back but I'm certain it was longer. I gave him a droopy glance, then shut my eyes once more as he sat down again. They didn't seem to want to stay open.

He was silent for exactly two seconds. "Know what you should do now?"

"Wha'?" I didn't open my eyes.

"Go to bed. Come on." I heard him push back his chair and stand up.

Go to bed? Great idea. I knew just who I wanted to do that with.

Before I could tell him, however, I felt his hand on my arm.

"Up you go, Gracie. You're almost out. Time for beddy-bye."

"Ri'."

He released me long enough to drop some bills onto the table, place the bottle on top of them, and steer me to the door. I forced myself to walk steadily when what I really wanted to do was drop to the floor and curl into a ball. Okay, so May was right and sleep was what I needed.

He frog-marched me outside and around the corner to his car. Ben was standing at the roadside. I gave him a sleepy glance as we passed. May pulled open the passenger door.

I fell onto the seat, managed to fasten my safety belt, then sat there, eyes closed, leaning against the headrest. As before, May didn't start the car right away, and I had a feeling he was sitting there studying me. When the engine finally came to life and we were moving, I forced my eyes open.

"I know m' sense o' d'rection's slightly off-center, but isn't th' Manor th' other way?"

"Give the girl two points. You're not going back to the Manor."

"Where'm I goin'?" I studied the buildings flying by.

May was driving pretty fast for the business district, but it was fairly late and maybe there were no cops lurking in one of McAllister's alleys just waiting for a certain red muscle car to zoom past. No prob for me if there were. I might be snockered but I wasn't driving.

Thank goodness.

"Home. With me."

My heart gave a jump but his next words knocked it back into place.

"You don't need to be alone tonight, Gracie."

That didn't sound amorous but more like someone offering to sit with a sick friend. *Okay, I'll take that.* At the moment, I wasn't sure what I wanted. The thought I'd just had, coupled with my continuing anger and hurt, was making all kinds of weird emotions coil inside me. Maybe friendship was what I needed at this point.

Nevertheless, something made me give him a lopsided leer.

"Oh? Just whatcha got in min', Mr. Donovan?"

"Nothing but your welfare, Miss McAllister."

"Not McAllister," I corrected, managing to squeeze out a tear that had survived being a victim of the other inundations. Now it was being sacrificed to self-pity. "I'm… Damn it, May. I dunno *who* I am now."

He didn't answer and I shut my eyes and stayed quiet. I didn't open them until the car stopped some twenty minutes later. What I saw was the now-familiar front porch of *Chez* Donovan.

****

He had to help me out of the car. Sitting still for so long had a bad effect on my muscles. They wanted to stay relaxed. After I'd twice taken two steps and had my knees buckle, he sighed and swung me into his arms.

"Don', May," I managed to protest. "I'm too heavy."

"Got that right," he answered with an exaggerated grunt. "What do you weigh, anyway?"

"Dunno…" I managed a drunken shrug and nearly flung myself out of his arms. His grip tightened. "Hunnert…ten?"

"Is that all?" He laughed. "Could've sworn it was at least a hundred and eleven."

He carried me up the steps.

There was an awkward bit of fumbling with keys to get the door open, with May pushing the screen out of the way a couple of times as it kept swinging closed to strike him on the shoulder. Eventually, we were inside and he set me on my feet in front of the stairs.

"Can you stand up while I get some sheets?"

"Gonna finally lemme see th' upstairs now? All four bedrooms?"

"There are *three* guestrooms, Gracie." He spoke patiently. "You can take your pick."

"Nope. I wan' th' one you're sleepin' in." There. I said it. No mistaking my meaning.

"Gracie…"

"Th'…whatchacallit?" I went on, determinedly. "Th' *master* bedroom. I wanna sleep with you, Master May."

I reached out, intending to pat his cheek. Instead, I swatted his chin.

"You're drunk, Gracie." Still holding onto my arm, he dodged easily.

Why was I surprised he was fighting it? Could it be he didn't want me as much as I was convincing myself I wanted him? At this point I didn't have to do much convincing.

"You don't mean that."

"No, I'm not, and yep, I do. Look!" I pushed away from him, holding up one hand, thumb and little finger pressed against my palm. "Three fingers." I closed my eyes and tapped the end of my nose. "Co'rdination fine." I opened my eyes again, looking up into those brilliant copper ones and flung my arms wide. "Take me upstairs, May."

I'm so damned eloquent. Guess I convinced him. He stared at me for one breathless moment that was so quiet we could've heard the beams shifting and the clock ticking on the mantel…if we'd been listening. All I could hear was May's breathing and a louder sound coming from inside me, the pounding of my heart.

It drowned out the world.

His hands slid to my waist.

Once again, as when we stood in front of the fireplace after dinner, I was overwhelmed by the man that was Mayfield Donovan. In that moment, everything about him seemed overpowering, though he wasn't moving or saying a word.

I could smell the faintest scent of aftershave, something familiar but elusive I knew I should recognize but couldn't, a fragrance giving his skin a fresh tang. There was smoke clinging to his shirt from the many cigarettes in the bar, and the barest hint of sweat, but the clean kind.

In the unlighted hallway before the stairs, he was nothing but a tall, dark shape looming over me, a single lamp in the living room making enough light that I could see the glint of that bronze hair. His hands were still at my waist, warm through the thin fabric of my sundress. Vaguely I remembered how worried I'd been that morning, wondering if I looked presentable.

Now? All I wanted to do was rip it off and throw my naked body at him. It hit me so hard I nearly cried out. *I want this man.* He might be a stranger, but he was one I'd known forever…and I wanted him.

What had happened to me to make that change?

Standing on tiptoe, I put my arms around his neck and pulled his head down, pressing my mouth to his. Our tongues touched. I tasted the residue of those three swallows of beer, mingling with all my Collinses. It should've been repulsive. Instead, it was arousing.

For just a moment, I felt him stiffen as if he'd pull away. Then his arms went around my waist and I was lifted off the floor as he straightened. I hung there, May's grasp all that kept me from falling. As he gently let me go, I slid down his body until my feet touched the floor again. May's hand on the back of my head pressed my cheek against his chest. He was breathing a little heavier now and his heart was pounding, too, and something else. His partial erection was pressing against my stomach.

"If you're sure?"

I nodded. There was so much heat flooding through me at that moment, I didn't dare try to speak.

May picked me up and started up the stairs. I kept one arm around his neck, resting my forehead against his cheek.

His room was at the end of a long, wide hall. The door was open and he left it that way as we went in. Some vestige of parental admonition still lingering?

He laid me on the bed as gently as he might a sleeping child. I thought of the many times he'd knocked me down. This was certainly an about-face. Had all that childhood bullying simply been a prelude to this?

When did we stop being enemies, May? Are we truly ready to be lovers?

He stood next to the bed now, looking down at me. The bedside lamp was on. It was in keeping with the décor of the rest of the house, fashioned to look like some kind of fuel lamp. I didn't bother trying to see the furniture, except to realize I was lying on a bed with massive posters, slowly sinking into a thick feather mattress. I was concentrating on only one thing just then. May. Who still hadn't moved. His expression was…odd…

My God. Is he afraid?

"I don't feel right about this, Gracie." He looked away. "I feel as if I'm seducing you."

"Feel right about it," I answered, making an effort to enunciate.

Fine time for May to become a gentleman. I wanted this and if I had to, *I'd* seduce *him*.

"I'm not drunk. I know what I'm doing. I'm not asking for comfort for today's disaster. Frankly, I don't know what I'm asking for, but let's not analyze it. Just let it happen."

"It's not like it isn't something I haven't wanted to do." He sat on the edge of the bed. That was a step in the right direction.

He leaned forward and kissed me again.

"From the minute I saw you standing by that little car." Another kiss, on my cheek, and a third, this one just under my ear. Hands touched the straps of my sundress. "Does this have any buttons?"

I shook my head, pushing myself up so I sat beside him. I reached behind me, fumbling inside the top of the dress.

"Built-in bra," I explained to his questioning look. I got it unhooked, wriggling the skirt from under me and he caught at the hem, pulling it over my head. It sailed into the darkness past the foot of the bed. My bikini panties followed.

Once again, he was silent. Resting a finger between my breasts, he trailed it downward, a featherlight touch making me shiver.

"Cold?" There was a quirk of his mouth.

"A-are you kidding?" I stuttered that word as the finger continued across my navel, my belly, and stopped. Gently, he touched the curls on my mound, fingers combing through them. He sat that way for several seconds before he smiled.

"What?"

"You'll find out. Later." He got up and began to undress, ridding himself of his boots first thing.

May's movements were matter-of-fact, not well rehearsed, no coy strip tease, titillating peeling, or hasty *just-can't-wait* stripping away of his garments. He just...undressed...as if it were something he did all the time when alone with me in his bedroom.

Like we'd done it often. Comfortable. Familiar.

He didn't have the typical redhead's skin coloring, all pinkness and freckles. The flesh showing above his jeans was evenly tanned.

For a teacher, he was buff. I nearly said so.

The revelation of all that dark bronze hair was dazzling, a brilliant mat of flaming curls forming a vee across his chest, then narrowing to a single love-trail divided by the deep dimple of his navel before disappearing into his button-fly jeans. They were low slung, revealing a narrow strip of untanned skin. He wasn't wearing a belt, and before his hand could touch that first button, I reached out, pulling it open. He let his hands drop, silently giving me permission to go on. I got the fly open. His erection sprang free. Maybe a penis isn't supposed to be called *beautiful* but this one was...thick, veins already pulsating but nowhere near fully engorged...

...*not yet*...

Another silent moment, this time no sound at all, no clock, no pounding hearts. I waited for him to make some facetious remark, ask me if I approved...did I think it could do the job...something stupid to ruin the moment.

He didn't say anything, didn't move except to slide off the jeans. I looked up at him. He was scowling slightly. Hands on May's hips, I leaned forward and kissed that delicate, smooth crown, then gently drew my tongue across the tip. He was still dry, but *very* warm.

With a gasp, May was on the bed, on me, arms around me, and I responded. It was a tangle of kisses, caresses, heated bodies, and his weight pressing me against the feather mattress. He touched me and I touched him, and we were both enjoying it. Soon, neither of us was dry…anywhere…he pushed away and sat up, gasping a little.

"Damn, Gracie!"

His hair was in his face. He was sweating, so it was sticking to his cheeks in wet little curls. I reached up and brushed one back, hooking it behind his ear.

"Are you ready? I sure's to hell am."

I nodded. He leaned toward me again, but this time I placed a hand on his chest.

"I hope you have a condom. I don't want to follow in my mother's footsteps."

That'd be the ironic end. I could almost hear it: *Well, like mother, like daughter…*

"Don't worry." He was reaching for the drawer in the bedside table as he spoke, feeling inside and holding up a little foil packet. "I'd never do that to you, Gracie."

"Mr. Boy Scout." I smiled. "All prepared?"

He sat up, swinging his legs and that magnificent erection over the side of the bed. There was another hesitation before he said, as he fiddled with the packet, "Don't think I do this often." He kept his head down, not looking at me. "I've been divorced four years, Gracie, but I've only brought two other women here. You're the third."

"You know what they say." I put my hand on his

thigh, gently stroking through the curly red hair. *Damn, the man's like a red teddy bear.* I wanted to kiss that thigh, run my tongue across his skin and discover if it tasted of sweat and that faint cologne I could still smell.

"What's that?" He did turn then, to lean over and kiss me again.

"Third time's the charm."

That made him laugh. He had the condom on now, crawling back to me. I moved my legs, making an avenue for him to lie between. He slid his arms under mine, lifting me slightly, and kissed me again. When he raised his head, his question was a whisper.

"Gracie, are you a virgin?"

"Would that matter?" *For God's sake.* I wanted to shake him.

He shook his head. "Only to make me go very slowly. I just want a heads-up if I'm going to hurt you. I did enough of that when we were kids."

He was deadly serious and it shook me a little.

"You aren't going to hurt me, May."

He reached between us, fumbling slightly. I felt the top of that most precious part of his body pressing between my legs. He pushed. There was that brief moment of discomfort. Then he was inside and I felt my own body expanding to encompass and make room for all of it, all of *him.*

My sharp inhalation made him ask quickly, "You all right?" and my soft, "I'm fine," reassured him.

God, he felt good. Nothing like the few other encounters I'd had. I'd always told myself all men were the same from the neck down, but not May. There was something different. I don't think it was his body. Maybe it was the heart and the mind within it, reaching out for my own heart and mind, giving me something I'd been wanting all my life.

Why the hell am I getting so poetic and philosophical at a time like this?

Arms stiff, he raised himself so he loomed above me, beginning that slow in-out. I lay still, passive until he set the rhythm, then I began to move with him. Suddenly he stopped, looking down with me.

"I don't know what the hell's happening. I just know from the moment I heard you were coming back I couldn't believe it. I wasn't in front of the Manor by accident that day. I love you, Gracie."

That stopped me cold. Something sliced through me that was freezing and searing at the same time.

This can't be happening.

"Are you sure you didn't sneak a couple of cold ones while I wasn't looking?" I tried to make it sound sarcastic when what I wanted to do was tell him the same thing.

Caution kept me from saying it. I was well aware words flung out during sex weren't always true. Emotions in bed make liars of us all.

"I'm stone cold sober. Only thing stiff is this." He reached down to cradle his latex-clad penis.

"Damn, May. I-I don't know what to say."

"Don't say anything. Say it's those three swallows of beer talking. Pretend I didn't say a word. Let's just make love."

We did. Make love. We didn't *have sex*. There's a world of difference.

I knew, in that moment, that whatever happened next, I'd finally found the *real* thing.

****

The next few hours were a maelstrom of emotion and sensation. We did things I knew and things I'd never known, with mouths, hands, other body parts. Afterward, we kissed and cuddled. May reached into the drawer again, lifting out the little box. As he extracted another packet, I asked, "How many are in there, anyway?"

"Six. I've five left."

So he'd used that particular box with no one but me.

"I bought it the day you arrived." It was as if he heard my thoughts.

"Pretty sure of yourself, weren't you?"

He laughed. "No, not at all."

What if *this,*" I motioned to our bodies, "hadn't happened?"

"In that case, they'd stay there until they expired."

"Let's save at least one for another day."

"I can always buy more." He tore the packet open.

Much, much later, May snuggled me against his side. I wrapped one arm around his waist, burrowed my cheek into his chest, and fell asleep to the steady beating of his heart.

Chapter 7

"Wake up, sleepyhead."

"Mmmm." I rolled over, yawning and stretching as I blinked and opened my eyes to the most mouthwatering sight I could've seen…a naked Mayfield Donovan lying next to me. His hair was mussed, hanging over his forehead and in front of his ears in bronze coils.

Oooh, baby. Man-candy. Yum.

I'd never say that out loud. Not yet, anyway.

May reached for me, pulling my body against his. I placed a hand on his stomach, studying that strip of white skin. It looked as if he'd been out in the sun a lot, with something very skimpy on. I envisioned him with a thong.

"May…?" I let my voice trail away.

"That's my name," he said cheerfully.

"Why?"

"Why *what*?" He was plumping pillows, settling against them.

"Why *Mayfield*. For a first name for a kid?" I'd always wondered about that.

"It was my mother's last name," he explained. "Christina Mayfield. Guess Daddy had delusions of grandeur, copying the way rich folks make their surnames into their children's first names." He laughed. "I sure didn't live up to that when I was a kid, did I?"

"I don't want to think about that right now." As far

as I was concerned, that red-headed hooligan of my childhood was gone forever.

"I'm sorry for that, Gracie." He kissed my forehead, the hand holding me against him starting to gently stroke my left breast.

I made a little purring noise. Honest to God. It felt good. I hoped he'd keep doing it.

"Hindsight's great, because now I know I *liked* you back then. *Really* liked you, but, being a child, I didn't know how to show it, or to get your attention, except to hit you or knock you down or… Afterward, I was always ashamed because I'd hurt you when what I wanted to do was the exact opposite." He laughed. "Thank God that was back then, because today I'd probably be labeled a bully, or worse."

"I have a feeling that, in a couple of years, you'd have grown out of it and we'd probably have started dating." I leaned into his hand.

"Through high school." He allowed himself to be drawn into the fantasy.

"And then you'd have gone away to college and we'd promise to write…"

"I'd ask you to come to Atlanta when I moved there, but you wouldn't want to leave McAllister."

"Then you'd meet Veronica and break my heart when you brought her back here." I said, letting reality set in. I looked away. "But I'd pretend I didn't care."

"And after she was gone, I'd discover exactly what I'd nearly lost by marrying her, and we'd be right where we are this minute," he finished.

"Are you suggesting all this was preordained?" I looked up at him.

He kissed me again, on the mouth this time. His

breath was minty, no morning-mouth. Had he gotten up and gargled and brushed his teeth while I was asleep? Should I have done the same?

"I'm suggesting there's a destiny that shapes our ends." He slapped my hip. "And it did a great job with yours."

As I laughed and rubbed the spot, he kicked away the sheets and got up. Okay, no early-morning nookie. Oh, well...

"Time to get up. Shower and meet the day. Time's a-wasting and we've got a lot to do."

"Like what?" I allowed him to pull me from the bed and lead me into the bathroom.

"Later." He was leaning into the shower stall as he spoke, spinning faucets.

****

While I dressed, May made breakfast. He had everything timed perfectly, appearing through the swinging door with two plates as I sat down at the dining table.

"Breakfast is served." The plate he placed before me held scrambled eggs, bacon, a mound of grits, and a slice of bread with a melted yellow rectangle spilling over its crust.

"You mean, dinner the other night wasn't merely a culinary fluke?" I picked up the bread, biting into it. Crusty wheat bread and melted mild cheddar blended sweetly on my tongue. "You even made cheese toast."

I slurped a string of cheese.

"I was taking a chance you'd like it." He poured coffee into a cup, dropping in three sugar cubes and splashing milk, then offered it to me. "There. A little coffee with your milk and sugar."

"How'd you know that?" I took a sip. Perfect. I could get used to this pampering. I wondered if it would disappear if I were around all the time.

"Mom and I spent a lot of time at your house, in spite of our one-sided animosity, and the fact that your fa— Benjamin Troup didn't like Daddy. Your mother didn't see anything wrong with giving children coffee, as long as it was greatly diluted."

"I like it fine." I indicated the toast as I picked it up again, returning to the original subject. "Mama used to make cheese toast for me all the time. I haven't had it in a while now."

I remembered how she'd always put it on a little saucer. I looked thoughtful.

"She said my father loved cheese toast. Why would she say that?"

"Because it was true?" he guessed. "Though, to my way of thinking, Benjamin Troup never looked like the kind who enjoyed much of anything except bossing other people around. Definitely not something as decadent and soul-satisfying as cheese toast." He bit into his, pulling it away so the cheese stretched into long yellow strings.

He gave his attention to his toast, lipping his way to the crust, sucking in cheese as he went. That gave me a little shiver, making me remember how his mouth had done the same thing to me last night.

"I mean, why would she tell me he liked cheese toast?" I stabbed eggs, shoveling in a forkful. "She was always saying something like that. *Your father...no, your daddy,* she always said *your daddy. Your daddy loved thunderstorms...you look so much like your daddy...you have your daddy's eyes...* I'd swear there was love in her voice when she said that. And then she'd turn around and rail about him. *Benjamin Troup is nothing but a power-crazy son of a bitch.* You could hear the venom." I thought about it. "Yeah…when she reminisced, she said, 'Your daddy,' and when she was angry, she said 'Benjamin Troup.'"

"Search me." He shrugged and kept on eating.

I nearly told him I'd like to. I was still enough under the spell of the previous night. I admonished myself to get serious. My self didn't want to listen. It wanted to drag May back upstairs and out of those jeans and jump his bones.

"It's obvious there was no love lost between them, else she wouldn't have left and he wouldn't have done what he did."

I sat there, mulling that over. Why had she said those completely contradictory things? *Your daddy*, one minute, *Benjamin Troup*, the next… *Oh, God.* I gasped, sucked in a morsel of cheese and bread, and choked.

"Hey!" May was out of his chair, pounding my back as I coughed and sprayed toast crumbs. He didn't stop until I held up a hand and waved him away.

"I-I'm okay." I wheezed. I drank coffee, taking a deep breath.

"Wasn't the cheese melted enough? Here." He held out his hand. "I'll put it back into the oven."

"The toast's fine. Hands off." I slapped his wrist but not very hard. "She wasn't talking about Benjamin Troup, May. She was talking about my *real* father. *You have your father's eyes.* I should've realized it the minute I saw that portrait at McAllister Place. Benjamin Troup had blue eyes."

"And so were your mother's. I remember. The prettiest sky-blue." He returned to his place at the other end of the table and picked up his fork. "Simple law of genetics then. You couldn't have been their daughter. Unless you're a freak of Nature or something."

He shoveled in grits as he spoke.

"Thanks a lot." I began to demolish my own grits. He'd stirred in at least half a pound of butter. *Delicious.*

"Don't worry." He shot me a bacon-greasy grin. "I love you, freak or not."

I threw the last crust of my toast at him. He caught it and stuck it into his mouth, making a big deal of chewing it.

"What are you going to do?"

"Finish my breakfast."

"About your father."

"You mean, the real one?"

He nodded.

I thought about it. "What can I do?"

"Find him." He made it sound so simple.

"I don't know if I want to." I stirred my fork in the remnants of my eggs.

"You mean to tell me you don't want to know about him?"

"I know enough," I answered. "I know he was a coward who got his girlfriend pregnant and wouldn't marry her so she had to find some other man to do it."

"You don't know that." He set down his fork. "There might be a very good reason why they didn't get married."

"Why are you playing devil's advocate?" I dropped my fork onto my plate also.

He didn't answer.

"A good reason," I repeated. "Okay…like what?"

"He… Well, he might've been in the army or

something, and got shipped to Afghanistan or Croatia or somewhere before she could tell him. Or…" He stopped.

"Go on."

"…or…they broke up and he left town and then she found out about you but couldn't find him. Hell, I don't know. It could be lots of things." He looked annoyed, as if I were putting him on the spot, when *he'd* started it. "Maybe he was already married."

"Good God, May." It came out before I realized it. "That makes it even worse. Now Mama's not only a whore but an adulteress too?"

"I'm sure it wasn't that," he backtracked. "I had to throw that in. Just in case."

"There's one possibility you didn't mention," I said slowly.

He gave me a questioning look.

"He could be dead. She always used the past tense when speaking of him. Maybe he died and that was why…"

In the living room, the mantel clock began to chime. *One…two…three…*

"Maybe not," he countered. "She might've just used the past tense because he was in the past as far as she was concerned. Think about it, Gracie. What if, somewhere in McAllister, there's a man who's your father, a man who doesn't even know he has a daughter?"

He looked earnest. The clock continued its melodic dings…*six…seven…eight…*

"You've got to try to find him."

"How can I? I've a plane to catch…"

The clock fell silent. I'd been half-listening to it, tuned in to what May was saying. Now, I realized there had been eleven of those little *dings. Oh, no.*

"…an hour ago." I looked at my watch, slapping the tabletop in anger. "Damn it, May. I missed my plane."

"No, you didn't."

"Of course I did," I retorted. "It left at ten. It's now eleven."

"I called this morning before you woke and changed the reservation. You're not flying out of here until a week from Monday. That gives us nearly two weeks to do some daddy-hunting."

He looked proud of himself. Briefly, I wanted to slap him. How dare he?

I knew the answer. *Because he loves me. Because he knows I want to know more but am just too hurt right now to admit it.*

"Where am I supposed to stay while we're doing this searching?" I didn't give him a chance to answer, in case we weren't on the same wavelength just then. "Jefferson Simmons told me the estate paid for three days at the Manor. Today's the last day. I can't afford to stay there for two weeks on my own."

"You can stay here." He said that very quietly.

"In one of the guest rooms?" I wanted there to be no doubt as to his meaning.

"Hell, no." The copper eyes crinkled at the corners as he gave me a grin. "In my bed. Now that I've got you there, I'm not letting you out."

He hadn't moved, as if keeping the distance of the table between us was important. Now he stood up, stalking around to where I sat. There was no other way to describe the way he moved just then.

"Besides, there's something else needing to be settled. Other than finding your father, I mean."

"Like what?" I tensed. *What now?*

"Like deciding what to do about us." Another very quiet, very simple statement, holding dozens of unspoken questions.

"May…" I stopped, mainly because I really didn't know what to say.

"I said it last night and I'll say it again, Gracie. I love you." He stopped, too. Waiting.

"How did this happen?" I asked, plaintively, meaning *How did you decide, after an absence of twenty years, that you love me? How is it I feel exactly the same? And how the hell can anything come of this when I'm supposed to be on my way back to California right this minute?*

"Just lucky, I guess."

I had a feeling he knew exactly what I was thinking but was agreeable to postponing the outcome for a while. He caught my hand.

"Finished?" As I looked confused, he went on, "With breakfast? Let's go check you out of the Manor."

****

Checking out had been easy. What happened while I was packing wasn't.

The phone rang while I was in the bathroom gathering my cosmetics.

"Would you catch that?" I called. Probably Tammy telling me I'd be charged another day for checking out past noon. I could afford that, but nothing more.

"Hello?" May sounded cautious as he answered the phone. There was a brief silence. "No, you've got the right room. May I tell her who's calling?"

So formal. There was a sudden stiffness in his voice, practically a bristle. Just a little too polite, with an edge.

"Gracie. It's for you. Someone named David

Clayton."

David? I was supposed to call him and let him know how the reading went. I completely forgot. What with all that went on last night, Mayfield-wise, I had a good excuse.

I hurried out of the bathroom, snatching the receiver from May's hand, ignoring the scowl he gave me. "David? I'm sorry, I forgot…"

"Gracie, who the hell was that who answered? Damn, kid, you didn't take my advice and latch onto that lawyer, did you?" He laughed as he said it, but there was a serious tinge to the words.

"That was just May," I began.

Calmly taking a couple of bikini panties from a drawer, May picked up my packing where I'd left off, moving to the bed and placing them in the suitcase. He turned to look at me, mouthing *Just May?* his scowl deepening.

"You remember? Mayfield Donovan. I think I've mentioned him…"

"You mean, the red-headed bully who used to regularly beat you up?"

"Uh…that's right."

I hoped David wasn't speaking loud enough for May to hear. May had turned back to the dresser, hands sweeping over a nightgown, another pair of panties. For a moment, his fingers brushed them lightly, then he scooped up both items and headed back to the bed.

"Since when do you let someone like that into your room?"

"Since we both grew up and buried the hatchet," I retorted.

"Sounds as if something else got buried," he shot

back. "But that's your business. How'd it go?"

It took me a minute to realize he was asking about the will. I hesitated, trying to figure out how to word it, but something went wrong.

"Oh, David…"

Abruptly, I was blubbering again, just as I'd done the day before, first, into the phone and then onto May's chest, as he stopped what he was doing and took me in his arms.

He pulled the phone from my hand, saying into it, "Hold on just a minute. Gracie needs to get composed."

Then he stood there, holding me and the phone until I raised my head and took it from him again.

"I'm okay now," I said to both David and May. In as few words as possible, I told David what Benjamin Troup had done.

"Shit, Grace. That's so…so harsh." He sighed. "Nevertheless, I think I'm glad. At least now you know you don't have any of that bastard in you."

Small comfort right then. I hurried on, telling him of my plan, of May's plan, to try and find my father.

"Might be difficult at this stage of the game," he warned. "Do what you have to. Sean can hold down the fort for another ten days, even if he *is* grousing. Do you need any legal counseling while you go about it?"

I wanted to tell him, yes…wanted him to drop everything and come to me immediately, but I knew he had more important things to do than hold his receptionist's hand.

"It's good of you to offer, but I think, just now, I need moral support more than anything else. Anyway, I've the Colonel…I mean, Jeff Simmons, if I need him."

"Keep me posted, then." He signed off with, "…and

hurry home."

I dropped the phone back onto the cradle and stared at it. May said something but I didn't answer, just keep staring at the phone. Finally, he touched my shoulder, shaking it slightly.

I looked around. "What?"

"Who's this David guy?" He looked furious. "Why's he calling you? What did you tell him about me?"

"Are you jealous?"

"Should I be?" He was holding a T-shirt and tossed it onto the bed with more than a little violence. "Damn it, Grace."

All of a sudden I was *Grace*?

"It sounds like you and he are pretty close. If I'm just a stand-in for the real man in your life, let me know so I won't make more of a fool of myself than I already have."

"You *are* jealous." I made pacifying motions with my hands. Of David? That shocked me—and delighted me, too, truth to tell—but, after all, May didn't know who David was.

"Damned right. Shouldn't I be?"

"No." I caught his hands, pushed the suitcase aside and pulled him to sit beside me on the bed. "First off, David Clayton's my boss."

"Didn't sound much like a boss. Anyway, secretaries have been known to get pretty cozy with bosses. Don't they call them *office wives*?"

"In the second place, I'm not his secretary. I'm his receptionist."

"That makes a difference?" Apparently May didn't think so.

115

"And third…David's gay." I finished in a rush. "He has a partner and a family and he's a good friend who's worried about me."

"Oh." He had the good manners to look ashamed and actually flush, a dull crimson sweeping through the tanned cheeks. "Well. I…" He looked away, then back, saying defensively, "He didn't sound gay."

"Ditch the stereotype, May." I let exasperation fill my voice, thinking back to my original meeting with David. "You'd like David if you ever met him. I think you two have a lot in common. Besides being concerned about me, I mean."

His look said he doubted it. "I'll take your word for that, since you know both of us but we don't know each other. Is he coming out here? To give you all that *moral support* you need?"

He threw my words back at me.

"You heard what I said. If I need legal backing, I'll ask Mr. Simmons. If he can't do it—conflict of interest or something, I'll ask for a referral. Surely this town has more than two lawyers."

"Oh, surely…" Copper eyes rolled heavenward, but he didn't say anything more on that subject. "You ready?"

With that, the quarrel, if it really was one, was dismissed. I got my makeup kit from the bathroom, tossed it into the suitcase, zipped it shut, and we were out the door.

As before, May insisted on carrying my luggage. He stood to one side as I checked out, which didn't take long since the room was already paid for. I kept expecting Tammy to say something about May being with me, but apparently, our association hadn't reached the gossips' ears yet.

Thank goodness.

I wondered how long it would take for that to happen. Perhaps a local schoolteacher sleeping with a former resident wasn't as hot a subject as a deceased citizen denying his paternity from the grave.

May suggested I turn in my rental and we'd use his car, so he followed me to the rental station located in that near-the-highway motel where I dutifully returned the car and keys and signed a few papers relinquishing it to the company.

In the convertible again, I thought to ask, "Is this going to interfere with your tutoring Tammy?"

"The date for the testing's getting close. Tammy's been studying hard. I think she needs a break for a while, say about ten days."

"That's convenient. What do we do now?"

"We go back home, sit down, and make a game plan." He floored the gas pedal and sent the car flying toward the city limits.

Chapter 8

May decided we should have coffee while we talked, so we sat on the sofa with our cups. He poured, then waited while I loaded my cup with sugar and milk before he spoke.

"You don't need a lawyer, Gracie." He was still negative about having someone else in on our plans. "I can hold your hand as good as anyone can."

As if to underscore this, he seized my hand, giving it a gentle squeeze. It was quietly possessive but also touching.

"Let's drink our coffee and get started."

"What do we do first?" I wasn't too proud to admit my ignorance. What did I know about ferreting out information? David had all kinds of people and places he used as sources, but he'd never shared any of them with me. That information went to Sean. I was only allowed to see the results as I prepared documents. "Hire a private investigator or what?"

"Sweetheart, this is McAllister, remember?" May looked pitying. "Where a good many people know almost everything that happens. Besides, I doubt if there's a PI here. I certainly never heard of one."

"Just as well. I doubt if I could afford him anyway." I'd better bring that up right now. "Guess we'll be our own leg men, then."

"With legs like yours, that shouldn't be much of a

problem." He gave me a grin, then hid it behind his coffee cup.

"Is that flattery?" I gave him what I hoped was a hard stare. "Somehow it sounds a little left-handed."

"Hey, I'm ambidextrous. I'll use any hand you want."

"Be serious." I wanted to tell him he was incorrigible, but I had a feeling he'd have an answer for that, too.

"I thought I was," he answered, and got that way. "Generally, when establishing an identity, the first place to look is at documents open to the public."

"You sound as if you know what you're talking about."

"I subscribe to one of those ancestry databases," he answered.

"Hey…why don't we do that?" I looked up, suddenly enthused. "Yeah…I send in a sample… specimen…whatever they call it, and they find a match…and save us a load of problems and a lot of time."

"Not saving a lot of time, you mean," he corrected. "It takes six weeks to get results."

I grimaced. "Strike that brilliant idea off the list."

"Besides…what if dear old dad's DNA isn't in the database? There's probably a fifty-fifty chance it isn't," he pointed out. "Not everyone is wild about having their genetic material available for public scrutiny."

"Yeah, guess you're right," I agreed. "But it was a good idea, wasn't it?"

He nodded. "One I'm surprised you thought of."

If I hadn't seen that quirk of his mouth, I might've been insulted.

I slapped his knee. "Okay, we go with your idea about documents."

"Not such a good idea now that I think a little further," he surprised me by admitting. "In this case, that'd only give us a marriage license and your birth certificate with Benjamin Troup's name on it."

"No help there," I agreed, and fell back on my usual source of information. "On television, the first thing the police do is interrogate the victim's family and friends."

"And solve the entire case in forty-seven minutes plus commercials at quarterly intervals," he finished. "This isn't a crime, but we could still follow that line of thinking."

He frowned, studying his now-empty cup. There were a few grounds floating in the single swallow left, and he tilted the cup, sending the contents swirling.

"Those aren't tea leaves," I reminded him. "You can't read my fortune in coffee grounds."

"I wish." He set down the cup. "Unfortunately, your grandparents are no longer with us..."

"...and they, like Mama, were each an only child, so I've no immediate relatives."

"So that leaves just friends, namely, the old school buddies your mother used to run around with. Her best friend, Angeline Ware, now my stepmother..."

Here his patted himself on the chest, then hesitated slightly.

"...and my father...and Carter McAllister."

"His brother?" I didn't even want to say Benjamin Troup's name. "I didn't realize he was Mama's age."

"Yep. Benjamin Troup was 'way older, almost thirty when he married your mother. She was twenty-two." He gave me a meaningful look. "Kind of like us."

"I'm nothing like my mother," I snorted.

I loved her dearly, but most of the time we didn't see eye to eye and many times she blamed our disagreements on my being *just like your father*. Generally, it was when I wanted to do something impractical, however. Like study art or spend a summer interning at a local community theater instead of getting a regular part-time job. Even then, there had been no anger when she said those things, more of a sad wistfulness, like those other times when she compared me to him…or occasionally to Benjamin Troup.

"*And I hope to God you never turn out like he who shall remain nameless,*" I quoted. "She made me feel like a certain boy wizard." I thought of something. "Carter wasn't at the reading."

"No reason he should be." May was still laughing at my reference to the boy wizard's nemesis.

"Wouldn't he be left *something*?" I argued. I chugged down the last of my coffee, grimacing as I realized it was now cold. "As the only brother, I mean?"

"Hardly. There had been bad blood between them for years, and I mean *years*. And it was no secret." He looked thoughtful. "Since right after your mother left, as a matter of fact." He raised an eyebrow. "Think that means anything?"

"Your guess is as good as mine." At this point, I had no idea about anything. "You don't suppose…" I left it unsaid.

"Shall we go find out?" He reached for my cup, taking it and his own back to the kitchen.

That little tidbit had my mind racing as I waited for him to come back. *Mama and Carter McAllister?* Was it possible? Maybe I was going to keep the McAllister name after all.

****

Carter had his offices at Gargoyle Central as I found myself thinking of the Seagram Building. Appropriate, if he was anything like his brother. He was also a lawyer, his door plaque reading *Criminal Law*. Did he get railroaded into studying law like Benjamin Troup attempted with Ben? As Ben might yet be?

I wondered how many clients he had in McAllister, which looked to be a fairly quiet place as far as I could tell. Especially since May grew up to be such a mild-mannered citizen. When I was five, if anyone had asked me, I'd have sworn he was going to become Public Enemy Number One.

As we drove to McAllister's less than bustling business district, consisting of a twelve-block square on the north end of town, I tried to remember my then-Uncle Carter. I drew a blank…absolutely nothing, not even an image.

How could that be?

If he lived in McAllister, and I was certain he did since he had offices here, and had been at McAllister Place while my mother and I were there, why didn't I have one memory of him?

His receptionist was cordial, didn't stare when I told her who I was, and informed me Mr. McAllister was free for a couple of hours. She whispered into the phone, then told May and me to *go on in*. I had a minor spell of nervousness as I knocked on the door and heard a deep Southern voice call out to us.

My hands began to shake and my stomach contracted. I felt as if I'd been hit with a fist. I couldn't move.

May didn't miss it, of course. "Gracie, what is it?"

"Nothing."

The moment passed. I shook my head and opened the door. He followed me into the room.

Carter was already on his feet as May pushed the door shut. I stopped just inside the office, barely leaving him room to stand behind me as I stood staring at the tall man coming toward us.

"Hello, May." He seemed a little surprised to see Mayfield with me, looking from him to me. "Grace, child."

He caught my hand, holding it just as Jefferson Simmons had.

Is this a custom among Southern men?

He was as tall as May, blue-eyed, of course—*well, that shoots down the idea he might be my father,* I thought—and still dark-haired with just the faintest smattering of gray at the temples. His hair was longer than May's, which surprised me, but it was well-styled, not just that awkward *I've-let-it-grow-long-now-what?* look some older men have. Carter McAllister looked enough like the man in the portrait at McAllister Place for me to know they were related. He was almost as handsome as Benjamin Troup, but his expression was a lot more…human.

For a moment, he just stood there, looking down at me as if trying to see something in my face. A resemblance to my mother? For some clue to my father's identity?

Before I knew what he planned, he crushed me against his chest in a tight hug. I closed my eyes, cheek pressed against the lapel of his jacket, inhaling the scent of his cologne. That elusive fragrance, the same one May wore. A sudden pang shot through me…safety tinged with confusion…something familiar and yet a great unknown.

He pushed me away.

"I'm sorry, Grace. I'd have been at the reading if I'd had any idea…" He didn't finish the sentence and the silence lasted a little too long.

May shifted behind me. That broke the spell and Carter released me.

"Please come in."

He waved us to the two chairs before his desk and returned to sit behind it. The desk became a barrier between us, though I don't think he intended that. He didn't have the cozy sofa-and-chair arrangement like Mr. Simmons did. Perhaps criminal cases didn't promote the same closeness as family law.

"How'd you find out, since you weren't there?" Did I really have to ask?

"Sammi called me. Poor child was very upset. She'd been counting on getting to know you."

"I'm sorry I won't have the chance now." I meant that. From the little I'd seen of the surviving McAllisters, including the belligerent Ben, I liked them. It would've been nice to say they *were* my relatives.

"But you did decide to come see your old *Unca Car* before you leave?" He leaned back in the chair, smiling at me.

It was certainly the smile of an indulgent uncle toward a favored niece. I wondered if Sammi was the recipient of that smile now. I also wondered about his age. He definitely looked to be younger than Benjamin Troup, but that may simply have been because he was so pleasant. May had said he was Mama's age, so that would make him around forty-eight, and his brother about fifty-three when he'd died. Not that I cared about *his* age all that much.

"If you talked to Sammi, you know you're not my *Unca Car,*" I told him, a little sharply.

"Blood doesn't always matter." He swatted away his brother's declaration with a flick of a hand.

"Thanks for that, anyway," I muttered and decided to get straight to the point. "I'm not leaving McAllister just yet."

"No?" He looked surprised.

"Gracie has decided she's going to find her father." Might've known May couldn't keep quiet any longer.

Carter didn't answer that, just turned to look at him. I thought his gaze was now a little speculative.

"And you're asking for legal advice?"

"I can understand how you might think that, but…no."

He looked surprised at that declaration but didn't speak.

"I'm here t-to…" I couldn't say it, just stuttered to a stop.

"Gracie wants to ask you about your relationship with her mother," May finished for me as if translating.

I shot him a grateful glance. He reached out and caught my hand resting on the chair arm, giving it a quick squeeze. That didn't escape Carter's attention.

"My…"

For a second, I thought I saw anger on his face, then it changed to the oddest expression. Sadness…and regret.

"My dear child." There was only the briefest hesitation. "I'm not your father." He smiled. "We dated…yes…and, I'll admit, we were…intimate."

I was startled to see the barest tinge of pink touch his clean-shaven cheeks as he said that.

"Believe me, if I were, there's no way I'd have let Benjamin Troup marry your mother. Fact of the matter, with the haste of their wedding, I always figured my dear brother actually slipped up for once. I thought that meant she really loved him, because she always insisted I use protection and since I cared for her, I did…" He paused as I looked away. "I'm sorry, that was indiscreet. I've embarrassed you."

He had, but discomfited himself more, I thought. I shook my head. It's one thing to be told you're a bastard, and another to listen to one of your mother's old boyfriends bluntly admit he'd slept with her and go into contraceptive detail. He might've been able to admit it in front of May without hesitation, but to say that to the daughter of a woman he'd cared for…?

"It's okay," I mumbled.

"I've always felt all this was my fault."

That made me look back. "How do you mean?"

"I introduced them." I must've looked surprised because he went on, "You didn't know? She never said anything about…us?"

I shook my head.

Carter seemed to settle into his chair, much the way someone would who was about to tell a long story. *May as well get comfortable,* his body language said.

"I was dating Mimzi at the time."

Mimzi? My mother had a nickname? A whimsical, silly little diminutive. It didn't fit the woman I'd known. She'd been tough, determined, serious. Nothing fanciful about her. Nothing *Mimzi.*

"Didn't know that, either?" At my second headshake, he went on, "I suppose it isn't telling tales out of school at this late date. We dated on and off from high school until I graduated from college. My last summer break, I asked her to go steady. As a prelude to something more, I was hoping." He laughed softly, eyes getting a faraway gaze.

Though he was looking at me, I had a feeling he was seeing someone else. A blonde, blue-eyed girl with a silly nickname.

"You could say we were a pretty hot item." That was delivered somewhat ruefully. "One night, I picked her up, then discovered I'd left my wallet at home. Since it not only had all my money but also my driver's license in it, I stopped by McAllister Place to get it."

His gaze dropped to the desk, avoiding both ours for a moment, a suddenly shy expression making me see that boy, younger than I was now, taking his girl on a date.

"That was the beginning of the end. I didn't want to have her sit in the car while I ran inside so I took her in with me, and then…Benjamin Troup came down the stairs." The shy look evaporated, replaced by hostility, even now. "I knew the minute he looked at her what was going to happen. Well, I hustled her out of there as fast as I could, and when I came home that night, he and I came as close as we ever had to actually fighting when I warned him to stay away from my girl."

Swallowing loudly, Carter looked up at the ceiling, as if he could still see that scene.

"He just sneered and walked out, didn't even dignify my threats with answers. And…sure enough…a couple of days later, he asked Mimzi for a date, and she accepted…"

Again, there was a silence, Carter staring at his desk, May and I being still as if afraid to break the spell. He sighed.

"Long and short of it, we argued, broke up, and I went back to school, angry and bitter."

"And Mimzi...I mean, Gracie's mother...started dating your brother?" May asked.

"That was the odd thing." Carter managed to look as if even now, he was surprised. "She had a couple of dates with him, but then she started keeping company with your father, Mayfield."

"Dad?" From his tone, May hadn't expected that.

"Beautiful Bill." Carter nodded. "He would've been in our graduating class if he'd stayed in school, and in spite of his less than sterling character at the time...sorry..."

May shook his head to show he was aware of his father's early reputation.

"...he and I palled around. By the time I graduated and came back home, they had broken up and your dad was dating Angeline and Mimzi was going with Marty, and then..."

"Wait a minute," I interrupted. "Marty?"

A new character introduced.

"Who's that?"

"Martes Salazar. He was the fifth member of our particular group."

"Not old man Salazar's son?" May spoke up. "The jeweler? Owns Keller's?"

"That's right. Though he wasn't the owner, then. Only one of the employees."

"I didn't know he had any kids," May said.

"Just the one son," Carter replied. "He was a

refugee. From Cuba. Came over in one of those boats, I think. One of the lucky ones who got a sponsor and stayed. Marty was born in Miami and was two when they arrived here. I was certain he and Mimzi were going to get married. It sure looked like true love to me."

"Why haven't I ever heard of him?" May asked. "I mean, I don't know every person in McAllister but I pass by Keller's all the time and, once or twice, I've spoken to Mr. Salazar, even been a customer, and I've never heard anyone mention his son."

"That's because he's deceased," Carter replied. "He was killed in an automobile accident a month after I got back to town. Mimzi defied her parents to go with him. They were pushing Benjamin Troup at her."

His tone became scornful.

"Real social climbers, your grandparents, Grace. They forced a break-up, and Marty couldn't take it." His words became clipped. "Got drunk and crashed his car into a telephone pole. Car caught on fire. Barely enough to identify."

He gave a long sigh.

"Mimzi was devastated, and Benjamin Troup stepped in to pick up the pieces. The next thing I knew, there was an engagement announcement and a wedding." He shrugged. "And that's it…Mimzi became Mrs. Benjamin Troup McAllister, Junior, moved into McAllister Place, and I had to watch the woman I loved with my brother, who never let me forget how he'd once more gotten what he wanted."

His voice dropped.

"And then you were born."

"H-how soon after the wedding?" That was all I could get out. This interrogation wasn't going as I expected. I figured I'd get a couple of straight answers and that would be it. Instead, I was getting a very complicated and slightly sordid story.

Carter didn't answer directly. "I'd been hoping he was sterile, so I could throw that up to him. No such luck. Still, none of us believed otherwise, so we accepted the story that you were premature." He shrugged. "They figured about six weeks."

"You were still living at home, then?" May sounded surprised.

"Our father stipulated in his will that I had a home at McAllister Place as long as I wanted it. There was nothing Benjamin Troup could do and I guess I was a glutton for punishment. I suppose I thought if I hung around, he wouldn't be too cruel to her. *Idiot.* He'd get angry and physical. The night she left, so did I. Told him he'd finally gotten what he deserved, and I hoped he never heard from either of you again."

Once more I felt a sudden sense of familiarity. I'd heard someone say those words or something similar. *Where? When?*

He fell silent. Just sat there as if exhausted by reviving old ghosts and telling their stories. Even May was quiet.

"I'm afraid that's all I can tell you," Carter summed up. "Benjamin Troup, Mimzi, and Marty are dead, and Angeline and Bill are all that's left besides myself. Looks like you're going to find nothing but dead ends, Grace."

"I imagine you're right," I agreed. "But I have to try." I got to my feet. "Thank you, Mr. McAllister."

"Carter," he corrected.

"…Carter…for speaking to me." I looked around the room then, as if seeing it for the first time.

Something on the shelf of the nearby bookcase caught my eye. A small framed photograph of a woman and a child. It was the only one in the room and I didn't have to guess who it was. I nodded at it. "Is that why you never married? Because of my mother?"

"No fool like an old fool, is there?" He looked at the picture and back to me. "I kept hoping she'd write and ask me to join her. Believe me, I'd have done it. I'd willingly have let Benjamin Troup name me as co-respondent in his divorce. Other than one letter, I never heard from her again."

"Is that how Mr. Simmons knew where to find me?"

"I've never let anyone see that letter, Grace. It's in my bank box and it's been there since the day after I received it. These days, it's fairly simple to trace someone, isn't it?"

"I guess it is." I had a feeling all the electronic data storage equipment in the world wasn't going to be much help this time, however. "It's not too late, you know," I went on, feeling saddened that he might've gone through his whole life alone because of Mama.

Had there been other women but he'd never gotten serious again?

"As I told myself recently," he said, surprisingly. "I felt lost when I learned Mimzi was dead, but something still held me. Now that Benjamin Troup's also gone... It's so odd. I suddenly feel *free*. You two can be the first to know. I'm going to take the plunge in a few months. At last."

"No shit?" May immediately backtracked. "I mean, congratulations. Who's the lucky lady?"

"Lydia Lynch."

"The librarian?" Apparently, May knew her because

he smiled.

"Congratulations from me, too." I held out my hand. "Goodbye, Carter."

He was up and around the desk, taking it gently. He leaned down and kissed my forehead. "Anything else I can do, don't hesitate to call me."

Nodding, I turned and walked out.

The receptionist looked up as we went past, adding her goodbye to his.

Once we were in the corridor, May put his arm around me. "Well? What's the verdict?"

I didn't have to ask what he meant. "He can't be my father. He has blue eyes."

"Right. Of course."

"Still, there's something…I don't know…I think there's something he didn't share, but I have no idea what it is."

"I guess you could've pushed it," he said. "Asked for a DNA test or something."

"Right…which would be like calling him a liar, and when it came out negative, I'd have to do it to every other man who's unlucky enough to become a suspect." I shook my head. "I'm going to take Carter at his word. Besides, I can't afford *one* DNA test, much less as many as I imagine I'd need." I gave a shaky laugh. "Mama was a busy girl."

"Let's get out of here." May pushed me down the hall toward the elevator.

We'd spent longer in Carter's office than I realized. It was now early afternoon. May was all for making an early night of it.

"Not that I expect to get to sleep soon, even if we do go to bed early." He gave me a grin as he said it.

"Seriously, you need to get unpacked and I've some bills to take care of.

****

While I carried my bag upstairs and made room in one of the dresser drawers and in the closet, he sat in his basement office with a handful of statements, accessing his bank's bill-paying app. By the time we both finished, it was dinnertime. I volunteered to cook.

"It's only fair." I bustled into the kitchen, finding an apron hanging on a hook in the little mudroom just off the porch, and then rummaging in the pantry.

I ended up with mushrooms and rice and some leftover roast chicken thrown together in a casserole. May declared it was great.

"You're almost as good a cook as I am."

"You think?" I couldn't resist adding, "It's certainly odd you can cook so well."

"I like to eat," he retorted. "Pizza and burgers got tired fast, so I told myself I was going to learn to cook good-tasting food, and did just that. However, if you want to take over that chore…"

"Why don't we share?" I suggested. "I wouldn't want to have all the fun." I got up to put the dishes into the dishwasher.

Later, in the bedroom, he had me out of my clothes before I could even suggest it. Guess great minds *do* think alike. About certain things. As he pulled me against his chest, I inhaled deeply, then looked up.

"May, do you use aftershave?"

"Doesn't any self-respecting man?"

"What kind?"

In answer, he released me and disappeared into the bathroom, returning with an opaque cylindrical bottle. I took it and pulled out the stopper. A fresh, tangy scent wafted out. The moment I smelled it, I recognized it as the same Carter had been wearing. I looked at the label, a picture of a ship on a crested wave.

"It's kind of a tradition," May said. "My grandfather used this brand and he bought it for Dad when he started shaving, and Dad got the same thing for me."

"Carter McAllister uses this." I thought about that. "Guess that's why I thought it smelled familiar."

"Let's forget about aftershave for a while." He took the bottle out of my hand and set it on the bedside table.

Lifting me in his arms, he sat down on the bed, pulling me toward him. I found myself straddling May's thighs. I looked down. We were pressed tightly together, pelvis-to-pelvis, pubic hair meshing, both brilliantly red. Remembering his remark the night before, *You'll find out,* I looked up, laughing.

"I understand now. We're the same color. Does that mean something?"

He looked down, too. "Definite compatibility." He kissed me and fell backward onto the bed.

I forgot about aftershave and everything else after that, for quite some time.

****

The wind was blowing and it was cold. Someone held me against his chest, the fabric of his coat rough against my cheek. There was a spicy, familiar scent on the cold air, coming from the tightly woven cloth.

"You aren't going to get into trouble for helping me, are you?" I recognized that voice. Mama, but so much younger...and afraid.

"Like I care at this point. You do understand why I couldn't go to the police, don't you?"

"Unfortunately, yes."

"Let the dead stay dead, Miriam." His voice vibrated through his chest and into my dozing ear.

"Passengers for Flight 425 to San Diego, please report to Gate A12. Passengers for Flight 215 to San Diego, please report to Gate A12."

"That's your flight."

"Are you sure he doesn't know?"

"Trust me, Benjamin Troup has no idea. I'm sending you as far away as you can go. Here…" I was shifted slightly as he handed her an envelope.

There was a papery rustle. "Th-there's a thousand dollars here. I can't…"

"Yes, you can. When you get there, let me know and I'll send you enough to get you started. Write me at the office."

"A-all right."

"I'll miss you, Miriam."

"I don't care if I ever see this damn town again, but I'll miss you, too." I was caught between them as she hugged him tightly. Then I was set on my feet. "Grace. Wake up, sweetheart."

Blinking, I rubbed my eyes as she took my hand. I looked up. A tall man in an overcoat loomed over me. The light was behind him and I couldn't see his face. He stooped and kissed my forehead. "Be a good girl, Grace."

"I will, Unca Car."

****

"Oh, my God." I jerked upright. The only sound in the quiet was a soft snore from May. I rolled over, punching him in the ribs. "May, wake up.'

"Not now, Gracie." He half-woke with a grunt. "I've

got a headache."

"I don't want to have sex, idiot." I shook his shoulder. "I just had a dream."

"And you woke me for that? Well…shit."

"Listen." I leaned over him. "It was Carter."

"What was Carter?"

"Carter McAllister was the man who drove my mother and me to the airport. He's the one who helped us get away."

"And you know this how?" He was wide awake now, rolling over to look at me.

"The aftershave. I think it triggered the memory."

"You couldn't wait until morning to tell me?"

"Sorry." I expected more of a response then that. "Go back to sleep." I lay back down.

"If you're wanting a reaction, I'll give you one, but it isn't going to be because of a dream. I'm a livin', breathin' reality, sugah." He reached out and wrapped an arm across my shoulders, pulling me on top of him.

"What about your headache?" I asked.

"What headache?"

After that, it was a delicious segue from loving to sleeping again.

Chapter 9

The next morning, however, instead of having a council of war at the breakfast table, May suggested an alternative.

"Let's go to the city park to have our talk. Remember how we used to go there as kids?"

I remembered, all right…and as usual where childhood memories of May and myself were concerned, the things I recalled weren't too pleasant. From my standpoint, anyway.

He must've realized that, for he said quickly, "We need to get out of here, Gracie, and the park's a pretty place…flowers, trees…sunshine… We can let our surroundings offset our grim reflections."

I started to argue that his home had a fairly pleasant atmosphere all its own, especially the bedroom, and the reflections there weren't so bad, either.

"Don't you want to see a little of McAllister while you're here?" He caught my hand, tugging insistently. "Let's go."

Before we could get to the car, however, his cell phone rang.

May pulled it from his pocket, glanced at the caller ID and said, "Get in the car, Gracie. I need to take this."

Not waiting to see if I obeyed, he turned away, walking a few feet from the car as he swiped at the phone icon. "This is May Donovan."

From the passenger seat, I watched him talking earnestly. He was too far away for me to hear, though. Darn it.

When he shoved the phone back into his hip pocket and slid under the wheel, I said, "Well?"

"Well, what?" He started the engine.

"Are you going to tell me what that was about?"

"Later..." He sent the gravel flying as we went down the drive.

****

McAllister's city park was located in the center of town and was once considered the town square, a one-block rectangle separating the main street from the one west of it. A cement strip surrounded by flowering trees and shrubberies divided its middle, while a sidewalk connected it with Cherry and Peach Streets at each end. Here and there, wrought iron benches glistened blackly, reflecting the sun.

May guided me to one of them.

"This place is beautiful..." I looked around as I spoke.

The bench sat in a grouping of Japanese magnolias, bright fuchsia darkening the underside of the petals, pale pink inside. They alternated with camellia bushes, the tallest almost five feet high, scarlet blossoms with peppermint stripes amid their dark green leaves. The walkway was bordered with pink and crimson azaleas. Birds pecked in the grass, *black* birds, though the sunshine made iridescent blue-green streaks on their wings and backs.

"...but those are definitely not pigeons."

"No?" He looked at the birds as if to assure himself they were.

"Come on, May. I know a starling when I see one."

"Guess the pigeons must be decorating the statue, then."

"Statue." I thought about that. "That's right. That's what's missing." I looked around. "Where is it?" I stood, pulling him to his feet. "It hasn't been pulled down, has it?"

"Are you kidding?" His voice was lofty, and sarcastic. "People in McAllister don't remove statues."

I gave him a quizzical look. "No?"

"No." He shook his head. "They're like traditions. They've always been here, so they'll always be here until you forget why."

He led me farther down the walkway, past a set of benches in the middle of the path. Odd place to put them, I thought. We went around them.

The statue was also in the pathway, on a five-foot square base with the sidewalk continuing around it on both sides.

A goateed man in mid-nineteenth century garb stared into the distance. He was holding a scroll in his hands. Around the edge of the base was a carved bunting. I could make out the *Stars and Bars*, forming the St. Andrew's cross of the Confederate flag. The inscription chiseled into the stone read, *Jefferson Davis, 1808-1889. President of the Confederacy, 1861-1865.*

"Good ol' Jeff D." I looked up at the statue. It was like May said. In all the time I'd remembered this episode, I'd never thought of whom the statue represented. It was simply *there*. And now…?

Without warning, a sudden swipe of fear washed over me. I took a step backward. A vision of a crying, terrified child. *Me*.

"Gracie?" May caught my hand.

"I'm afraid." I whispered the words. "Why, May? I remember crying. Why should looking at this statue frighten me?"

"Damn it." He pulled me onto a nearby bench. "My fault." Releasing my hand, he looked away. "Again."

"Care to explain?" I was plainly puzzled. I sniffled away a runaway tear.

There was a sigh of irritation. At himself, I thought. He looked back at me.

"I seem to be stuck in Step 9 of a 12-step program, with only one person I need to make amends to. Do you suppose I could just give a general apology covering everything I ever did to you and you could give me an all-encompassing forgiveness and that would settle it once and for all?"

"You can try." I was still wondering what he'd done involving the statue. Whatever it was, it had certainly scared me.

"Right." Taking a deep breath, he went on, "Grace McAllister, I humbly apologize for any and all cruelties, hits, punches, shoves, and whatever else I did to you when I was a benighted and completely stupid little shit, and beg your forgiveness for same."

I swallowed and frowned. "I don't know, May. That covers a lot of territory and a lot of years. I may yet remember some things I can't forgive you for."

His expression changed, becoming as anxious as I'd ever seen it. In all seriousness, I couldn't go on.

"I'm kidding," I assured him. "Of course, I forgive you."

"For any and all?" he persisted.

"For any and all," I repeated. "Now, would you

mind telling me exactly what you did that concerned me and Jefferson Davis's statue, so I can regret forgiving you?"

He pretended to think about that. At least, I hope he was pretending.

Taking a deep breath, he leaned against the bench. "It was when I was around eight, I guess. Your mother called mine…Angeline, I mean. She wanted to meet her somewhere Benjamin Troup couldn't hear. To complain about the way he was treating her, I suppose. Angeline was Miz Miriam's confidant and probably the one person keeping her from doing something like shooting Benjamin Troup or offing herself."

I must've looked horrified because he went on, quickly, "Anyway, your mother asked me to watch you. Guess she wanted to get us out of the way so we wouldn't hear, either. Little pitchers, big ears, you know. Wanting to make sure we didn't hear and say something to the wrong person."

He gave me a smile, reaching for my hand again.

"You can imagine how that went over. The last thing I wanted to do while in the park was babysit a three-year-old, especially when there were birds to chase and fallen camellia buds to pick up and throw at them."

"I remember she was always asking you to tend me," I said. "And you usually did the opposite."

"Did it that day, too," he admitted, having the grace to look ashamed, even now. "I tolerated you getting in the way for a while, then picked you up and set you on the base of the statue at old Jeff's feet, and went on my merry way while you screamed your head off."

"You didn't."

"I did, and I've said I'm sorry, and you forgave me,

so don't go getting angry."

I didn't answer.

"It wasn't long before everyone in the park could hear you. You had a good set of lungs on you back then, Gracie," he said, admiringly. "I figured I'd better get back and shut you up before Miz Miriam found out what I'd done. I'd just gotten you down when she and Mom showed up."

"And you came out smelling like a rose as usual, I'll bet," I muttered. "What lie did you tell her?"

"That you'd just started crying on your own and I couldn't make you stop no matter what I did. She commented you were just too spoiled for your own good." He grinned. "Which was the truth, so I didn't correct her."

"You rat." I hit his shoulder. Not too hard.

He winced anyway, and rubbed it.

"Lucky for you I don't remember."

"I really am sorry, Gracie. After you left, I missed you."

"Missed having someone to pick on, you mean."

"Missed *you.* Once you weren't here, I realized I actually liked you, and I think that's when I stopped being a bully. I got it into my head Miz Miriam took you away because I was so mean."

"That sounds so weird."

"What? That I thought I was the cause of your going away?"

"No, your calling my mother *Miz Miriam.* You did that with Abigail, too."

"McAllister is still *Old South* in some ways, Gracie, and we call married ladies by their titles and their first names, like we have since forever. Traditions.

Remember?" He glanced at his watch. "What say we just sit here and enjoy the scenery and talk, and not think of slights or injuries, past or present, for a while?"

"Fine with me," I agreed. "What shall we talk about?"

"Oh, I don't know…food's always a safe subject. Do you still like peach ice cream, or has your taste changed? I remember you could eat a whole dessert dish of that stuff even when you were barely big enough to handle a spoon."

"I still love it," I admitted, his description making me visualize a baby waving a spoon and covering herself with melting ice cream. "Although my tastes have enlarged to include gelato and sorbet now."

"Well, aren't we cosmopolitan? Which do you like best? I'm a frozen yoghurt man, myself."

We spent the rest of the time comparing our tastes in desserts.

Chapter 10

Discussing the merits of frozen yoghurt and other palatable after-dinner treats soon reminded me that breakfast was long gone.

"Is there somewhere we can get some lunch?" I interrupted May's poetic description of the homemade peach ice cream served by a certain restaurant in Macon. It was amazing how enthusiastic the man could be about food. "All this talk has made me hungry."

I wondered if one day his obvious sweet tooth would catch up with him and he'd balloon into twice the man he was now. It definitely indicated the way to his heart was partially through his stomach.

We got to our feet, strolling leisurely to where the car was parked. On the way, we passed Kyle, minus his bellhop's jacket, seated on a nearby bench. A comic lay open on his lap and he was busy reading while munching on a burger and scooping fries from a paper bag on the bench beside him.

I didn't speak to him. He was so immersed in the comic as well as the next bite of burger that I don't think he knew we were there.

"The Manor's dining room has a buffet lunch..." May began, but I nixed that before he could finish.

"Too fancy. I want something rib-sticking and calorie-loaded. How about Shedd's?" I suggested as we climbed into the car. It was the only place I knew besides the local franchises and I imagined those places were overrun about now.

"If the sheriff hasn't closed it," he agreed.

"Can we hurry?" I made my request plaintive. "I'm a city girl. I have to have my three-squares or I'll get faint."

"I've noticed you've a good appetite," he agreed.

This from the man who'd just bragged of eating an entire ice cream cake by himself.

"They don't have much of a menu selection," May seemed to be trying to talk us out of going there. "Just burgers, chili, and barbeque."

"I'm a fan of all three from 'way back," I said. "Step on it, May. I can feel malnutrition setting in."

His answer to that was a laugh as he floored it.

****

I wasn't kidding when I said I was hungry.

May watched me tuck into barbeque, Brunswick stew, and French fries as if someone had told me a famine was scheduled an hour from now.

"Do you always eat like this?" He bit into his own burger.

I nodded. My mouth was too full to answer.

He shook his head. "I was teasing about your appetite, Grace, but after this… Keep it up and I may have to take back what I said about you not weighing much."

"Hah." I reached for a French fry, swirling it in catsup and stuffing it into my mouth. I sipped some more of my soft drink, then wiped barbeque sauce from my mouth with a paper napkin.

"Finished?"

I nodded, wadded the napkin, and dropped it into the

plastic basket that had held my lunch.

Pushing both baskets out of the way, May said, "Now…to business."

Just then, the screen door opened. Someone wearing a camo jacket and cap came lumbering through the door, heading for the bar. Older, his five o'clock shadow making him scruffy-looking, what my mother would've characterized as "trash." He wasn't a fat man, but *big,* and that was the only reason I noticed him…his size.

A few minutes later, two more appeared, calling out to the bartender and going over to one of the pool tables. Then three others walked in—with their wives? girlfriends?—going to a nearby table.

The waitress hurried over to the pool table, pencil out, pad ready.

Until now, Shedd's had been relatively deserted except for us. Abruptly, it was getting downright crowded, and noisy, as someone shoved some coins into the jukebox and a country-Western singer began serenading the pool players.

"First off, do you intend to change your name as requested in the will?" May raised his voice slightly to be heard over the singer's.

"I don't think 'request' is the right word," I answered. "It was more like a royal command, but I haven't decided. If we find my real father, maybe. If not…do I *have* to?"

"I doubt anyone in the family's going to force it. Except for the undearly departed, probably no one else cares." He nodded. "Let's table that problem for now. We can ask Jeff Simmons if we have to. I thought of something else while you were scarfing that barbeque. Have you ever thought that Benjamin Troup could be lying? That you really *are* his daughter?"

"Except for my eye color, there's no way I can prove it," I answered, glumly.

"Stranger things have happened in the gene pool." May waved that aside. He gave me a mischievous squint. "Come to think of it…maybe you *are* a freak."

He laughed as I swatted his shoulder.

"Wouldn't it be his word against mine? And guess who people are inclined to believe? Especially since it's in a will… Isn't that kind of like a deathbed confession or something?"

"That's a defeatist attitude." May scowled. "Anyway, it's easy to prove these days. Good ol' DNA. I'm sure there's plenty of his still available. I doubt the grieving widow has thrown out his belongings yet. A strand of his hair from a comb…a quick swab of the inside of your cheek… If there isn't, we can check yours against his *real* kids'. That'd be easiest, and it'll settle once and for all and maybe you won't have to go daddy-hunting."

"Right." I fell back on my previous argument. "Who's going to pay for that? I've seen some of the bills my boss forwards to clients and I don't have that much to fork over. Unless you plan on my asking David for a raise?"

"I imagine you're paid very well," he retorted, "but I do agree, a fully extensive test for legal use would probably be expensive. To save money, we could try one of those genealogical websites, but it'd still take time for the results, and it might be questioned…so…okay, that's out for now. Anyway, investigating's more fun. Second question… What do you do if you find daddy dear and he doesn't want to own up he was the happy little farmer?"

That stopped me. May's encouragement had me envisioning a joyous reunion with tears and relief on both sides that the story was finally in the open. Now, the spoilsport was bringing up the negative aspects.

"I guess I'm hoping he'll be so glad he won't deny it, but if he does, and there isn't much doubt, I'll go away quietly and leave him to feel guilty. This is for my own benefit, anyway. Not his." I'd said that before, so I was repeating myself, tough, if half-heartedly. Would I really give up so easily?

At that moment, I thought I would.

"Good enough answer, if you can stick to it." May's nod set that question aside, too. "Okay…on to that phone call I received. It was from Carter McAllister, adding a couple of exceptions to what he'd already told us. Essentially, he readily admitted driving the getaway car when you left town. He says he didn't tell you because it doesn't really matter. He isn't your father and his helping you and your mother get away doesn't change that. I let it go."

"You said a couple of exceptions," I pointed out. "What's the other?"

"It's not so much what he said, but what he didn't say," May went on. "I got the distinct feeling there's something he isn't telling, and I think it has to do with that allusion your latent memory says he made about your mother knowing why he didn't go to the police about something."

"He didn't tell you?"

"I brought up the fact that you remembered the conversation between him and your mother, but he says you're mistaken. After all, it was twenty years ago and you were half-asleep and only five. He could be right, but…" He shrugged. "Wish we'd been face-to-face so I could've seen if there were classic signs of lying…eyes shifting to the left, plenty of hesitation before answering, and such. Since we weren't, I didn't push it."

"I'm not wrong," I said. "I know what I heard."

"You know what you *dreamed*," he corrected. "Besides, it may not have anything to do with *you*."

"But you don't think that."

"I'm saying we should consider any and all possibilities. Besides, there are other ways to get information."

"Is that all he said?" I asked.

"Except for his mentioning Marty Salazar…but something about the way he said it…I'm going to have to think about that a bit."

I frowned.

"I don't like that look. What are *you* thinking?"

"That I didn't imagine what I heard. *Let the dead stay dead*. Who died?"

"Lots of people. Someone dies every day."

"In McAllister? That would empty the town fast."

"Carter might've just been using a cliché, you know. He could just as easily have said something like, *Let sleeping dogs lie*."

"*…if you can't make them tell the truth*. Right."

I laughed at his puzzled expression, changing to a grin as he recognized the old pun.

"Maybe we should go to the newspaper office and ask to see papers from that time. Ask specifically to see any articles concerning someone dying around the time we left."

"You're really determined to make this into

149

something bigger than it is, aren't you? It doesn't necessarily mean someone died, Gracie."

"You've said that already."

He had been nursing a ginger ale rapidly becoming diluted with melting ice. He slurped the last drops, shook out the remaining chips of ice and crunched for a bit, then swallowed, "Say, I'm still thirsty. You want something else to drink?"

I glanced at my cup. Nobody warned me a medium soft drink at Shedd's held twenty-six ounces. The half-full cup still sat in front of me, its plastic lid impaled by a straw. "Maybe some more ice?"

"Be right back." May picked up both cups and headed for the bar.

There was only one person at the bar, the camo-wearer. May stopped next to him, speaking to the bartender, who poured him another ginger ale and refreshed my ice, replacing the lid and straw with new ones. As he turned to go, Camo said something. May stopped, looking back. For a moment, they spoke, rather heatedly, I thought, before he turned and came back to where we sat.

"A problem?" I asked as he sat down, handing me my drink.

"Nah." He downed a third of the drink in one gulp.

"Do you know that good ol' boy?" I nodded at the man at the bar.

"Why do you ask?" May looked in that direction.

From his expression, I thought he not only knew him, but also, he wasn't one of his favorite people.

"He strikes me as a charter member of *Rednecks Anonymous*," I answered. "Straight out of some grade-B movie about the South. What did he say to you?"

May shifted his attention. The man had taken out his cell and was speaking into it. He'd turned so he could see us as he talked.

"Nothing much."

"Mayfield…" I put that warning lilt in my voice a Southern mother always used to warn a child she knew he was lying.

He hesitated, then sighed as if deciding to tell the truth and get it over with. "Just wanted to know how much longer I was going to hang around the McAllister slut since she wasn't getting any of the old man's money."

"Of all the nerve." I was half out of my chair before I realized it.

"Gracie, sit down." May's voice was so sharp I obeyed without argument. His hand tightening on my forearm also helped a little.

I don't know what I thought I was going to do. The jerk was almost as tall as May and probably outweighed him by fifty pounds, and he looked like the type who'd hit back even if struck by a woman…*especially* if struck by a woman.

"What did you tell him?" I made my answer quiet, struggling to hide my anger. News of my humiliation was spreading faster than I expected, if a total stranger already knew about the will and referred to me in such a way.

"I told him I'd heard stupidity ran in his family and was glad to see he was keeping it alive and well." He raised his cup and took another swallow. "I don't think he appreciated that too much."

"Oh, God…May, who is he?

"Taylor Dix." May straightened. "A sonofabitch

with a hair-trigger temper. Not simple-minded—too smart for his own good, in fact—but an ignorant roughneck and a bully. He's kind of the town handyman as well as the local bootlegger. When we were teens, it was a show of manhood to get close enough to taunt Dix, then run away before he could react."

"That sounds stupid."

"Yeah…as I found out. The hard way." He ran a hand through his hair, lifting it off his neck. "That's how I got this. I wasn't as fast as I thought."

At his hairline just behind his left ear was a long, thin, very pale scar. A little lower and it would've gone across his carotid.

I managed to hide the shiver that thought produced, turning to look back at Dix, who finished his conversation and returned his phone to his hip pocket. He glanced at his watch and said something to the bartender, leaning against the bar and raising his drink.

"I hope your parents had him arrested."

He shook his head. "Didn't happen."

"Why not? If he tried to kill you…"

"The only witnesses were a bunch of underage teens who'd had too much to drink and were therefore in danger of being arrested themselves…and a certain Benjamin Troup alibied Dix. Said he'd hired him to work on one of his cars at the time he was supposed to be trying to cut my throat."

"…and he was believed, because the great Benjamin Troup McAllister never lied," I finished, bitterly.

"It was probably just as well. I was a bit of a smartass myself back then and the sheriff knew it. With Benjamin Troup's backing, it could've ended with Dix proving I'd provoked *him* and *me* being the one going to jail."

I shivered.

"Quit worrying. He doesn't look as if he's going to cause any trouble. Relax, Grace. Nothing's going to happen." He slid back from the table, reaching behind him. "Funny, I was sure I put my phone in this pocket…"

"You did," I said, glad for a change of subject. "I remember. Maybe it fell out when you got out of the car."

"In that case, I'd better backtrack and see if I can find it." May stood up. "Give me your phone a minute, Gracie."

I held it out to him. He punched in a number and handed it back.

"Call me. If the phone's outside or in the car, I'll find it by the ring."

"Good idea." I did as asked, listening to its trill.

"If I'm lucky, this won't take but a minute." He pushed back his chair and headed for the door.

I got up, too. "I'll go with you."

"No, stay here and finish your drink. I'll find the phone, and then we'll go."

"Okay." I sat back down.

At the bar, I saw Taylor Dix watch May walk out, then look at his watch. A chill went through me, though I didn't know why. When he turned back to the bar, I relaxed and gave my attention to my drink.

After a couple of swallows, I looked at the clock behind the bar, thinking May should've been back by now. He only had to go around the corner of the building. The walk from here to the car didn't take five minutes.

At that moment, Taylor Dix looked at his watch. Again.

That was the third time.

Maybe he was expecting someone. I pitied anyone he had a date with.

Once more, Dix consulted his watch.

That did it. I didn't know what was wrong, but something definitely was. I got to my feet, running for the door.

Behind me, I heard the waitress call, "Hey, wait…you haven't paid…" as the screen slammed and I headed for the corner.

That was when I heard the first grunt of pain.

I rounded the corner, slamming into the guy so hard I rebounded. He staggered as I interrupted his aim of a kick at a body lying in the gravel with someone leaning over it.

As I regained my balance, the man on the ground caught his attacker's foot and twisted, levering himself onto his knees.

I realized it was May. That made me stop stock still.

His assailant toppled but didn't stay down, scrabbling across the gravel on his backside until he was out of reach. "Let's get outta here!" he shouted as he scrambled to his feet. He ran around May's car, heading for a rusted pickup on the other side of the parking lot.

Still on his knees, May spun, reaching for the other one, fingers catching at his arm. That one got in one more kick and broke away, following his companion.

Staggering to his feet, May started after them, then stopped.

By this time, I came out of my freeze.

"May, are you all right?" I tugged on his arm.

I heard a truck engine starting up.

"Hell, no." He whirled, looking down at me. There was blood on his face, a broken star of an impact wound on his cheek. He was panting loudly.

"Can you breathe all right? Is anything broken?" I danced around him, hands fluttering, afraid to touch him.

Except for the blood, he didn't really look hurt. He looked more angry...and resentful. For being caught off guard? For my seeing what happened?

I heard squealing tires and a loud thump as the underside of the truck hit the broken pavement at the back of the parking lot where it entered the street.

May ran around the car, staring after them. I told myself he couldn't be very hurt if he could move that fast.

In a moment, he was back., "Couldn't get the tag number. They were too far away."

One eye was now so swelled I don't know how he'd managed to see out of it. Blood trickled down his cheek onto the front of his T-shirt.

I slapped my hip pockets, pulling out a wadded tissue that I attempted to press to his cheek.

"I'm okay, Gracie." He swatted me away. "Quit fussing."

Yep, he was all right, and acting the he-man.

May bent and scooped something off the gravel. The missing phone. Luckily it hadn't gotten trampled during the struggle.

He tapped in a number, then winced and rubbed his free hand across the knuckles of the hand holding the cell. His fingers were skinned and bleeding.

Walking a few feet away, he spoke into it so I couldn't hear what he was telling whoever answered. I hoped it was 911. When he came back to me, his face was so pale and he gave me such a look of pure fury, it frightened me, though I knew he wasn't actually angry with me. At that moment, I don't think he even saw me.

"Sheriff should be here in a few minutes." He headed back around the building.

"Where are you going?"

"To get some ice. To put on my face."

"Did you call an ambulance?"

"Don't need one."

I ran after him. I wasn't going to stay out here alone. What if those animals came back? I'd be no match for them if they decided to finish what they'd started. Exactly what had they started, anyway? Was this a robbery? Was May in the wrong place and a likely victim, a lone man in a deserted parking lot, even if it was in broad daylight in the early afternoon?

I still clutched the blood-spotted tissue. As I looked down, something fell onto it, making a clean spot in the blood. It took me a minute to realize it was a tear. I blinked back the others.

Save them for later, I told myself. I knew if I let another fall, there'd be a downpour.

I stamped back inside.

May was sitting at the table we'd both vacated, holding a small rolled-up bar towel to his cheek. The bartender was hovering nearby, looking worried, while the waitress cleaned May's free hand with another towel. An open bottle of rubbing alcohol sat on the table, filling the air with its medicinal smell.

She looked as concerned as the bartender.

I glanced around. Surprisingly enough, no one else seemed to notice May's condition. Everyone else was still eating or drinking or chatting calmly. Apparently patrons with blackened eyes and bloody faces were a common enough sight.

Only one person was on the move.

Taylor Dix was no longer at the bar. He was fast-walking down a little hall where a sign on the wall read *Restrooms*.

"Those bastards." May gritted and jerked his hand from the waitress's. "That's enough, Megan, thanks. That alcohol hurts worse than the actual wound." He glanced at me, lowering the towel-icepack. "Are you okay?"

That's my tough guy, more concerned about me than himself.

I nodded.

In the distance, I heard the scream of a siren.

Chapter 11

May might not have wanted an ambulance, but whoever he'd spoken to decided he did. An Emergency Medical Team arrived three minutes before the sheriff.

The EMTs were quick and efficient. After learning what happened and getting May's vitals, one properly cleaned the impact wound while the other spoke to Megan and the bartender.

By now, Shedd's was nearly deserted.

It was amazing how quickly it emptied once that first siren sounded. Only a few customers stayed behind. *Probably because they don't have police records,* was my cynical thought.

I was glad only a couple of people were there. I didn't want to see any more than I had to, unless it was the two who'd hurt May and that I hoped would be as they were dragged away to jail in chains with me kicking them every step of the way.

By now, Tracy Crockett, Junior, the sheriff, had parked his car and ambled over and inside. He stood a moment, watching the EMT work, before he pulled a small notebook from a hip pocket. Extracting a pen from the holder on its side, he stopped next to the medic talking to the waitress and the bartender. There was a muffled conference in Shedd's entrance with the sheriff writing down whatever they were saying.

Afterward, he ambled over to where we sat. With

pen poised over a clean page, he looked silently from May to me, and began his interrogation. "I need to get a little information."

Neither of us spoke. He seemed surprised, then began again, reading from the little pad.

The EMT ignored him, continuing with his work.

"I have the victim's name as Mayfield Donovan." He looked at May. "That's you, right? Teacher, aren't you?"

"Yes, sir," May answered.

That polite answer surprised me until I reminded myself where I was. In McAllister, at least, law enforcement, those in authority, and our elders were still accorded some respect. Sheriff Crockett was all three, as well as having more or less inherited his current position. I later learned he'd succeeded his father, Tracy Crockett, Senior, as sheriff.

"You know it is, Sheriff," May added, quietly, but with a slight smile.

Crockett gave him an answering one.

"Just following Standard Operating Procedure, May. Okay...what happened? You start your drinking a little early in the day, take exception to something said and decide to settle a difference of opinion outside?"

He sounded so much like a smalltown sheriff from a television show, I nearly laughed in spite of the way I felt. In the next moment, however, anger set in.

"Hey! Don't try to say this is May's fault. He was *attacked*."

"Gracie..." May dropped the towel onto the table. The ice had long melted and was dripping down his hand. The fabric made a wet slap as it struck the table, water immediately puddling beneath it.

The EMT caught May by the chin, turning his head so they faced each other. He began applying butterfly strips to the wound on May's cheek. "This doesn't need stitches."

"Well, May…" I flicked a glance at him before glaring at the sheriff. "Whatever happened to hearing your side of it before he makes up his mind?"

"This is Miss McAllister, I take it," the sheriff said.

That made me angrier. Of course he knew who I was. Didn't the whole world know?

Then, he had to add, "…or are you still calling yourself that?"

That did it.

I drew in a deep breath. May squeezed my hand.

The medic produced some gauze pads smelling of alcohol and began swiping down May's jaw and across his chin, cleaning up the dried blood there.

"Excuse Gracie, Sheriff," May interrupted. "She's a little upset."

"Upset?" That hurt. Why was he apologizing to the sheriff about *me*? "You better believe I'm upset. We were minding our own business, and then those two…those…"

That was all I got out. I looked up at May, realized I was seeing him through a blur of tears and then my forehead was pressed against his chest.

That got in the way of the medic's ministrations and he stopped cleaning May's face.

I knew I was giving everyone—the remaining two couples, the bartender and Megan, even the sheriff—a show, something more to gossip about but I couldn't help it. I let go and just…bawled.

"Give us a minute, Sheriff. Gracie's had a hard time

of it recently. She…Well, I guess you've heard about Benjamin Troup McAllister's will." May seemed to take extra care choosing his words. I was grateful he didn't say "her father's will."

"Goes without saying," Crockett agreed.

"We were having lunch and discussing what to do next."

"Yeah, I heard about that. Doubt if there's anyone in McAllister who hasn't." Crockett made what I considered the understatement of the year and looked sympathetic. "Really sorry, Miss McAllister. Shouldn't be surprised, though. Benjamin Troup was a sonofabitch and that's a fact."

My head came up. With a sniff, I studied the sheriff's tear-blurred image. I guessed he was about my erstwhile father's age or a little younger, so that meant he'd known him. Naturally.

The medic made a couple more dabs at May's chin with the gauze, then tossed it into a small plastic bag. He dug around in his kit and produced more plastic bags and some cotton swabs.

Would he never get finished? He wasn't exactly doing brain surgery.

"Fact is," he went on, "I was surprised he managed to die of a heart attack and not from a bullet between the eyes." He nodded as I reacted to that. "Yep. Thought he'd push someone a little too far one day and…*Boom.*" He made a firing gesture with thumb and forefinger. "I was tempted to do it myself a time or two." He managed to look a little shamefaced. "Yeah, I know. Shouldn't be saying that, with me the sheriff and all, but I've known Benjamin Troup longer than I've been the Law in McAllister, and he was a bully from the get-go. Guess that's why Carter's so nice. To make up for it."

He tapped the pen point against the page on which a few lines had already been written. He studied those sentences a moment.

The medic caught May's hand, running one of the swabs under the nail of one finger.

"That's neither here nor there, now. Which means I'd better quit mean-mouthing one of our recently-deceased prominent citizens and get back to the case at hand. How about telling me what happened leading up to the…uh…altercation?"

"As I said," May began. "We were discussing the will…"

"Unh-huh." Crockett nodded. "And…?"

"All done, Sheriff," the medic interrupted. He held up three small plastic bags, a cotton swap in each one. "I'll give these to your deputy.:

I guess all of us looked surprised. We'd been more or less ignoring him and not paying attention to what he'd been doing.

The sheriff nodded. The medic packed up his equipment, called to his partner, and gave May some last minute instructions. "Since you didn't lose consciousness, I don't believe you have a concussion, but if you have any vision problems, feel dizzy or extremely sleepy within the next twenty-four hours, get over to McAllister General ASAP."

May nodded and we watched as they went out the door, leaving Megan and Jake to return to the bar.

As the doors swung shut, May picked up the thread of the conversation. "Benjamin Troup stipulated he wanted Grace to stop using the McAllister name. She's decided to try and find her real father."

Crockett thought about that a moment. "How does Shedd's tie into that?"

"It doesn't," I cut in before May could reply. "That's neither here nor there." I began to reel off information as unemotionally as possible. *Just the facts, ma'am.* "May and I were deciding where to start."

"And you thought Shedd's would be that place?"

"No…" Was he being deliberately obtuse or what? "We sat in the park a while, and discussed places to go and people to see, and then I was hungry…I'd been to Shedd's previously and suggested it, so we came here. We had lunch—do you want to know what we ordered…or had to drink? No alcohol, I assure you."

I didn't try to keep the sarcasm out of my voice, making May wince slightly.

Crockett was obviously accustomed to waspish women because he merely said mildly, "No need for that. I'm familiar with Shedd's menu. Please go on, Miss McAllister."

"I…uh…" I floundered a moment. He was so amiable I was immediately embarrassed…as he intended, I don't doubt.

"We had lunch," May interrupted. "Then I thought I'd lost my cell phone and went outside to look for it."

"When he didn't come back," I cut in, "I went out, too, and…found him." Taking a deep breath, I continued in a friendlier tone, forcing a smile. "I hope I'm not a suspect, Sheriff."

"If the way you're acting's any indication, I doubt it," Crockett answered, and smiled back at me. "Did either of you get a good look at the assailants?"

"We did." We spoke together.

"They were in their early forties, wearing camo

hoodies and jeans, and drove away in a rusty old-model black pickup," May supplied.

The sheriff wrote that down. "Did they say anything?"

"They called my name," May said. "I looked around, said, 'Do I know you?' and got a fist in the gut for an answer."

"Did you talk to anyone outside or in here?" He directed that question to May.

I realized I'd been deftly elbowed out of the conversation.

"Megan…when she took our order." He nodded at the waitress who was hovering nearby, pretending to wipe down the table behind us. She'd been doing that since Crockett came in so it should've been spotless by this time. "Jake…when I got refills. Soft drinks," he added, before Crockett could ask.

"Hm. Don't think they're suspects, either. That's it? May nodded.

"Wait a minute." I remembered. "What about that guy at the bar? Taylor Dix."

"You spoke to Taylor Dix?" Crockett frowned.

"Shit. That's it." May slapped his forehead as if he were the biggest dunce in the world.

"What's it?" I looked at him.

"Taylor Dix is related to one of the bellhops at the Alhambra. He's Kyle's second cousin. Kyle probably told Taylor about that little scene we had in the lounge… Remember what he asked me?"

"…and what you said to him," I finished for him. "That has to be it. He called someone, remember? And he kept looking at his watch. Sheriff, he's the one."

I caught Crockett's arm. He looked down at my

hand and I released him.

"You've got to arrest him." I had to get in the last word.

Crockett didn't seem impressed by that. "Did Dix follow Mr. Donovan when he left?"

"No." My heart sank. He hadn't left the bar, not until after May was back inside getting first aid from the waitress." I shook my head, reluctantly admitting, "He was still here when I went out."

"Then he's got witnesses he was nowhere near Mr. Donovan when he was attacked.

"But he made a phone call," I protested.

"No law against that."

"Can't you subpoena his phone records?" I knew I was grasping at straws. "Find out who he called?"

"I could," Crockett admitted, then quashed that idea by adding, "with just cause, but unless we can identify the person he called as one of the two who attacked Mr. Donovan—"

"Just call me 'May,'" May put in.

"—May," Crockett nodded agreement, "that won't help. So far, I don't have much of a description of either them or the truck." He flipped a couple of pages in the notebook and read, "…'camo hoodies and jeans and a rusty old-model black pickup.' That fits two- thirds of the men and vehicles in McAllister."

"Aren't you even going to question him?" My voice reflected the helplessness I felt.

"Of course. When we find him." He glanced around the near-empty room. "I notice he's not here now."

"When May came back inside, he went down that hall," I gestured toward the *Restroo*m sign, "He never came back. Probably went out the back way, the coward."

"I'm afraid I can't arrest him for leaving afterward. In case you didn't notice, quite a few others did the same." The corners of his mouth quirked a little. "We'll question everyone who was in Shedd's this afternoon…that we can find. My deputy's outside, rounding up any who haven't already driven away."

I envisioned the deputy, probably a doofus who'd merely nod and let them go.

"Why don't you save time and just arrest Taylor Dix? *Now?*" I wasn't giving up.

"Because if I do that with as little evidence as I've got," Crockett said patiently as if he were speaking to a five-year-old, "he'll simply lawyer up and be out in ten minutes. It's not enough to hold him, especially since he was in sight at the time of the attack."

"You aren't going to do anything?" I knew I was being unreasonable, but I couldn't shut up. This was May who'd been hurt, not some stranger. "You're just going to write this off as an attempted mugging and let it go at that?"

"I didn't say that." It's to his credit Crockett took no offense at my accusations.

"What *are* you saying?" I demanded.

Why didn't May shut me up? Maybe he realized I needed to get it out of my system.

"We'll get a forensics team in from Savannah. Don't have one here. They'll check the evidence in those bags the EMT's leaving with my deputy. If he managed to hit back or maybe scratched one of them—"

"I got in a couple of swings," May admitted. "They did some kicking and hitting, too."

"—then we should be able to get DNA, and if either

of his attackers is in the system, as I expect they are, we may be able to tie them to Taylor Dix."

"Will you need my clothes?" May asked.

"Not unless there was close contact."

"There was a lot of scrambling going on. That's about as close as we got, a lot closer than a fist."

"...or a boot," I added.

"Guess you'd better swung by the station and leave them then."

May nodded. :Okay if I go home and change clothes and bring them in?"

Crockett shrugged. "If you'd gone to the hospital, they'd be bagged there, but we can't have you leaving here in the altogether, so guess that'll have to do."

I don't think I've ever felt so helpless in my life. I was accustomed to meeting problems head-on, facing them then and there, not sitting around waiting for something on a cotton swab or a bit of skin from under a fingernail to be analyzed and give up its answers.

Crockett pulled his radio off his belt. "Mel? You there, copy?"

It squawked back an answer.

"If you're finished taking names, swing by the Manor and see if Kyle Chandler's still on duty. If not, find him and bring him to me at Shedd's. Out."

The fact he knew Kyle's last name and neither of us had mentioned it should've told me something.

"You're bringing him here?" May asked.

"I can question him as well here as at the jail." Crockett managed a slight smile. "McAllister isn't such a hotbed of crime the sheriff has to be out patrolling the streets every minute. The forensics team should be here pretty soon. Savannah's not that far away. How good did the medics clean your hands?"

May held up his hands. His knuckles were badly skinned, a couple bruised and blackened.

Crockett caught one of his hands, studying his fingers, as well as the red-rimmed fingernails. "Looks like you've got plenty of blood under your nails. Hopefully it isn't all yours." He released May's hand and pulled out a chair. "In the meantime, mind if I sit down?"

He put the notebook into his breast pocket and dropped into the chair.

"Anyone want some coffee?"

I shook my head. May nodded, mumbling, "I'd like something stronger, but since you're on duty…"

"None for me, thanks," I put in.

Crockett waved a hand at the bartender. Jake took a glass carafe from a little coffeemaker behind the bar, poured out two cups full of steaming black liquid, and called to Megan who brought it to us on a little tray.

Crockett handed one to May and sipped at the other.

"Tastes better than it looks," he said.

May tasted his and agreed. Crockett looked at me and made chitchat.

"So you're Mimzi's daughter."

"Did you know my mother?" I asked hopefully. "Can you help us find out anything?"

"'Fraid not. Mimzi Baker was 'way out of my league. She had her own little clique of friends and I wasn't in it. I'm afraid I can't give you any information that'll help you in finding your father."

"You're not much help at all, are you?" It came out a lot nastier than I intended.

"Gracie." May's scold bounced off me.

"Well, May…" My retort had a whine in it. "He

can't arrest Taylor Dix for arranging to have you beat up for who-knows-what reason, and he knew my mother but can't help us there, either. Some sheriff."

I flounced around on the seat, facing away from them. If I'd stamped my foot and pursed my lips in a pout, it would've completed the picture of a disappointed, spoiled brat.

"Grace, honey…" May set his coffee on the table.

"No, May." Crockett was understanding.

Damn it, I didn't want understanding. I wanted results.

"She's disappointed. Lots of people get that way when they find out the law doesn't work like they see it on the television. Considering what this little lady's gone through lately, I guess I should be grateful she's not throwing things."

At that moment, the door opened and a uniformed deputy appeared with Kyle the bellhop in tow. "Here you are, Tracy. He was just getting off work."

"Am I under arrest?" Kyle blurted before Crockett could say a word. He looked panic-stricken, gaze wavering from Crockett to May and back again. "He says Mr. Donovan got beat up. I didn't do it. I swear."

"No one says you did." Dismissing the deputy with a nod, Crockett waved Kyle to the fourth chair. "Sit down, son."

"I've been behaving myself since I got that scholarship to the U, Sheriff. I'll lose it if I get into trouble," Kyle fell into the chair, protesting his innocence.

So he was another bad boy gone good?

"Calm down." Crockett laid a fatherly hand on his shoulder and, remarkably, some of Kyle's apprehension very visibly fell away. "I need you to answer a couple of questions and then you can be on your way."

"Yes, sir." He straightened, leaning back in the chair.

"Good." The notebook and pen came out again, but this time something new was added. Crockett pulled his cell from another pocket, pressed a button and set it on the table. "Going to record this, if that's all right with you."

"Shouldn't my ma be here?" Kyle eyed the phone as if it were a coiled snake.

"You're twenty-one, aren't you?" Crockett asked.

"Yes, sir, last month." Briefly, the boy looked as if he wished it weren't true.

I felt sorry for him, until I reminded myself it might be his fault May got hurt.

"Then we don't need anybody but you," Crockett told him, and got down to business. "Now... Did you tell anyone about Miss McAllister being a little under the weather yesterday at the Alhambra?"

"No," he answered promptly. "Who would I tell?" He answered his own question. "Well, I mean...I did mention it to my cousin Taylor."

"When?" Crockett didn't show by even a flicker what that meant, though I caught May's arm.

"When I went to lunch." Kyle's answer was completely guileless. Obviously, he had no idea what he'd done. "I stopped to get a burger, and he was there..."

He paused as a sudden thought struck.

"Please don't tell Ma I talked to Tay. She doesn't like him. After Pa left, she told him not to come around anymore. Told us kids not to talk to him, either. Said he was a bad influence."

Ma Chandler was a good judge of character, I thought.

"If you tell me the truth, you won't need to worry about your ma knowing you spoke to Taylor," Crockett assured him. "Now then, what did you two talk about?"

"Just...stuff, you know..." Kyle shrugged. "...where the crappies were biting...how hunting season couldn't get here fast enough, an' things like that...then he said he'd heard Mr. Ben's will had been read..." He looked at me. "That's what he always called your daddy...I mean, not your daddy..." His expression showed he wasn't certain what to call Benjamin Troup. "...anyway, he'd heard the will had been read and wasn't it a hoot how he'd put Miz Miriam's brat in her place?" He glanced at me. "I'm sorry, Miss McAllister, but that's what he said."

"It's okay, Kyle," I murmured, though it really wasn't.

"Go on," Crockett encouraged.

"Well...he mentioned Mr. Donovan...said it was a joke on him, if he expected Mimzi's brat to be an heiress, but it served him right after the way he put on airs...marrying that model and all..."

He gave May an apologetic glance.

"What else?" Crockett steered him back to the conversation.

"He said he hoped *she*—that is, *you*—" Again, he looked at me. "—wasn't going to try anything about the will, because if she did...well, he'd helped Mr. Ben with some problems before, like that business with Tuesday, and if he had to, he'd do it again since this time Mr. Ben wasn't here to defend himself."

He paused.

I drew in a quick breath. If that didn't sound like a threat, I don't know what did.

Kyle obviously thought so, too. "I told him I didn't care how much he liked Mr. Ben, Miss McAllister didn't deserve to be embarrassed like that."

"What happened then?" Crockett asked.

"He went off on a toot about how he owed Mr. Ben…how good he'd been to him…hiring him for odd jobs, and letting him keep a still on his property and only asking for ten percent of what he sold…" He stopped. "I guess I shouldn't have said that. You won't tell Taylor, will you?"

He looked more anxious than he had when he asked Crockett not to talk to his mother. I guess Taylor Dix was more to be feared than Mrs. Chandler.

"Right now, I'm not worried about Dix's bootlegging business," Crockett answered. "What happened next?"

"He kept getting louder and louder and everyone around us was staring, so when my order came, I took it and left. As fast as I could…went to the park to eat it."

"That's right," I confirmed. "We saw Kyle while we were there."

Kyle looked relieved, as if somehow that exonerated him of any wrongdoing. "I didn't see you."

"That's because you were too busy reading that comic."

"Yeah," he nodded. "That was a new issue. I got it in the mail this morning. It was the latest—"

"Kyle," Crockett interrupted quietly, putting a hand on the boy's shoulder again so he had to meet the sheriff's eye. "You do know your cousin Taylor's a

172

badass and a no-good from the get-go, don't you?"

"Well, yeah, but…" It hit him. "Oh, God, you don't mean…he beat up Mr. Donovan?" He swiveled in the chair, looking from May to me to Crockett again. "I swear, Sheriff, I didn't… Are you going to arrest him?"

"At the moment, we aren't arresting anybody. Not enough evidence."

Those damnable words. My anger resurfaced. I struggled to stay quiet and subdue it and nearly choked.

"I'm going to let you go. From now on, be careful what you say about people and to whom. I'll have Mel drive you home."

"If you don't mind, Sheriff, I'll walk. Ma won't like seeing one of her kids being brought home in a squad car…even innocent-like."

"As you will." Crockett dismissed him.

Before he could finish speaking, Kyle was out of the chair and heading for the door. He couldn't get out of there fast enough.

He passed a man coming in, carrying something like a tool box. He was wearing a jacket with SPD in a little shield on the left breast pocket.

"You got here fast," Crockett said.

"Crime in Savannah's slow today," the man said. "Thanks for getting me out of town for a while." He nodded to May, taking in the butterflies and the black eye. "This the vic?"

Crockett nodded and he got to work, setting down the case and opening it. "Too bad you were treated before I got here…all that alcohol and wound-cleansing probably did away with most of the evidence."

"I didn't call the ambulance," May defended himself. "The dispatcher did."

"Never mind. What's done's done." That sounded fatalistic enough. "I'll make do with what I've got."

Muttering to himself, he began swabbing May's hands, including the knuckles, and scraping off some of the blood under and around his nails.

I wondered why no one mentioned that the EMT had done something similar. Maybe this guy was more thorough?

Crockett continued talking while the technician worked. "If what Kyle said is true—and I've no reason to doubt it—and taking Dix's hero-worship of Benjamin Troup into account...he probably saw you in the park the same way you saw Kyle, followed you here, and then decided to have a little fun with May before he did whatever he planned on doing. Dix always did love a good fight. Sometimes I think he started a few just so he could hit someone."

He shook his head.

"Don't want to imagine what he thought he could do to Miss McAllister in broad daylight..."

That sent a chill through me.

"...but guess it doesn't matter now."

"Do I need police protection?" I asked.

"I doubt it. You're warned now. Besides, Dix is too much of a coward to plan anything elaborate. Anyway, I've only one deputy and I can't spare him to follow you around for...how long did you say you were going to be here?"

"I didn't," I said, shortly.

"In that case, I'd suggest you settle up whatever needs settling and get back to...where was it? Los Angeles?...as fast as you can."

"Are you running me out of town, Sheriff?" I tried

to speak lightly but it came out sarcastic. "Isn't it usually, '*Don't* leave town'?"

"Just making a suggestion," he answered mildly.

At that moment, the forensic tech said, "All done."

"I know this may seem a minor crime compared to anything happening in that big city of yours," Crockett told him, "but I'd appreciate it if you could rush this."

"I'll see what I can do." With that vague promise, he put his samples into separate glass tubes, put each tube into a baggie, scribbled something on each and packed up.

"EMT gave some stuff to my deputy," Crockett said. "Ask him for it."

The tech nodded and was gone.

Crockett's radio crackled to life again. He pulled it off his belt and walked a few feet away, talked for a couple of minutes, then came back.

"Got to leave. There's a three car pile-up at the exit ramp from I-75. My deputy needs help directing traffic away from it."

Nodding, he left, following Kyle through the doors, leaving May and me there.

May waited until the sound of Crockett's car had died away before he said, "Let's get out of here."

****

Outside, the heat hit us like a hot, sultry curtain. June weather was out full force. As we went around the corner of the building, something moved out of the shadows. I jumped, cowering against May, expecting to see Taylor Dix come charging at us.

"Mr. Donovan?" It was Kyle. He'd been leaning against the side of the building.

"I thought you'd gone."

"I wanted to apologize."

"No need for that," May said. I don't know if I could've been so generous. "Like the sheriff said, I hope this teaches you to think before you speak from now on."

"Are they going to arrest Taylor?"

"I doubt it." May let his disgust show. "He was in plain sight inside the whole time."

"Go home, Kyle. Try not to think about it." I surprised myself by saying that, especially since I was certain I'd do nothing but think about it all night.

"How are you going to get home?" May asked. "I know you usually ride with Chad, but he's probably home by now, and you turned down the sheriff's offer…"

"Guess I'll be walking." Kyle glanced toward the road running past the parking lot.

"That's a long way."

"It's no more than I deserve for what I did."

"Now that's plain stupid talk," May gestured to the convertible, the only one in the lot other than the sheriff's patrol car. "Come on, I'll give you a ride."

"Would you?" Kyle looked as excited as a kid being told Christmas came early.

May aimed the fob at the door. As it chirped, he said, "Get in."

While I sat silent in the front passenger seat, he and May spent the length of the drive extolling the muscle car's merits. I wondered if May was simply steering the talk away from Taylor Dix and Kyle's innocent involvement in the whole mess. The conversation wound down only when May stopped in front of the house.

It was a small cement-block cottage, not too humble-looking but nothing fancy, either. Just a lower middle-class home in a lower middle-class neighborhood, similar to the California one I'd grown up in, I realized.

"Do you think I'll ever be able to afford a car like this?" Kyle asked as he opened the back door and got out.

"Probably." May didn't even think about it. "Tell you what…get that diploma and a job and I'll sell this one to you."

"You mean it?"

May nodded

"Thanks, Mr. Donovan." With a wave, Kyle ran to the house.

May backed the car out of the drive.

"You do realize that when he graduates, he's going to expect you to live up to that promise," I said.

"And I will," he answered. "That's two and a half years from now. By then, I'll be ready to trade this one in for a newer model."

I couldn't tell if he was serious or not, so I let it go.

Instead, I said, "You're certainly being nice to him after it was his fault you got hurt. I don't know if I could be so forgiving."

"Now, Gracie…"

"I mean… I truly didn't expect any of this when I decided to come here…not what was in the will…certainly not all that's happened between you and me…and most especially not you getting beat up by someone who apparently has a misguided loyalty to my dead legal, if not biological, father."

I gave a halfhearted giggle that had a bit of a hysterical lilt.

"If I didn't know better, I'd say it was some kind of

conspiracy…but I *do* know better." I paused. "Don't I?"

"You had no way of knowing what was in the will," he answered. "As for Taylor Dix…I think Sheriff Crockett's right. He won't try anything else because we're now on the defensive. Let's try to forget it."

As I started to say I couldn't, he went on, "I know it won't be easy, so tuck it away and maybe after a while it'll slink off somewhere and be ignored."

"I can't." I was ready to cry again. All I needed was an excuse to start, and our conversation seemed like a good one.

May must've thought so, too. "I hope you're not going to start crying," he said, not looking at me. "Because it's going to be awfully difficult to comfort you and drive at the same time."

I sniffed loudly and leaned back. "I wouldn't dream of it."

"That's my girl." He sent the car roaring down the road.

Once we got home, I fiddled around in the kitchen, assembling sandwiches and coffee. Neither of us was hungry, so we sat at the table, staring at the bread and ham slices I'd slapped together. I think May's cheek was beginning to throb a little, because he winced every time he took a bite.

In fact, he was stolidly chewing on the sandwich as if he wasn't tasting it at all.

Finally, he said, "Okay, I know what I said in the car, but…want to talk about it?"

I shook my head and got to my feet, gathering plates and glasses. "Nope. It's tucked away in that little mental cubbyhole where I stash things I don't want to think about, and it's staying there."

I hurried into the kitchen, scraping breadcrusts into the disposal.

"Matter of fact, I think I'll stuff them in here along with the remnants of our sandwiches." I turned on the faucet and flipped the switch, listening to the grate-and-grind of the disposal. As I turned it off, I dusted my hands together. "All gone. I've too much other stuff to worry over to waste time on Taylor Dix."

While I was talking, May put the dishes in the dishwasher.

"Come on." He put an arm across my shoulders. "You look as if you're ready to drop."

"You don't look much better," I mumbled.

"Flattery will get you everywhere." The arm slid to my waist.

Gently, he pulled me out of the kitchen and guided me up the stairs. I leaned against him, feeling my eyes beginning to droop. If I relaxed, I was certain I'd fall asleep.

In the bedroom, he pushed me into the bathroom and caught the hem of my tank top, pulling it over my head in one smooth movement. He tossed it in the direction of the clothes hamper. It missed, landing on the floor in front of it.

When I didn't move to pick it up, he pulled off my sandals, unzipped my jeans, and slid them off, picked up my top, and stuffed both inside the hamper. Then he shoved back the shower door and turned on the water.

"Hop in."

I staggered rather than hopped. He pulled the door shut and left me there. A soap-on-a-rope hung from the showerhead. I rubbed it between my palms, halfheartedly working up a lather, scrubbed my face, then stood under the streaming water and did what May told me not to do…thought about what happened.

I realized I'd never seen anyone hurt before. How would I have reacted if I'd walked around that corner and found May dead? I didn't doubt they'd have killed him before they were finished.

But he didn't die, and he's here, with me, now. I turned off the water, shoved back the door, and stepped out.

May was waiting with a towel. He threw it around me and rubbed me dry, so vigorously I shook from the movement of his towel-covered hands over my body. Then, he dropped it to the floor and led me back into the bedroom.

The bedspread and sheet were turned back, pillows fluffed.

Still not speaking, I climbed into bed. He got rid of his own clothes and got in beside me. For a moment, we lay there in silence.

"Come here, sweetheart." He reached for me and cuddled me against his chest.

That did it. Snuggled against his bare warmth was the last straw.

One tear trickled down my cheek, then another. I began to cry. I burrowed my face against May's chest and sobbed and he patted my back and held me close and let me cry it out.

"This is all my fault."

"How do you figure that? Just a little while ago, you were blaming Kyle."

"It's his fault, too, for telling his cousin," I answered. "But it's more mine. If I hadn't come here, and heard what Benjamin Troup wrote in his will, and decided to find my real father…"

"Following that logic, blame me, too. I was the one who convinced you to try to find your father. Hell, blame your mother. She's the one who ran away. Or Carter for helping her. Or… It's everyone's fault and no one's fault, Gracie."

My only answer was a watery sigh.

"Now, repeat after me: This isn't my fault."

"Th-this isn't m-my fault…" I mumbled, then asked, "Why do I feel like it is?"

"Oh, my Gracie-Wacie…" Rolling me onto my back, he leaned against me, kissing my forehead. He did the same to my temples and my eyelids, licking away the tears wetting my cheeks. When he touched his lips to my mouth, I responded with a desperation that wasn't so much wanting love in that moment as needing reassurance…

It was an exhausted, violent coupling born of the realization of how fragile and tenuous human life is. Short and a little rough and determinedly frantic, and when it was over and May ripped off the condom and flung it into the wastebasket, he fell back onto the bed with a deep groan and gathered me to him, holding me tightly.

"It'll be all right, Gracie. Say, did I hear correctly somewhere a couple of hours back…you *are* going to try to find your real father?"

I didn't answer.

Curling together, we both slept.

Chapter 12

"Gracie." Someone shook my shoulder. "Time to get up."

"Go 'way." I swatted at the hand and rolled over, burying my nose in the pillow.

"Sorry. No can do." He rolled me back. "It's seven o'clock. I've let you sleep in long enough. Time to hit the ground running."

"Seven o'clock?" I opened my eyes.

May was leaning over me, fully dressed and looking much too alert for that time of morning.

"What are we? Dairy farmers? I've slept later than this when I'm working."

"You're not in California now, sweetheart." He caught my wrists and hauled me upright, slapping something into my hand. "Get dressed. I'll make you some breakfast."

With that, he jogged to the door and went out. I glanced down at the garment I held. A bra. With a sigh, I slid it on and searched for something more to wear.

May met me at the foot of the stairs with a travel cup filled with hot coffee and a sandwich plate holding two pieces of cheese toast hugging a fried egg between them. I accepted it with thanks.

I studied him as I took a sip of coffee, thinking his eye looked a little less purple and his cheek a little less battered.

"Since you seem to have taken control, what's on the agenda today?"

"First stop, we're going to see my dad. After that…we'll see." He held the door open for me, nodding at my sandwich. "Bring that with you and let's go."

I went through the door and he locked it behind us.

"If we're going to your folks' place," I hurried down the steps and to the car, "…do you want something to hide all that…" I nodded at his black eye, "…so they won't ask questions?"

"Like what?" His voice held a suspicious note as if he thought I was about to play a trick of some kind.

"I don't know…" I fumbled mentally and came up with, "I could put some makeup on it…"

"Nothing doing," he interrupted, hastily. "I'll go *au naturel*, thanks. Anyway, I imagine by the time we get there, Daddy'll know all about it." He came down the steps, aiming the fob at the convertible. "Get in."

We got into the car.

I was quiet while we drove along, busily working my way through the egg-and-cheese sandwich.

"Not still thinking about Taylor Dix, are you?" May asked, as I finished my coffee and put the travel mug in the cupholder on the console.

"Not about Dix specifically." I shook my head.

"What then?"

"Something he said…about Tuesday…he said he'd helped Ben with some problems before, like that business with Tuesday…remember?" I glanced at him. "I don't know why but that phrase has stuck itself in my head, and…"

"…you're trying to figure out what he meant?" May finished.

"Yes, and I'm coming up with a big, fat blank. Tuesday? A day? A specific date? What does it mean?"

"Maybe that was a day his still broke down or something." May shrugged it away. "Probably nothing important."

"Then why did I take note of it?"

"How should I know? You didn't mention it at the time. Why remember it now? It probably just popped up. A random thought. I doubt it has any significance at all."

"I don't think so," I argued but I didn't sound certain. "Why would I pick up that one phrase when I didn't react when Kyle mentioned it?"

"One of Life's Little Mysteries." May sighed. "Perhaps one of us will have a sudden insight and, as they say, *all will be revealed.*"

"If only..." I sighed, too.

We were at the outskirts now, heading down the road leading into town. We had to pass McAllister Place on the way. Since the house was visible from the road, I turned away so I wouldn't have to see it.

A few minutes later, May said, "Grace, I think we're being followed."

"You're kidding." I looked back.

It was another hot June day, and the dust the car's wheels were throwing up made a crimson cloud of good old red Georgia dirt behind us. Through it, I could make out the faint shape of another car, low-slung and sleek. A yellow sportscar.

"Ben?" Why would he follow us? "It's probably just a coincidence."

"Let's find out." At the next side road, May turned off without signaling. So did the sportscar. He picked the next turn to take, onto what was almost a footpath. The other car did the same. "Okay, let's see what's up."

Flipping on the turn signal, he slowed and pulled over to the shoulder, easing the muscle car to the edge of a steep ditch overgrown with kudzu, the other side of which became an abandoned cornfield. The wind rustled through what was left of the dried yellow stalks. The sportscar followed, stopping behind us and waiting for the dust to settle.

Both of the sportscar's doors opened. Ben and Sammi got out. They walked to where May stood.

"Hey, Mr. Donovan. Thanks for stopping. I was afraid we'd have to follow you all the way to town." Ben's greeting was as innocuous as could be. He gave May an ingenuous grin. "I heard about your fight with Taylor Dix. Hope that black eye is healed before school starts. Otherwise you're going to get tired of explaining."

"The gossip mill in McAllister beats any jungle telegraph by a mile," May muttered. "Don't tell me you saw us passing and followed us just to tell me that?"

"No, sir, but I am curious… Did my dad really take part of Taylor's moonshine profits?"

I laughed before I could stop myself.

"Answer: According to Dix…yes." May's answer was abrupt. "Next question: What do you really want?"

"We wanted to see Grace again before she left." Ben bent so he could look into the car. He waved. "Hey, Grace."

"Hey, Ben." I waved back.

"Grace?" Sammi put a hand on the door, peeping in at me.

"What's happened, Sammi?" I sounded a little brusque, though I didn't mean to. I softened my voice and went on, "Is something wrong?"

"Other than losing our sister, you mean?" She shook her head dramatically.

Ben was speaking to May in an undertone, so she opened the door and caught my arm, tugging on it. I let her pull me out of the car.

"I meant what I said at the reading, Grace. I don't want us to lose touch. When you get back to California, will you please call me, or at least email once in a while?"

"Sammi, I don't think…"

"Sometimes people *shouldn't think*, Grace. That's when they start complicating things. Ben and I both want to get to know you. Even if it's long-distance. Please?"

Why not? They were both good kids, in spite of having a bullying sonofabitch for a father. If they wanted to pretend I was their sister…I admit I liked the thought.

I pulled my phone from my pocket. "Here. Enter your number and email addy."

"You too." She took it, giving me hers in exchange.

We entered information, then handed them back. Sammi looked at what I'd texted and smiled as she slid the phone back into the little pouch on her belt. Then she hugged me. That surprised me, as did the fact that I hugged her back just as strongly.

As we separated, she said, "I'm going to call you every week, and if you don't answer, I'll leave a voice mail, and if you don't call me back, you may find me walking through your door. We're not letting you go, Grace."

"You make it sound like a threat." I laughed. "Don't worry. I'll answer, Sammi. I promise."

I followed her around the car to where Ben and May stood. May broke off to look at me.

"I think your brother has something to say."

Ben said, "Whatever Sammi said goes double for me, Grace. I've always resented being the eldest so I'm not going to let a little thing like paternity give you an excuse to wiggle out of being my older sister."

Before I could answer that, I was engulfed in another tight hug and released.

Ben caught Sammi's hand. "Come on, Sam. These people have places to go and things to do."

"Whenever you leave, have a safe trip, Grace." With that, Sammi got into the car.

Ben climbed in, slammed the door, and started the engine. Somehow, he managed to turn the car around on that narrow road and send it zooming back the way it had come.

"Those are good kids," May said. "I wonder if they're really Benjamin Troup's?"

"It should happen." I laughed.

We got back into the car and May turned the convertible around, too, heading it back to the highway and on to his dad's. In that moment, I felt better than I had since the reading of the will.

****

May's father's home was more modern than the old farmhouse, being what was termed a split-level ranch back in the '70s. It was a neat brick building on an acre of land. There were plenty of pine trees surrounding it and, at one corner, I could see a couple of towering pecan trees, one with a very frayed rope hanging from a limb.

Since this was the house Bill and Angeline moved into after Billy was born, I wondered if that was where May's brother once had a swing. The walkway to the front door was edged by a narrow border of limestone chips, with green and white striped liriope and variegated caladiums filling the flowerbeds on each side of the steps.

May didn't knock, just swung the screen wide, opened the door, and went in, calling out, "Mom? Daddy? We're here."

I followed, stepping from Georgia heat into a near-frigid atmosphere. Goosebumps popped out on my bare arms. I was rubbing them before I realized it.

Footsteps sounded from somewhere in the back and a woman appeared. *Bustled,* I should've said, for that was the way Angeline Donovan moved, as if she were in a tremendous hurry to get somewhere because she had so much to do.

Perhaps years of running after May and his brother made her that way, though she certainly didn't appear harried. If anything, she looked extremely happy, as well as small and plump, with faded blonde hair pulled back in a short, curly ponytail that didn't look out of place.

The first thing she said was, "I heard about that little fracas you had with Taylor Dix. Oh, May."

A small hand hovered over the bandage before patting his wounded cheek but she didn't say anything else. Instead, she hugged May and was given a loving, if dutiful, filial kiss.

It was obvious Angeline wasn't the wicked stepmother type. Because she'd been married to Bill since May was about five, the love I sensed between the two was mutual. She was probably the same height as I, and to see the towering May bending over and hugging this little woman made me wonder if he and I looked as comical together. As he released her and stepped back, he touched my arm.

"Mom, this is Gracie."

"Oh, my dear…"

I barely had a chance to brace myself before I was enveloped in a hug also.

"I'm so glad to see you," she whispered into my ear.

Angeline stepped back, and took my hand.

"Come in and sit down."

I followed her into the living room. This was a homey place, nothing like May's showcase, a room where children once played on the floor and watched television, though probably not on the plasma TV now adorning the wall. I could imagine a lanky teenaged May sprawled on that sofa while little brother Billy drove his toy cars across the floor and generally got underfoot.

"Where's Daddy?" May asked, as I settled myself on the sofa and Angeline sat in what I imagined was *her* chair, an overstuffed recliner.

There was a knitting basket on the floor, overflowing with balls of yarn skewered with knitting needles of various sizes. Nearby, an identical chair was probably Bill's. A magazine basket sat on the floor beside it, filled with sports magazines and Western paperbacks.

"He's out in the shop." Angeline didn't look in May's direction. She appeared to have eyes for no one but me. "You know how he is," she went on as May started to speak again. "He probably got started on something and can't bring himself to stop."

"Guess I'd better go out there and remind him." May headed through another door. He looked a bit peeved by his father's nonappearance.

"While he's doing that…would you like something to drink, Grace? Tea, coffee?" Angeline was the perfect

Southern hostess, offering her guest a refreshing beverage.

"Tea would be nice, if it's sweet," I added.

"Is there any other way?" Angeline got up, following May. "I declare, I don't know how anyone can drink it otherwise. I'll be right back."

She was gone only a minute, not even long enough for me to get a good look around, though what I did see was comfortable, and I knew this was the kind of place I could be comfortable in, too. Not that I didn't feel all right at May's, but I still got the sensation I shouldn't set down a glass without a coaster under it and should always wipe my shoes before I came inside.

Angeline didn't offer a coaster but set the glass, its outside already beaded with moisture, on the coffee table. I could see several white rings on its surface, evidence many other glasses had been set that way over the years. She placed her own tea on the end table near her chair and leaned back as I took a sip.

It was perfect and I told her so, then managed to stifle a shiver as the chill of the ice in the glass added itself to the cold in the room.

"Let me say right off, I've been so anxious to meet you," she said. "I never heard from Mimzi after she left and I always wondered how you turned out."

"Well, here I am." I set down the glass. "What's the verdict?"

She laughed. "From what I see and from what May's told us, I'd say you turned out just fine. Just fine, indeed." She leaned forward, voice dropping slightly. "He really likes you, you know. More than *likes*, I think."

I leaned forward, too. "I kind of think so, too," I whispered.

We both laughed.

"Tell me, where's Billy? May hasn't mentioned him."

"I daresay since you came into his life again May hasn't thought about his baby brother." Angeline laughed. "Billy's attending summer session in Athens. He wants to graduate early. Speaking of May..." She looked in the direction of what I was assuming was the kitchen. "I wonder what's keeping them?"

"Maybe Mr. Donovan roped May into whatever he's doing?" I suggested. I got up. "Why don't I see if I can get them in here?"

I was impatient to meet Bill Donovan and tried to keep from showing it.

"Would you?" Angeline looked relieved. "It's so hot out, and I'm afraid I don't do well in this weather, now that I have a bit of a heart condition. That's why I keep the house so cold." She waved a hand as if indicating the air. "The doctors told me being out in the heat's bad for me."

"No problem," I said. Frankly, I'd welcome that June heat for a little while. I felt as if frost was forming on my nose. "Just point me in the right direction."

"Go through the door to the kitchen. It opens into the back yard. You can see Bill's workshop from there."

Nodding, I did as she instructed, giving the kitchen a glance as I passed through.

It was modern but not cutting-edge. The stove, refrigerator, and under-the-sink dishwasher matched, a chrome set. The cabinets were painted white with yellow trim and the window over the sink, looking out onto the back yard, had yellow print café curtains. A Fifties-style chrome dinette set rounded out the décor.

I opened the kitchen door and stepped through. Outside, I stood a moment, welcoming the rush of hot air around me.

The workshop was a small add-on to the garage situated behind the house. There was a window, and I could see lights inside and two figures. A flagstone path led from the back stoop to the workshop door. As I followed it, hopping from stone to stone, I noticed a patio to the side with a roll-out grill and a picnic table, more flowers in pots, and past that, a vegetable garden now wilting in the sun.

The door was open and I could hear May and Bill talking as I got closer. I suppose I should've just barged on in, but for some reason, I stopped outside the door. It opened outward, so they couldn't see me where I stood. I figured May was telling his father about me and I wanted to hear what he had to say.

"I told you I didn't want you bringing that girl here, May. I don't want her in my house."

That first sentence brought me up short. Don't they say eavesdroppers never hear anything good?

"I don't know why you're acting this way, Daddy. I thought you'd want to see Gracie. After all, you and her mother were friends."

"Mayfield, we were more than friends. I don't want your mother reminded of that."

"Is that what this is all about? You think Mom's going to be embarrassed because you dated Gracie's mother? Hell, Daddy, she was Miriam Baker's best friend. Don't you think she already knows?"

"She doesn't know *everything*."

"So this is about *you* being embarrassed? You don't have to worry, neither of us is going to asked probing questions. We won't give you the third degree." May laughed.

Bill muttered something I couldn't understand.

"Be that as it may, you're going to have to get use to Gracie being around, because she's going to be an important part of my life from now on."

My ears perked up at that. I felt my heart beat a little faster.

"What's that supposed to mean?" There was so much suspicion in Bill's voice it shook me.

"I think you can figure it out."

"My God, boy, you're not sleeping with her? Oh, damn, May."

"What we're doing is none of your business. Suffice it to say I love Gracie and I'm going to ask her to marry me."

I put one hand to my mouth. *Oh, May.*

"Son, you haven't known that girl long enough to want to marry her."

Was that a cliché or what? Even if it were true, I resented his saying it.

"I've known her all my life, Daddy, even if we haven't seen each other for a while."

"*A while?* You call twenty years '*a while?*' Remember what happened last time. *Marry in haste, repent in leisure.* You don't exactly have a good track record where women are concerned."

"Gracie's nothing like Veronica."

"You can't marry her, May. I forbid it."

"Last time I looked at my driver's license, I was over twenty-one, so you can't forbid me anything."

"You young fool…"

This sounded as if it was about to turn ugly. I

decided it was time I broke it up.

"May? You out here?" I pulled the door open.

They were both standing in a deer-in-the-headlights freeze-frame. May had his back to the door, Bill was facing him. My first glimpse of Bill Donovan confirmed the way I'd pictured him. Tall as May, an older version of his son, he was solid but not fat, and those good looks earning him his nickname were still very much in evidence. The red hair was mellowed out by the white in it, but it still managed a coppery gleam. The only difference between Bill and May were their eyes. His were hazel, not the reddish copper of May's.

"Gracie…" May breathed my name as if in relief. He held out a hand and I came inside the shop. "Daddy, this is Gracie," he said unnecessarily and hugged me against his hip.

He kissed my temple. A little defiantly, I thought.

Bill made a sound halfway between a choke and a protest, then regained control. Taking a deep breath, he held out his hand.

"Hello, Grace."

"Mr. Donovan."

Cautiously I placed my own in his. It lay there a moment before his fingers closed about it. He released me and walked past us to the door.

I half expected him to brush his hand against his jeans as if swiping away my touch.

He didn't.

"Shall we go back inside? I think it's getting too hot to stand out here and talk."

I wondered exactly what kind of heat he meant.

****

Once inside, Bill calmed down. Maybe he was still

leery of what he might say about the time he'd dated Mama, or of how his wife would react. I personally didn't see the problem. After all, as May said, Angeline was Mama's best friend, so they'd probably shared more than one gabfest extolling Bill's vices and virtues and other features.

Deciding they were already caught up on the will-reading and May's 'bar fight,' as Angeline called it, May told them what Carter said, and what we'd deduced from the scene I remembered.

Through it all, Bill nodded agreement, then said, "I don't know if I can add anything. Benjamin Troup was older than we were, and even if he'd been our age, I doubt he would've associated with us mere mortals."

His voice when he said that was so much like May's, I had to smile.

"Carter was so damned different. I sometimes wondered if they were really brothers." He laughed at that.

I agreed Carter was definitely a nice guy.

"I'm mighty sorry you came all this way to be insulted like that," he added.

I thought that was odd since he'd insulted me, too, though I wasn't supposed to know that.

He continued, "That was completely uncalled for. Benjamin Troup always was spiteful. Guess death hasn't changed that."

"I'll survive," I told him.

"What we were really wondering about," May said slowly, and I knew he was about to broach that very touchy subject, breaking his word about the third degree.

I hoped Bill wasn't going to react as he had in the shop.

"…is if you could tell us of anyone else who dated Gracie's mother. Besides yourself, I mean."

"May, I told you…" Bill began.

"Oh, for goodness' sake, Bill," Angeline exclaimed before he could get out more than that brief protest. "I hope you aren't going to think you have to be delicate because I'm in the room."

"Well, Angie, I don't feel it's proper…"

"Proper? Sugah, I was Mimzi's best friend. We shared everything. And one of those things we shared was what we thought of our boyfriends. She told me about most of her dates with you, gave me blow-by-blow descriptions."

Bill winced as she said that and closed his eyes. I had a feeling he was praying Mama hadn't gotten *too* detailed.

"I did the same. That means you can be completely truthful, sweetheart," she finished.

"All right." He opened his eyes, giving her a look so full of love it shook me.

I'd seen that same expression on May's face. I knew then and there Bill had no intention of being completely truthful, not as long as Angeline was present.

"I dated your mother, Grace. When she wasn't dating Carter. From about the time May was three until he was five. Off and on, nothing serious…at first. Then, while Car was away at school, we got *really* serious. At least, I did. I was actually thinking of asking her to marry me. Sorry, honey."

He shot Angeline an apologetic look. She smiled back and shook her head. Apparently, she already knew that.

"As soon as I mentioned that, Mimzi's parents were

at me with both barrels. She broke it off on our next date."

"Carter mentioned they were social climbers," I said.

"They were using Mimzi to get where they wanted to be on the McAllister society ladder." There was bitterness in his voice, even after this long. "Her marrying a former numbers runner wasn't the way to do it."

At least he didn't mince words about his alleged profession. I noticed May didn't even blink as he said it, so it must be common knowledge in the family. Was that good or bad?

"I'd gotten myself straightened out by then and was trying to turn myself around. After all, I had a kid to take care of and I knew I couldn't do it from a jail cell, even if my folks took May. Hell, if I'd gotten arrested, he might've ended up in a foster home somewhere, and I was determined that wasn't going to happen. So I decided to be a good father and make a home for myself and my son, and I wanted Mimzi to be part of it, but as I said, her parents couldn't see that, so…"

He made a vague, useless gesture.

"What about Marty Salazar?" I spoke up.

"Marty?" Bill looked surprised. "What about him?"

"Wasn't he part of your group?"

"Damn, I haven't thought about Marty in years." He looked ashamed at forgetting someone who must have been a good friend.

"Carter told us Marty dated Mama a while."

"I don't know that you'd call it a *while*," Bill corrected. "More like twice. After Mimzi and I broke up, she went back to Carter, then Benjamin Troup moved in on her. She went out with him a couple of times, then, as far as any of us knew, she gave him the cold shoulder."

"That's right." Angeline nodded. "Said he was too overbearing. And too stuck on himself. Besides, she thought he was too old."

"Then Marty showed an interest in her. Her parents deep-sixed that, too. Fast." Bill looked angry. "Marty was a good kid...funny, smart, and talented...but Mr. and Mrs. Baker didn't want a *cubano* hanging around. Hell, Marty couldn't even speak Spanish. That relationship was doomed from the start."

"Carter seemed to think they were serious," I persisted. "He thought they were going to get married."

"Don't know why he'd say that." Bill frowned. "Like I said, they went on maybe two dates. After her parents chased him away, Mimzi didn't date anyone for nearly a month."

"Don't forget you saw her a couple more times," Angeline reminded Bill. "After Marty died."

"That's right." He said that grudgingly. Showing a little surprise that she knew?

"And she did have a few more dates with Benjamin Troup," she went on.

Bill ignored that. "We were all shocked when Marty died. It was so unexpected."

"How do you mean?" I asked. "Other than sudden death always being unexpected."

"Because of the way it happened," Bill said. "I guess you know about that?"

"Just the barest facts." I nodded. "Nothing more."

"Marty drove his car into a telephone pole. At the inquest, it was determined he'd died instantly and not when the car exploded. A whiskey bottle was found in the wreckage, so they decided he'd been drunk-driving and lost control of his car."

"They couldn't do a blood alcohol test?" May asked.

"Not enough left. The identification was done through dental records."

I shuddered and looked away.

"It was all so weird. Marty didn't drink. When a bunch of us went out together, we'd see who could get the most potted, but he was always the designated driver. We used to tease him about it. If he was drunk that night, something must've happened to really upset him, though damned if I know what it could've been. He'd just graduated from college, he was young, healthy, and while his parents weren't rich, they were well off enough to pay for him to go on to get his Masters."

He stopped, looking away a moment.

"Someone started a rumor he was a secret alcoholic, and he'd let his drinking get away with him that night. That was a bunch of bullshit. Sorry, Angie." Bill sighed and looked from May to me. "I remember the four of us went to the funeral, then afterward, we drove out to the site of the wreck. Carter and I were being all stiff-upper-lipped and Mimzi and Angie were crying, and had been all through the service. I didn't want to go but Mimzi insisted. She wanted to see where it happened, she said, so we went. She just stood there, looking at that broken pole. It had cracked in half and was lying on the side of the road with the wires still strung through it. There was a big scorched place on one side and an even bigger burned spot on the ground. She was the first one of us to turn around and get back into the car. She never mentioned Marty again."

We were all silent a moment. What could we say?

"After that, I hung around a while. She seemed so upset I felt she needed comforting, you know. She and I had a couple more dates. I was hoping maybe I could get into her parents' good graces, and then…bingo, she was announcing her engagement to Benjamin Troup, and that was that."

"Do you know anything about something that happened on a Tuesday? Was that the day Marty had his accident?"

"Tuesday? Nope. It was on a Saturday, as I recall. But…Tuesday was Marty's nickname. He used to recite that old nursery rhyme. You know, *Monday's child is fair of face…*"

"Why? Was he born on a Tuesday?"

"As far as I remember, he was born on a Friday. But the poem goes *Tuesday's child is full of grace*, and Marty was a great dancer. He was in all the school musicals, and whenever we had a dance, all the girls would line up to be his partners. He used to joke that, combined with his name, he was so damned full of grace the girls couldn't help themselves."

"What about his name?"

"Marty's full name was Martes Esteban Salazar. In Spanish, *Martes* means *Tuesday*. So he was *Tuesday, full of grace*…get it?"

"Yes." I was disappointed. Just a kid's joke, a childhood nickname.

"I'm sorry, Grace." Bill looked apologetic. "That's all I know. I'm afraid I haven't been much help."

"Truthfully, Mr. Donovan, I didn't expect to learn this much, but it doesn't really matter. I've decided I'm keeping the name McAllister because I think Benjamin Troup is really my father. I think he was just trying to get in one last stab at my mother from the grave." I stood up, preparing to make a graceful exit. "I'm not going to let him have it."

"It doesn't really matter," May repeated.

I turned to look at him. His expression was determined, as if he realized he'd better say something now or lose the chance forever.

"Because if I have my way, Gracie's going to be changing her name to Donovan pretty soon."

"Oh, May." Angeline was out of her chair, hugging him and then me.

Bill, on the other hand, looked as if his son had just rammed a fist into his belly. He went white, then red, but didn't say a word. He appeared to be choking slightly. I hoped he didn't have a heart condition like Angeline did.

"If I say this is so sudden, will anyone believe me?" I managed a smile that came out slightly sickly, not because I wasn't happy, but because of Bill's expression and what I'd heard as I eavesdropped. "May, let's talk about this when we get home, and then…"

"And then?" He looked anxious.

"Then you can ask me again. Officially."

I didn't bother to act coy. I'd say *yes,* we'd plan the details later, and I'd work on winning Bill Donovan over, and try to find out why he was so set against May and me being together.

Chapter 13

We'd driven about ten minutes before May spoke. "You're awfully quiet."

I stirred slightly but kept my gaze on the mounds of kudzu rushing past the passenger window. "I'm thinking."

"About what? You aren't angry because of the way I asked you, are you? I mean, I didn't really intend to do that. It just seemed like the right time and it kind of came out."

"I'm not angry." I turned to look at him. Seeing how anxious he appeared made me feel guilty I might've made him worry. "It was romantic, in a way, but when you give me my ring," I shook a finger at him. "I expect you to do it right."

"I promise." The way he relaxed was comical, that Donovan smile back in place. "Candlelight, flowers...the whole she-bang. I'll even get down on one knee."

"That I want to see."

"I'll have someone from the *Daily News* record it for posterity."

"And I'll have it enlarged and put over the mantel." That made me laugh. Then I got all mushy. "I love you, May Donovan."

"And I love you, too, Soon-to-be-Mrs. Donovan. If you're not mad about that, what were you thinking?"

"That what I said to your father is true. I think Benjamin Troup is really my father."

"What made you change your mind?"

I could tell it was old news, as far as May was concerned. He didn't care and probably never had.

"Some of the things your father said."

He frowned at that, no doubt remembering Bill's outburst.

I hurried on, "Look at the facts. Benjamin Troup dates my mother. She lets him know fast she isn't interested…it's all her parents' idea. A month later, there's a very quick wedding. What does that tell you?"

"You're plotting out this scenario."

I could tell he had an idea where this was headed.

"Suppose *you* tell *me*," he said.

"I think he seduced Mama, maybe even forced himself on her. She didn't tell anyone because she figured no one would believe her. She finds out she's pregnant and gives him an ultimatum…marriage or she goes to the police."

May shook his head, but whether he was denying it or saying he hated to think that was true, I couldn't tell.

"He realizes there's a rare chance someone might believe her and he could be facing a rape charge, so it's a fast, quiet marriage. That's probably why he treated her so badly, because he'd finally been forced to do something he didn't want to do. As for Mama? She tried to make the best of a bad situation, put up with it as long as she could, and then she'd had enough. She got what she wanted…a name for her child, and she didn't really love him, so she asks former boyfriend, now brother-in-law, Carter to help her get away."

"And the thing Carter wouldn't tell the police was

that his brother had raped the woman he married. It fits."
He reached over and caught my hand.

"Hands on the wheel, eyes on the road." I replaced
his fingers gently back on the steering wheel. That made
him smile.

"Does it bother you? Knowing your father was
probably a rapist and your mother his victim?"

"Not as much as the fact that he's Benjamin Troup."
I laughed. It felt good. With May beside me, it really
didn't matter.

"Oops...." He shook his head. "We're forgetting
one minor detail."

"What's that?"

"Blue eyes...brown eyes..."

"Maybe you were right," I said desperately. I didn't
want my bubble of well-being burst so fast. "I'm a-a
sport...an anomaly...one of those freaks that happen in
spite of the laws of genetics.

"If we accept your theory, we have to accept that,
too," May conceded. He was silent a moment, nodding,
then shrugged. "Okay. What do you want to do now?"

"You really want to know?" I nearly went limp as I
saw he acknowledged we were both going to believe
what I'd said.

"I wouldn't have asked if I didn't." He leered and
softened it with another smile. "I hope it involves getting
naked and rolling around on my bed."

"Sorry." I was, but in that moment, there was
something else I wanted to do that was more important
than making love with May. "Much as I hate to
disappointment you, what I'd really like to do is go to the
newspaper office and find out more about Martes
Salazar."

"Why?"

"Just plain old curiosity, that's all."

"I won't say I'm disappointed." He definitely was, and didn't attempt to hide it. "But I can be brave about it…as long as there's some fooling around going on later. We'll have to go to the library, though. That's where the old editions of the paper are kept on file."

"Before we do that, let's get something to eat."

"Don't tell me," he gave a theatrical groan. "That Inner Woman who needs her three-squares is wide awake and hungry?"

"You know it."

"Okay." He sounded more resigned than eager for lunch, however. "Where…?"

"We could go to…" I paused. "…Shedd's?"

"Do you really want to go there?" He said it as if I'd asked him to take me to the Black Hole of Calcutta. "After our last less than favorable experience in that place?"

I shrugged. "I doubt if Taylor Dix'll be showing his face there for a while. Besides, I like the barbeque."

As if on cue, May's phone rang.

Fumbling it from his pocket, he glanced at the caller ID.

"I don't believe it." He pressed a button, saying, "Well hey, long time no hear."

I went by the house but you weren't there… The reply was loud enough to hear, if somewhat mechanical-sounding.

"We're on our way to Shedd's for lunch." A reaction of surprise floated from the phone. "That's right, *that dive*. Say, why don't you meet us there?' The speaker didn't hesitate but gave a rattle of agreement. "Good. See you in a few."

He disconnected the call, dropping the cell into one of the cupholders in the console. For a few minutes, he simply stared at the road in front of the car. "Damn…"

"May… May?"

I said it three times before. He reacted.

"Hm? Sorry, Grace, what?"

"Who was that? Are they meeting us for lunch at Shedd's?" I added, amused but at the same time somewhat puzzled by his reaction, "I hope it's not an old girlfriend."

"Don't worry yourself about that," he laughed, also. "No, that was my cousin, Dylan. Remember him?"

"Dylan?" I searched my memory. *Did I remember a Dylan?* Nope. "I'm sorry…I don't…"

"Oh, sure you do," he replied, supplying facts. "That summer before you left? He, his brother, and his folks came up from Estonko and we went out to eat? At Joyner's Steakhouse? Benjamin Troup was out of town, so we had a great time, at least Dyl and I did. You were a general nuisance, as usual, because we didn't want you and your high chair sitting on our side of the table…"

I thought about that, tried to envision it…a family restaurant setting with my mother, May and his parents, and a family of strangers, one of whom was a boy May's age… I was about to remind May that I'd been four at the time, and no, I didn't remember his Cousin Dylan, but by that time, we'd arrived at Shedd's.

Chapter 14

There was a pickup truck parked near the entrance, a man in jeans and dark blue T-shirt standing beside it. He might not have red hair, but his height and something about his features bore enough of a resemblance to May's that I knew this had to be Cousin Dylan.

I had been fairly quiet on the drive over, trying to remember anything I could about him, but so far, nothing had gelled in my mind yet...only that his name rang a bell that had nothing to do with his being May's relative.

May stopped the car beside the truck, cut the engine, and slid out, running around to open the door for me.

As I got out, Dylan was there. "Hey, Cuz."

He and May shook hands, then swooped in for a semi-hug, stepping back and acting as if they hadn't seen each other in years, which, if I remembered correctly, was a typical Southern greeting, even if their last time together had been the day before.

Dylan immediately noticed the butterfly tape. "Say, what happened to your face? Run into a door or something?"

"Or something." May glossed over any explanation by demanding, "What the hell are you doing here, and why haven't I heard from you before now? That wife of yours keeping you chained to the bedpost?" Turning to me, he added, in an undertone, "Dyl's still a newlywed. Got married last summer."

"Oh?" I offered a hand as his cousin's attention turned to me. "Congratulations." I added, "I'm Grace McAllister."

Now that I'd seen him, I realized he looked familiar. What was the thing I was struggling to remember?

"Thanks." Dylan reached to take my hand. Hearing my name, he paused slightly before taking it. "McAllister? Not little Gracie? Daughter of...?" He waved a hand as if indicating the entire town.

Obviously, *he* remembered *me*.

"Yes and no," I answered, and to his raised brows, added, "It's complicated."

"Well, let's go inside and you can uncomplicate it for me." He gestured to Shedd's front door. "Hope they've got plenty of barbeque, because I'm totally empty."

****

Today, there were quite a few people in the bar, construction workers, people on the town's road crews, and others, stopping at their favorite place for lunch. Hard hats lay in empty chairs and chartreuse highway safety jackets brightened the crowd. Though it wasn't noisy, there was a high hum of voices.

I could see there were two other girls moving between the tables, helping out. Noon was definitely a busy time.

Megan took our requests, giving a quick study of May's still-visible bruises, before asking in a low voice, "Get everything cleared up with the sheriff, May? When do the bandages come off?" She also smiled at Dylan, remembering him, and asking about his folks and "How's things in Estonko in general?"

"Same old same old," Dylan replied.

As she left the table, May asked, "So what brings you up this way? It wasn't just to see me, was it?"

"Sorry, no." Dylan shook his head. Unlike May, his hair was dark though just as curly. "Had to fly to New York. Meeting with my publisher."

"Oh?" May sounded interested but not exactly impressed. "Books doing okay?"

"So far. Working on a new one now. I got in a couple of hours ago, planned to drive back home and thought, since I was passing McAllister, I'd stop by. Was Christmas really the last time we saw each other?"

"Christmas Day," May affirmed.

"May tells me we've met before," I told Dylan with a smile. "But I don't remember, so I apologize."

"No prob." He returned the smile. It was almost a duplicate of the Mayfield Donovan charmer. Guess it's genetic. "It was a long time ago and you were a lot younger." He laughed, as if remembering. "We both were, though I definitely remember you, Gracie."

I didn't correct him about my name.

"I can't believe it's been over a year. Eighteen months," May went on, as if I hadn't spoken, shaking his head. "We used to be inseparable."

The idea I should remember something about his cousin kept niggling in my brain, so I fell back on the old Southern custom of getting to know someone by being a snoop. "Tell me, Dylan, what do you do? You mentioned books. Are you also a teacher? Like May?"

That question was usually the first of two any stranger Down South was asked, the second being, *Who are your people?* To establish a connection through mutual friends.

"Dyl used to be an investigative reporter," May cut

in before he could answer. I detected pride in his tone. "In Washington. In D.C.," he added. In case I thought he meant the state, I guess.

"Oh?" That single word was supposed to encourage more information, though it elicited a grimace from Dylan.

"But now I'm in construction, with my dad and brother." He pulled a card from the T-shirt's breast pocket, offering it. "In Estonko.

I accepted it, reading *Roth and Sons, Contractors and Construction*, while thinking that construction work in a small south Georgia town was far, far removed from being an investigative reporter in Washington, D.C.

Then, something clicked.

"Dylan Roth," I said aloud, looking up at him. I remembered where I'd heard the name. Or *seen* it, rather. On the cover of a book. A bestseller, as a matter of fact. I pointed a finger at him. "Dylan Roth."

May was staring at me, frowning slightly as if he didn't understand why I was repeating that.

"That's my name," Dylan agreed, amiably.

"You wrote *Glory of Princes*." I declared, stabbing the finger into the air, as if emphasizing each word.

"Guilty." He nodded, adding, "Unfortunately."

"…and *Wicked Waits Forever*," I continued.

"…and the first earned him a messy divorce while the second won him the prettiest girl in Georgia," May put in, looking as if he was coming to Dylan's rescue though his cousin seemed to be holding his own fairly well. When I gave him a mock glare, he caught my hand, raising it and pressing a kiss against my fingers. "With the exclusion of one currently visiting from California, I mean."

I smiled at him and a sudden image popped through my mind… May seizing my plate, holding it in the air, while I stretched to retrieve it. Someone saying, "Quit it, May. Stop picking on her. You're making her cry." That someone pulled the plate from his hands, setting it before me. "Here you are, Gracie," while May muttered, "Aw, you're no fun."

"I remember now. You save me from a May-ambush. Thank you…if a little belated."

"You're welcome." He nodded. "Also belated…but enough about me." Dylan looked eager to leave the topic of his literary career behind. "What's been happening with you, Cuz?" His eyebrows raised as he gazed at our entwined fingers. "Or do I have to ask?"

"You mean, you don't know?" May looked surprised. "You're here, in McAllister, and you haven't heard?"

"Hey, I've only been in town twenty minutes," Dylan protested. "Not long enough to get hit with the latest gossip yet."

"Allow me to bring you up to date." Releasing my hand, May leaned forward, elbows on the table, as he launched into a surprisingly brief but very fact-filled synopsis of everything happening in the past few days.

"Damn," Dylan breathed as he finished. "I'm almost sorry I asked." He looked at me. "And now, you're going to try to…"

"Say, since you were an investigative reporter, maybe you could stick around and help us," May cut in, before he could finish.

"Oh, no…my reporting days are over." Dyl shook his head. "Scarlett's expecting me home in time for supper, and if I don't show up…" He let the rest trail away.

"Your wife's name is Scarlett?" I wondered if I should've been surprised.

He nodded. "And has the hair, and the temper, to prove it."

"Come on, Dyl," May urged, flashing that prizewinning smile. "You can use the material in your new book."

'Nothing doing," Dylan said. Obviously, the Mayfield smile didn't work on male relatives. "My next novel is a romance."

"Plenty of material right here." May wrapped his hand around mine and brought it to his lips for an exaggerated kiss. "Well?"

"Don't tempt me." Dylan laughed. "Seriously, I can't stay, got work waiting for me. I just wanted to stop by and say 'Hello' while I was up this way."

"Damn it, Dyl." May looked disappointed. "We could sure use some help."

"What have you done so far?" Briefly, it looked as if he was going to give in.

"We've talked to people who knew Mama," I supplied. "After lunch, we plan to see if we could find anything in back issues of the newspaper, and then…" I shrugged. "I don't know…talk to the sheriff?" I glanced at May as if for corroboration.

Dylan nodded, looking satisfied. "Sounds like the same thing Scarlett and I did when we were trying to figure out what happened to our great-grandfathers. So you've got it covered. You don't need my help," he concluded.

At that moment, Megan appeared with our orders, and that cut short any talk for a very long time.

She brought a repeat of our previous order, but for three, and I tackled mine with an equal enthusiasm. May didn't say much, just kept giving me some amused and tolerant glances. I noticed he didn't exactly stint on chowing down on his own sandwich or Brunswick stew, however. Neither did Dylan.

Five more minutes, and we would've finished and been gone, but then...

A laugh behind us made me look up...and freeze. Either I hadn't paid much attention or he'd been more or less hidden in the crowd...and quieter, but the person I saw as I looked toward the bar sent a chill through me, followed by anger.

Taylor Dix stood there with two men. Neither was wearing a camo hoodie, but I'd have bet every cent I had they were the two who'd beaten May. He was talking and gesturing and they were grinning and nodding.

Behind the bar, the bartender stood to the side, looking anything but happy. He glanced my way, saw that I'd seen Dix, and his gaze went from them to the phone on the wall behind the bar. It was almost as if I could read his mind.

He wants to call the sheriff but he's afraid.

Had he heard them admit what they'd done to May? Maybe that's what they were laughing about.

May picked up his cup. "Empty. You two need a refill?" That was when he saw I was turned away. "What are you looking at, Gracie?" He followed my gaze. "Oh, shit."

Dylan looked up. "What is it?"

"I was hoping you wouldn't see him." In that moment, as much as I'd like to see Taylor Dix lying unconscious on Shedd's floor, I didn't want May hurt

213

again.

"In that case, you shouldn't be looking in his direction," May said. The odd thing was, he didn't seem worried. If anything, he appeared to be accepting something. With a sigh, he pushed back his chair.

In the meantime, Dylan had looked over at Dix, and gave his own sigh, a near-duplicate of May's.

"May, please don't start anything." I caught his hand, squeezing it to emphasize my words. "Let's pay our bill and go."

"Don't worry, Grace." He patted my arm. "What would I do?" He shook his head and held up his cup. "I'll get some more soda, and then we'll skedaddle. Do you want any?"

Déjà vu all over again, but this time, I shook my head.

"No? Okay." He got to his feet.

"May…"

"Don't worry. I'll be right back."

"Wait." As May stopped, Dyl pushed back his chair and stood up. "I need some more soda and so does Gracie, don't you, Grace?"

"No, I…"

"Of course, you do." He talked over my denial. "…and…" He picked up my cup, handing it to May. "…you're going to need help carrying three cups, Cuz. Come on."

He headed for the bar. With a grim smile, May followed.

Without looking at Dix, Dylan pushed between him and one of his buddies, gesturing to the bartender, then waited as Jake took the cup, added new ice and refilled it. May elbowed his way in beside him.

Jake returned Dyl's cup to him and reached for May's.

By this time, Dix had glanced his way. His expression changed as he elbowed his friend and nodded at May. The only way to describe his expression was *calculating*. When he smiled, his face became almost feral.

The two friends glanced at May and nodded expectantly.

Dix said something.

Accepting the cup's return from Jake, May half-turned away, before he stopped and looked back. It was so much like the night before I felt sick.

He glanced at Dylan, who looked around him at Dix, then nodded.

May answered Dix, not loud enough for me to hear because of the noise in the room, but Dix heard it well enough.

May walked away.

With a roar, Dix flung himself at May, landing on his back. May staggered, sending the drink he held flying, liquid erupting into the air as the cup landed on a nearby table, bounced off, and crumpled on the floor.

"Hey!" someone shouted as the people at the table were spattered with ice and cola.

With a crash, May flung Dix over his head onto the floor. Dix didn't stay down but scrambled to his feet, arms swinging. Behind them, his cronies launched themselves at Dylan.

Dyl wasn't standing there simply watching, however. He caught one of Dix's buddies by an arm, swinging him into the air, then dropping him. His leg bent. The man's body straddled that upraised knee, then slid off. With a wheeze of pain, he doubled over, hands clutching protectively as Dyl's knee came up again, catching him under the chin.

Blood and spittle sailed through the air, splatting a nearby table as May sent Dix sprawling full-length on the floor. One of his buddies caught May's arms, swinging him around.

By this time, the two guys who'd gotten the cola shower and some of the other patrons had formed a circle around them, not joining in, thank God, but definitely interested. Someone dragged the downed man out of the way, dropped him to the floor, and put a foot on his chest.

There was a bright flash as an overhead light reflected off a knife appearing in Dix's hand. Other hands reached out and wrested it away, keeping the fight fair.

May hit the knife-wielder with his fist, then gave him three more short, quick raps in the face. I actually saw the man's nose flatten as blood sprayed. He went limp and May let him go, jabbing backward with his elbow and catching the remaining bully in the belly. Dylan whirled, brought up his other hand, and sent that one sailing about six feet into the crowd.

Two of the construction workers caught the body and let it slide to the floor.

Through it all, I watched in shocked silence, amazed by the way the two cousins moved, almost coordinated. Did I dare wonder if, in their teens, they might have been in enough scraps that they could work as a team?

I wondered if I dared ask May about that.

For several moments, there was stunned silence, broken only by Dylan and May's harsh breathing as both stood there, hunched over slightly, hands fisted. Then...

Someone clapped.

In a moment, there was applause from everyone in the bar, except Dylan, May and myself. I was still too stunned to move. Then, in a single movement so smooth it looked choreographed, everyone turned and went back to whatever they were doing, as if nothing had happened, leaving the cousins standing in the midst of the still-unconscious trio.

"Hey, Jake…" May's call made a couple look back. "I spilled my drink. Can I have another?"

That brought a laugh as Jake reached for a fresh cup, filling it with ice and soda. He handed it over the bar. May accepted it, said something more and got a nod. Jake presented two more to Dyl.

Taking a swallow out of one, he followed May and returned to our table.

The bartender picked up the wall phone, hit three numbers, spoke into it, then ended the call. Pulling something from under the bar, he came around the counter with a small bucket and began sprinkling sawdust on the splash of blood as well as on the dark spot where the spilled drink was soaking into the wood.

"Did you know they were going to do that?" I asked.

"Believe me, Grace, I had no idea. I simply saw an opportunity and took it."

"You deliberately provoked him," I accused. "You could have been killed."

He gave me his most innocent look.

"Of course, he didn't." Dylan put in. "I doubt there's anyone here who'll say May did…if that applause meant anything."

I shook my head, not certain the Mayfield luck would hold out against Sheriff Crockett.

Setting down the cup, May held up his hand, opening and closing his fingers. He drew in a quick, short breath.

"If asked, I imagine they'll all agree that Mr. Dix, who is very drunk, attacked a customer. Without provocation. And said customer—and cousin—simply defended themselves." May raised his glass. "The sheriff's on his way. Jake kindly placed a call, asked for an ambulance, too, I think…not for us," he added quickly as I started to speak. "I don't think Dix is going to get away this time."

I shook my head and gave my attention to his hand. "Oh, May, your poor knuckles."

The barely-formed scabs were broken open. Blood trickled between his fingers and onto his palm.

He pulled a napkin from the dispenser on the table and dabbed it away, then wiggled his fingers again.

"They're all right, Gracie. Nothing's broken…I think."

I noticed he winced a little as he said it, however, but if he wanted to play Mr. Tough Guy, who was I to say otherwise? As long as he didn't stand up and fall flat on his face.

A sudden quick inhalation of breath made me look back at Dylan. I'd been so worried about May, I'd ignored him. Now I saw he was as bad off as May. Maybe worse.

He was sporting not one black eye but two rapidly forming empurpled ones. The corner of his mouth was bleeding slightly and his upper lip was puffy. One hand was bleeding and a finger thrust out in the wrong direction.

"Oh, Dylan…" I breathed out sympathetically.

"Think that finger's broken," he grunted. "How the hell am I going to type with a finger in a splint?"

"Better worry more about how you're going to explain it to Scarlett," May muttered, wincing as he tried moving his own fingers.

At that moment, we heard a siren, getting closer.

"Guess that means we'll be staying a while longer," May muttered.

"Looks like it," Dylan agreed.

More *déjà vu*.

****

May's second interview with Sheriff Crockett was short, sweet, and to the point. To my surprise, Crockett bought it. *All of it.* Or appeared to. All he did was shake his head, despairingly.

"See you brought in reinforcements this time," Sheriff Crocket said, nodding to Dyl who sat with one hand cupped around the other, protecting that broken finger. "Hello, Dylan. Haven't seen you in a while."

The sheriff listened to the bartender's terse explanation, hauling one offender upright as he regained consciousness and asking him if that was the way it happened. He got a slurred and reluctant, "Yeah," and had all three handcuffed before the ambulance arrived.

By that time, a deputy was there, busy speaking to the other patrons, who this time appeared very eager to get on record as to what they'd witnessed.

"I knew some day Dix'd meet his match. Just glad it was while I'm sheriff so I could enjoy it. You'll be wanting to press charges, I assume."

I hope, was the unspoken thought.

Behind us, the same two EMTs who'd tended May previously were treating the three who were now conscious and sitting up.

I wondered if they saw the irony in the situation.

"Damn right I will." May answered with a tinge of outrage, suggesting the sheriff shouldn't think otherwise.

Dylan echoed his words.

"This time I've got Dix dead to rights."

Crockett looked amused. "Witnesses say you handled yourself pretty well. Where'd you learn how to fight? I didn't think an English teacher would be a good brawler."

"My daddy taught me. He didn't know I was going to become a teacher."

"That's right," Crockett nodded as if being reminded of something. "He's Beautiful Bill Donovan, isn't he?"

"Guess you know him, too?" May said, and for the first time, looked a little worried.

"I do." Crockett surprised both of us by adding, "Admire him for how he turned his life around. Glad he taught his son how to defend himself before he became completely law-abiding, however."

He glanced at Dylan.

"Not going to ask you where you acquired your fisticuffs ability. I'm well acquainted with your daddy, too. Tell him I said 'hello.'"

Dylan managed a half-grin and a nod.

****

A few minutes later, Sheriff Crockett told us we were free to go, except for Dylan, who needed his hand looked after. Not so with Dix and his friends. The last we saw them, one was being loaded into the ambulance and the other two were ushered separately into the squad cars.

As we drove by, I wanted to shake my fist and shout, "Good riddance!" and smirk, but I managed not to, giving myself a mental pat on the back for not being vindictive. Much.

We'd stop by the station later in the afternoon and fill out the complaint forms. Dylan said he'd do that after his hand was looked after.

I settled in the back seat of the convertible, Dyl in the front because of his injury. May turned the car onto the road leading to the hospital and the emergency room.

The public library would be visited later in the afternoon.

****

We waited until Dylan's finger was set and splinted and he was on his way to the McAllister sheriff's office.

"Told you we'd get you some material for your new book," May reminded him as he settled behind the wheel of his pickup.

"If I were writing a mystery noir novel," Dylan retorted. "Don't know how I'll fit a bar fight into a romance."

"You'll think of something." May looked confident "You're a writer. If Scarlett says anything, just blame me."

"Don't worry, I will," Dylan promised. He leaned around May, looking at me. "Good luck, Gracie. In finding your father...*and* if you're going to stay involved with this guy. You'll need it."

He smiled as he said it, though.

Chapter 15

The librarian gave May a shocked glanced as she took in his old bruises, his new ones, and his re-skinned knuckles. She was a small, blonde woman who seemed vaguely familiar, though I was certain I'd never met her before. She didn't say anything, however.

"Ran into a door," May muttered.

"Looks like the door wasn't too happy about that. How does *it* look?" She gave him a short smile and without giving him time to answer, said, "How may I help you two?"

Could it be she didn't know who I was? If so, she was the first and only ignorant person in McAllister.

I explained what I wanted. She led us to a set of carrels in the back corner of the library. I was surprised microfilm was still in use, expecting to see computers and other more up-to-date storage equipment.

"We've found microfilm to still be the best media for information storage," she told me.

As I settled into the chair before the screen, she began making adjustments to the machine.

May seated himself next to me as I thanked her.

"The papers for the date range you want should all be on this roll." She indicated the screen in front of the machine. "If you need anything else, just ask."

She went out, shutting the door. May waited until she was a few feet away before he spoke.

"That's Carter's fiancée."

I looked back at her through the glass paneling on the side of the door. Of course. Now, I could see it…a faint resemblance to Mama. I wondered if either of them realized that although Carter thought he had recovered from loving my mother, her replacement was a vague copy. Same as his older brother had done with Abigail.

I hoped neither woman ever realized that.

"It's been a while since I've used one of these." I turned back to the screen, looking at it as if it were an antique from two centuries before instead of just one. "I thought maybe it'd be digitally-converted or something."

"I'm afraid McAllister's library doesn't have enough money for one of those," May replied. "Or enough people who'd want to use it even if the funds were forthcoming. Around here, generosity goes to medical facilities and business concerns."

He was silent while I played with the controls, rolling images back and forth, zooming in for close-ups and back again until I had it figured out. Once I started searching, he got up.

"Gracie, I'm going outside. You don't need me for this."

I didn't answer, just nodded. He went out, closing the door. I watched him walk away, and then my attention was on the images of the printed pages as the story I was looking for flashed onto the screen.

UNIDENTIFIED MAN DIES IN AUTO ACCIDENT

EMTs were called to the scene of a one-car accident near County Road 30 in the early morning hours. There were no witnesses, but a driver was found in the burning wreckage, which was off the road, resting against a telephone pole that had snapped upon impact. The lone occupant of the car was pronounced dead at the scene. No identification has been made at this point and sheriff's deputies are investigating. This is the first automobile fatality in McAllister in three years.

That short, almost curt, single paragraph shook me more than I cared to admit. Bill's words had painted a picture of Marty Salazar as a young man as happy as anyone else at that time, someone he'd liked, though they were more or less rivals for the same girl. This, however...*the first fatality in three years*...those words reduced Marty Salazar to a statistic.

For some reason, that angered me.

I forced myself to send the pages speeding past, looking for specific words and phrases. Soon, another headline jumped out at me.

ACCIDENT VICTIM IDENTIFIED

Dental records have identified the victim of Saturday's early-morning auto fatality as Martes Esteban Salazar, 23, a resident of McAllister. Identification was partially determined by tracing the registration of the car involved. Tentative notification to the victim's parents was given so dental records could be obtained and identity confirmed.

A coroner's inquest will be held.

I scrolled further.

VERDICT OF INQUEST ON AUTO ACCIDENT

The verdict of the coroner's inquest on the death of Martes Esteban Salazar has been rendered as accidental death while under the influence of alcohol, Sheriff Tracy Crockett, Senior, announced today.

Salazar, 23, was killed in an early morning accident on County Road 30 when he apparently lost control of his car and crashed into a telephone pole. Medical information indicates he was killed instantly and didn't die in the following fire. A broken and melted whiskey bottle was found in the wreckage. Investigators state they were told Salazar was an alcoholic. Salazar's father, Alejandro Salazar, employee of Keller's Jewelry, protested the verdict, saying, "My son didn't drink. There has to be some other explanation for that bottle being in the car." Without information to the contrary, however, the coroner's verdict will stand.

The body will be released to Pender's Funeral Home. Burial arrangements to be found on page 12.

I worked the lever, found page 12.

MARTES ESTEBAN SALAZAR

Funeral services for Martes Esteban Salazar, 23, killed in an early morning auto accident four days ago, will be held at Pender's Funeral Home, with interment to follow at McAllister-Woodside Cemetery.

Mr. Salazar was a resident of McAllister, having moved here at the age of two with his parents. He attended McAllister High School, graduating in 1991, and was a recent graduate of the University of Georgia with a major in history. He was to have entered the University's Master's program in the fall. He is survived by his parents, Isabella Rodriguez y Soledad de Salazar and Alejandro Salazar.

Visitation will be between 10:00 and 3:00 with graveside services to follow.

That was it. I flipped through a couple more issues.

Nothing else. Four short articles, a combined total of eight paragraphs, to sum up a man's life.

I felt a sudden devastation, though I'd only known about Marty Salazar for a few days and only then through others' descriptions of him. I remembered how I'd felt after my mother died. Of having to handle all the arrangements myself, trying to keep myself together to do the things I'd never had to think about before. It was bad enough to lose a parent, but to lose a child...

I felt myself wishing I could tell Mr. and Mrs. Salazar how sorry I was. I remembered May hadn't mentioned Marty's mother, just his father. Perhaps she hadn't survived her son very long? Had grief killed her? I know there was a short period when I thought it was going to do the same to me.

My curiosity satisfied, I turned off the machine and left the carrel. May was standing at the checkout desk, talking to the librarian. They both looked up as they heard my footsteps.

"Did you find what you were looking for?" she asked, with a bright smile.

"Yes." I took a deep breath, trying to shake off the gloom hovering over me. "Thank you very much." I caught May's arm. "Let's go," I whispered.

Obediently he turned to go, but I stopped, releasing his arm. He waited as I looked back. "Carter McAllister told me you and he are going to be married," I said to the librarian. "Congratulations."

"Why, thank you." She dimpled as she smiled. "You know Carter?"

"He's an old family friend." I smiled back, caught May's arm, and walked away.

He waited until we were outside before he spoke. "What happened? What was in those stories that's upset you so?"

"What makes you think I'm upset?"

"Because you're holding my arm so tight you're cutting off the circulation."

"Sorry." I let go.

There were finger marks on his upper arm. I waited until they faded before I spoke.

"It's just..." I shook my head. I couldn't find a word to describe how I felt. At last, I burst out, "It was just so damned depressing, May. What your father said and then reading about it in cold newsprint. It made me think of Mama dying and...I guess it shook me up more than I expected."

I looked away.

It was a bright day, so hot I could see little waves of heat spiraling off the sidewalk. As usual, coming outside from an air-conditioned building was a welcome change for a few minutes. Now the June day was reasserting itself.

"Sorry to be such a weeping willow."

"Don't be." May bent and kissed me. Right there in public. "It's one of your more endearing qualities."

"What? Being a crybaby?" I snorted as I swiped at my eyes.

"That's right. Because you're *my* crybaby." He wrapped his fingers around mine. "Come on, willow, let's go home and I'll see if I can figure out some way to cheer you."

It was halfway in my mind to ask May to take me to see Marty Salazar's parents, but I soon talked myself out of that idea. What would I say to them, anyway? Besides, at this late date, they might not want to be reminded of what they'd lost on that early morning. I knew I wouldn't.

As it was, when we got back to May's place, I had little time to think about grieving parents or anything else. The phone was ringing as he opened the door.

****

May ran into the living room to answer it, having a short conversation with whoever was on the line. As he set it down, he turned to look at me and smiled, hammering his fist through the air.

"Yes!"

"Good news?"

"God's looking out for us. That was Sheriff Crockett. They pegged one of the assailants from today's fracas from the blood type from that other unpleasantness, and he rolled over on Dix so fast it wasn't even funny. And, get this..." His smile went wider as he continued. "That idiot Dix waylaid Kyle this morning, bragging how he *fixed that stuck-up teacher good...* that's a quote by the way...and little Kyle ran straight to the sheriff."

He burst into delighted laughter as he caught me and swung me around. "Crockett's adding up the charges as we speak."

I was laughing, too, in relief that Dix would be cooling his heels in the local jail until he was transferred to prison. I hoped he got a very long sentence.

May scooped me off my feet and carried me up the stairs and into the bedroom, where he proceeded to make love to me in such a vigorous and inventive fashion it drove any other thoughts from my mind.

Chapter 16

A muffled series of thuds jerked me out of a sound sleep.

"Wha...?"

I raised my head, staring blearily. May lay on his stomach, one arm flung across my chest, a leg pinning my thighs to the bed.

"May? May, wake up."

He roused slightly, moving his head.

"What's that?"

"What's what?" He opened his eyes as the sound stopped.

The doorbell began to ring. Stridently, frantically. *Ding...ding...ding-ding-ding...*

"Someone's at the door," I muttered unnecessarily as I struggled to sit up.

"I'll get it." He was already climbing over me, pushing me back onto my pillow as he slid to the floor.

Pulling his jeans off a chair, he stepped into them as he started to the door. I heard the metallic whisper of the zipper as it slid upward.

I glanced at the clock. "It's five o'clock in the morning. Who could it be?"

"Whoever it is, I'll take care of it." He went out the door, pulling it shut. "Go back to sleep, Gracie."

Like that was going to happen.

People don't ring doorbells at five in the morning

without good reason, and that reason didn't usually have anything remotely *good* about it. An illness, a death, something that couldn't wait for the sun to come up. I don't know why, but I thought of Marty Salazar again. Had they waited before notifying his parents? Or had they pounded on the door before sunrise, jerking Mr. and Mrs. Salazar from sleep and into the nightmare of a door opening to a uniformed deputy bearing words they never expected to hear?

I hoped they hadn't used those words that had now become a cliché, *Sorry for your loss.* I agree with David. Those have to be the most insincere-sounding words in the English language.

Whoever was outside was still leaning on the doorbell. Reaching for the nylon robe matching the nightgown I had yet to wear, I wrapped it around myself. I was in the hall before May could reach the front door.

"All right. I'm coming." He muttered, more to himself than to whomever was outside.

I stopped at the head of the stairs as he pulled it open.

"Daddy? What are you doing here?"

Bill?

"I need to talk to you, May." Bill brushed past his son so roughly May had to jump back to keep from being knocked aside as he rushed into the living room.

"It couldn't wait until daylight?" May followed him inside.

"No. It can't." Well, that was plain enough. "I've been thinking about this ever since you left,, and I have to talk to you before it goes any further."

"Before what goes any further? Daddy, you aren't making any sense."

He certainly wasn't.

"Where's Grace?" Bill asked.

"Upstairs asleep."

"In your bed?" Bill asked, in a way saying he hoped he was wrong.

"Daddy, are you going to start that again?"

I could hear the exasperation in May's voice, the struggle not to become angry.

"Did you have sex with her?"

"That's none of your business." The outrage in May's tone was echoed in my own thoughts.

Where does he get away asking a question like that?

"None of my business?"

I don't think Bill could've sounded more shocked if May had hauled off and slugged him.

"My God, boy, do you know what you've done?"

"Exactly what have I done?" The question might've sounded impertinent but May was plainly confused. "Daddy, what ails you?"

I decided I'd better get in there. Bare feet making as much noise as possible, I came down the stairs, pausing in the living room doorway.

Bill glanced my way. Whatever the problem was, he certainly looked as if it had kept him up all night. He was wearing the same clothes he'd had on the day before but they were wrinkled now. His eyes were bloodshot, and he looked, for want of a better word, haggard. He shot me a glare holding downright hate as he took in the hastily thrown-on robe, my tousled hair, and bare feet.

"Gracie…" May made an attempt to keep his voice mild. "I thought you were asleep."

"How could I be when I can hear you two all the way up the stairs?" I decided to pretend I didn't know what they'd been talking about. "May, what's happened? Is it your mother? Her heart?"

"My wife's fine," Bill snapped. The look he gave me told me he hadn't been fooled. "If you could hear us upstairs, you know we weren't talking about Angeline."

He turned so he was facing me. A confrontation. If he'd snorted and pawed the ground, I wouldn't have been surprised.

"Gracie, go back upstairs," May ordered. "I think Daddy wants to talk to me. Alone."

I hesitated. I didn't want to leave May to face whatever it was by himself.

Bill held up a detaining hand. "My son won't listen to me, Grace, but I hope you will."

"Listen to you about what, Mr. Donovan?" I came into the living room, walking over to stand near May.

"I want you to leave McAllister and my boy," Bill said.

He began rocking back and forth on the balls of his feet, hands clenched. I wondered if he was getting ready to take a swing at me. In all I've ever heard about Bill Donovan, it was never said he was violent toward women, but now I wasn't sure. There's always a first time.

"I don't understand." I didn't have to pretend to be confused because I really was. "Why do you dislike me, Mr. Donovan?"

"Dislike you?" His expression changed, filled with so much despair it shook me. He looked stricken. "Grace, I don't dislike you. I... Oh, God... I swear I never expected anything like this to happen."

He put his hands over his face and began to cry. The heartrending sobs of a man so full of grief he was barely able to stand it. May and I stood there, shocked into silence. What was there we could say?

Finally, Bill took a shaky, watery breath, snuffled slightly, and raised his head. Staring directly into my eyes, he spoke eight words that changed my life.

"You can't marry May, Grace. He's your brother."

Chapter 17

The world stopped turning.

Time stood still.

No one existed in the entire universe but Bill Donovan, May, and me. We stood there, the three of us, staring at each other. I felt as if I no longer understood spoken language. I was stricken with a brain-damaging lack of translation.

He didn't say that. I misunderstood. Oh, God...

If Bill had picked up one of the pokers from the fireplace and struck May across the face with it I doubt he could've been any more shocked. And Bill? He looked as if he wished God would shove a lightning bolt through the ceiling and incinerate him then and there.

May was the one to break the silence. "What the hell are you saying? Benjamin Troup's Gracie's father. We've decided."

"You decided wrong," Bill bit off the words. He looked from May to me, then went on, "Your mother was the most passionate woman I've ever met, and when we were together, we spent more time in bed than out of it."

I didn't want to hear that. Couldn't he see he was making Mama out to be more of a tramp than I'd already been told? I didn't want to look at him, but I couldn't turn away. All I could do was stare at him, meeting those clear hazel eyes, so much like my own, and for just a moment seeing a younger man. *Beautiful Bill*, a man who'd played the field until he met his match in Miriam Baker.

"When she broke up with me, I didn't think I could take it, and then, after Marty died, and she needed comforting..." He laughed. "I certainly did my best. I'd always been careful, used protection, but that time... I don't know if it was the reminder of how mortal we all were or what, but she said she didn't want me to, and I was glad to oblige. Then, she started seeing Benjamin Troup, and that quickie wedding followed..."

Now I was the one wishing I could be obliterated. I felt myself falling, everything getting black. My ears were ringing.

Please don't let me faint.

I wanted to simply dissolve into nothingness and get away from those unbelievable words. My hands clenched, nails cutting my palms. The pain pulled me out of it.

"Then you were born. They said you were premature, but I knew better...nine months after the last time we made love...with all that red hair...and I understood. She didn't know which of us was the father and she'd chosen the wrong one. There was nothing we could do because by that time I'd married Angie, and Miriam would never hurt her best friend. She did the only other thing she could. She put up with Benjamin Troup for as long as she could, and then she ran away...and took my daughter with her."

"No." I felt so weak I fell against May, but as his arm tightened around me, I pushed him away. At the same time, however, I wanted his warmth, his body, to console me. I wanted to use his presence to prove Bill's words a lie even as I knew they weren't.

"Gracie." May reached for me again.

"No! No, no, no…" I slapped at his hands, then turned and bolted for the stairs, scrambling up them as fast as I could.

"I don't care what you say," I heard him say.

He sounded like someone whistling in the dark. *Pretend nothing's wrong and it'll be all right.*

"I love Gracie and I'm marrying her."

"Christ, son, you've already broken the laws of God," Bill choked out. "Don't make it worse."

I didn't hear any more. As I reached the bedroom, I slammed the door behind me, cutting off the sound of their voices.

May's my brother?

I was like a hamster in one of those exercise wheels, running around in circles, aimlessly frantic. Bill's words kept flying around in my head, smashing against each other, each collision as painful as a jolt of electricity. I didn't know what to do.

May's my brother! I've been to bed with my brother…had sex with my brother…

I thought of the things we'd done, how I'd enjoyed them…enjoyed *him…my brother… It can't be…no…*

What am I going to do?

There was only one thing I *could* do. Get out. Go back home. Forget May. Forget everything we'd done. If I could. Bury the secret deep inside my soul.

I threw off the robe and grabbed yesterday's clothes off the chair where they lay next to May's T-shirt and boots. Somehow, I got them on. I dragged my suitcase and overnighter from under the bed and threw them onto the rumpled covers.

There were sounds from downstairs, the front door

slamming, a car starting up, driving away. By the time May came in, I was half-packed.

"What are you doing?"

"What does it look like?" I didn't stop, moving from dresser to bed and back again as I shoved a wad of underthings into the case. "I'm getting out of here."

"Gracie, listen." He reached out, fingers brushing my arm.

"Don't touch me." I jerked away so violently I nearly lost my balance.

"We need to talk about this."

"Oh? Which part should we talk about, May?" I whirled around. "The times I let my brother fuck me? Or the part where I decided to marry my brother and have his children? Oh, I know…when your father told us both, so very plainly, we've committed incest."

"It isn't so, Gracie. I think I'd know if you were my sister."

"Then why didn't you?" I demanded. "It was right there in front of us the whole time. Maybe we just didn't want to admit it, but…"

I swung around, looking into the full-length mirror that made up the walk-in closet's door.

"Look at us." I gestured at our images. "Same hair. The same color…*we're compatible*, you said. More than compatible…and…his eyes…"

"What about Dad's eyes?"

"They're the same color as mine. Not like yours. *Like mine.*"

"It isn't so."

"Saying that doesn't make it a lie, May."

"And saying it is doesn't make it the truth. Hell, by that logic, maybe he isn't *my* father. I love you, Gracie.

and I'm not letting you go."

"I don't think you have a choice." For a very long moment, we stared at each other. I broke eye contact first, turning back to the bed. "I have to finish packing."

He made a little sound, a whimper of near-defeat. "I'll get your things from the bathroom."

He was only gone a few seconds, appearing again with my makeup kit. He threw it into the suitcase. I zipped it shut with such a violent gesture it's a wonder it didn't rip out the stitches. Hauling the bags off the bed, I headed for the door.

"You can't get a flight today." He spoke so reasonably, not a quaver in his voice.

"I'll stay at that motel outside town…re-rent a car…drive back to Atlanta." I'd had a few minutes of sanity to think. Maybe I could and maybe I couldn't do any of that, but I wasn't going to argue.

"How do you plan to get to the rental office?" He sounded as if he were taunting. "It's fifteen miles from here, Gracie."

"I'll walk."

"You'll never make it. Look…" That one word told me he'd given up. "If you're determined to go…"

"I am."

"I'll take you."

He reached for the suitcase. It took three tugs before I let it go. He stalked through the door. I followed.

****

Neither of us spoke on the drive. I sat huddled against the door, as far from May as I could get and still stay in the car. He'd thrown the overnight bag into the foot area on the passenger side, but shoved the suitcase between the seats so it protruded, a protective barrier between us. He didn't look at me but concentrated on the road. The couple of glances I shot in his direction told me his jaw muscles were tight, as if he were gritting his teeth to keep from saying anything.

At the car rental, he pulled into the spot marked *Customer Parking*. He didn't get out, didn't even set the brake, just stopped the car and sat there, the engine idling.

I opened the door and got out, reaching in to catch the handle of the suitcase and struggled to drag it across the seat. I set it down, then leaned in to pick up the overnighter. I started to shut the door.

"I'm not giving up, Gracie."

I didn't answer, slamming the door so he couldn't say anything else.

It wouldn't take much to get me to stay, and I didn't want to think what would happen if I did. I wanted to fling the door open. Throw myself into his arms.

I love you, May. God forgive me. I can't think of you as a brother. Never as my brother.

Whirling, I hefted the cases and dashed for the entrance, not looking back. Behind me, I heard the car drive off.

Where would I stay in the meantime? I couldn't go back to May's and couldn't afford the Manor's rates. At the motel? Would the McAllisters take me in? More questions flooded my brain as I stalked to the desk where the same clerk who'd received back the keys to the car looked up, recognizing me.

****

Twenty minutes later, I was back again in the same little car. I'd asked if it was still available and, luckily, it was. I'd also decided to throw myself on the McAllisters' mercy and see if they'd give me shelter until I could leave.

Abigail herself opened the door. "Grace? My goodness? What's happened? You look as if you just lost your best friend."

Not a good greeting.

"Mrs. McAllister...Abigail..." I couldn't get the words out. All I could do was stand there, blinking and swallowing tears. "I..."

"Has something happened between you and May?"

I nodded, managing a mumbled explanation. "I need somewhere to stay...until my flight."

"Of course, dear." She didn't ask for more information, instead pulled me into a comforting hug. She must have seen I wasn't in any condition to talk and wouldn't want to if I had been. Frankly, that motherly embrace nearly did me in.

She released me, pulling me inside.

"I'll make up one of the guest rooms."

****

I was able to change my flight again—I'm certain the airlines people thought I was the most undecided customer they ever had. A day later, I was on my way back to LA. Ben and Sammi took me to the airport in the quickest drive to Atlanta ever. Ben even promised to return the rental for me.

Back in LA, everything returned to normal. To all outward appearances, that is.

After managing to tell my boss what Bill had confessed, and enduring his shock and sympathy— "God, Grace, if I'd had any idea, I wouldn't have encouraged you to go"— I was once again safely ensconced behind my desk, answering the phone, welcoming clients, and typing forms.

Back to normal life. Business as usual…even if, inside, I felt as if I'd died.

Every week, for a month, I got a letter from May, letters I tossed into the trash, unopened.

I didn't want to read what he'd written, didn't want to see those words begging me to come back, telling me what his father said wasn't true…simply because he didn't want to believe it. I won't say how many voicemails were deleted from my cell.

Luckily, Sammi didn't write. Perhaps she knew I wouldn't open her letters, either.

It was a cliché, but I left my heart in McAllister, and every night for that same month, I cried myself to sleep as I remembered May and missed him, missed the feel of his body against mine, in mine…and still wanted him, even as I asked myself how I could dare such a thing.

Chapter 18

Six weeks passed.

This morning when I got to work, David was already there, sequestered in the conference room.

New client?

I was surprised. The day before, he'd told me he was planning catch-up work. There had been no mention of anyone coming in and the calendar was pristine clear. As far as I knew, he intended to finish some things he'd been neglecting and then was leaving early. His mother was coming over to babysit, so he could take his husband out to dinner.

David and Lee felt they needed some time away from the kids for a few hours, now that Davy was fighting pre-school and Kerri was entering the Terrific Threes. Mrs. Clayton encouraged them because she wanted some time with her grandchildren. Lee had also been threatening to begin practicing law again, once Kerri was in nursery school, and I was expecting any day for him to stroll through the door and take up residence in the until-now empty office down the hall.

If David had taken on a new client, that was well and good. He certainly didn't have to ask my permission, though he already had a heavy *clientèle*. I had my own work to do. I was busy plowing through some typing that had built up. During my absence, Sean had tried his best, but he simply wasn't secretary material. It was mostly busywork, but it served to keep my mind off other things.

The intercom buzzed.

"Yes, David?" I flicked it on.

"Grace, would you come back to the conference room? I'm sending Sean up to man the desk."

"Okay."

Sean came around the corner as I spoke. I stood up, relinquishing my chair. He settled into it.

"Shall I save this?" He indicated the letter on the screen.

I shook my head. "I just started. I can type it again."

I left him pecking away at the keyboard as I made my way down the hall to the conference room. I knocked, and to David's call went in. He was standing by the long table. I didn't see anyone else.

Where's the new client?

"Come in, Grace." He motioned me to a chair, then walked to the door.

"Where are you going?" I didn't sit down.

"I'll be back later." He went out. As the door swung shut, I saw someone standing behind it, partially hidden.

It took me a minute to recognize him, since he was wearing a suit and not his usual T-shirt and jeans.

"What are you doing here?" My tone could've been for my worst enemy.

"Is that any way to greet the man you love?" May's grin was as cocky as ever, but I sensed anxiety hovering behind it.

"You're not the man I love," I corrected. "You're my brother."

"I'm not your brother, Grace, and I'm never going to accept that I am."

"Then you're a fool." Being rude was the only way

I was going to survive this.

I wanted to throw myself at him, cover that smiling face with kisses. I took a step back to keep from doing exactly that.

"*You're* the fool." He took a step toward me. "For giving up so easily. Why didn't you answer my letters? Or return my calls?"

"What would've been the use? There's no sense in beating a dead horse, May."

"So now I'm a dead horse? That's not very flattering."

"I'm getting out of here." The best way to get rid of temptation...and May was definitely that...was to remove myself from its presence.

"No, you're not." He caught my arm, pulling me away from the door. "You're going to stay and listen to what I have to say."

"Let me go, May," I thrust out my chin, trying to look tough, "or I'll scream."

"And make a scene in your boss' office?" His own look was contemptuous, but he released me. "I don't think so. Wouldn't want to upset the clients, would you?"

I didn't point out to him it was too early in the morning for clients, and we didn't have any scheduled anyway.

"Sit down." Too startled by this sudden aggressiveness, so much like the mean child I'd known, I obeyed, dropping into the chair David had indicated earlier. "You're going to listen to what I have to say...what you might've learned if you hadn't run away."

"David won't like you bullying his receptionist..." I

began.

"David's the one who suggested this, so I doubt he'll complain," he snapped.

That startled me. David was siding with May? How could he?

"What could you possibly…" I began, only to stop as he held up a hand.

"I did a lot of thinking after you left, Gracie. Brooding, plotting, hating Daddy for what he'd said, even hating you a little for accepting it so easily. I haven't been to my parents' since you left, and that's worn Mom to a frazzle, trying to placate both of us. Finally, I decided to do more than think. I've some things to show you and more to tell you, and then… If you still want to walk out of here, you're free to go."

"…and what'll *you* do?" I asked.

"I'll go back to McAllister." He made it sound so simple. "School starts in three weeks, and I'll settle back into the routine and try to forget the woman I love. But I'll never call you sister. *Never.*" He held up something he'd been holding. A file folder. "Deal?"

"If that's the only way I can get rid of you. Deal," I conceded, grudgingly.

"All right, then." He dropped into the chair next to me, placing the folder on the table. "First…"

He opened the folder.

There were several sheets of paper inside, as well as a small, clasped 5x7 manila envelope. He set the envelope aside and picked up the first sheet. I reached for it. He jerked it away.

"We should've done this right away and the cost be damned. This is a DNA paternity report, a full, detailed one. *Mine.*"

He laid the sheet in front of me. I looked down at it.

"Read this carefully, paying special attention to the third paragraph."

Picking up the sheet, I began to read.

Sixteen genetic loci were tested... The process used was given, three sets of analyzing software. Then came the interpretation of the analysis and the probability of paternity of one *Mayfield William Donovan* to *Subject 13579*, with the statement: *With the mother's exclusion, probability of paternity is 99.9942%.*

I dropped the paper, pushing it aside.

"Doesn't tell me anything I didn't know. You're your father's child. So what?"

"*I'm* my father's child," he agreed, and took the second sheet out of the folder and handed it to me. "But *you* aren't."

Those words sent a jolting hope through me.

I took the second page, and went directly to that third paragraph, skipping the rest this time. Results of analysis: *Grace Stephanie McAllister and Subject 13579. With the mother's exclusion, probability of paternity is 0.0%.*

The paper fell from my hands, floating across the table to rest against the first. I looked up at May. He was attempting not to smirk and failing miserably. I didn't say anything. I was so relieved I couldn't.

I didn't ask where he got my DNA. I suppose I'd left plenty of it around his bedroom. Was that why he'd offered to get my makeup case for me as I packed? To take hair from my brush?

"And..." He pulled out a third page. "Neither are you related in any way to Benjamin Troup."

Once more, I scanned for that specific sentence.

Grace Stephanie McAllister... Subject 24680. With the mother's exclusion, probability of paternity is 0.0%.

I was relieved but once more confused. "All this does is prove who I'm *not*," I pointed out. "Who am I?"

"Contrary as always," May made a statement of fact, giving it an affectionate tinge. "Who, indeed, is Grace Stephanie McAllister? I could say, *Who cares?* I love her whoever she is, but at this point, you want more than that, don't you? You want it in black and white if you can get it."

"You're damned right."

"Don't be rude, Gracie." That came out in his disapproving schoolteacher voice. "Be patient, and the answers will come."

He took out a fourth paper. Handed it to me. And waited.

All I saw was that one sentence: *With the mother's exclusion, probability of paternity is 99.9942%.* My heart gave such a lurch I was certain it must have been visible. I looked at the number. *Subject 12354.*

"Who is he? Who's 12354?" I felt another jump inside my chest. "Not Carter?"

It would be nice to have Carter McAllister as my father. Even if he had denied it. Quite plainly. I didn't think he would've lied about that, even if he did about other things.

"Not Carter," May agreed. "Not blue-eyed Carter."

"Where did you find him?" I caught his shoulder, shaking him slightly. "May, who is he?"

He gave my hand a stare, one eyebrow raised. I released him.

"Let's set that aside for a moment." Pulling the paper from my hand, he gathered the others and stacked them neatly together, placing them back into the folder. He put the envelope on top of it.

"But I want to know *now*." I gestured at the papers.

"Patience." He closed the folder, pushing it aside so I couldn't reach it. "First, I want to tell you what else I learned after you left. About the crime Benjamin Troup committed."

"I don't give a damn about that," All I could do was look at that folder.

Out of reach. To get it, I'd have to lean across May and I knew he'd never let me near it.

"Who cares what he did?"

"Everyone should." May said. "Are you going to sit still and be quiet and listen, or shall I gather my toys and go home right now?"

I knew he'd do it. I nodded.

"Good." May settled back in his chair and began to talk...

Chapter 19

"…after I left you at the motel, I drove home in a fury. I barely kept the car under the speed limit when what I wanted to do was send it down the highway as fast as it would go. All I could think of were the words Daddy and I threw at each other after you ran upstairs…"

****

Why have you waited until now? Why didn't you say something before?

Because I never thought I'd see Grace again. I certainly never expected you'd fall in love with her.

For God's sake, Daddy…

There had been a brief, crazy moment as he pulled out of the car rental's driveway when he thought of driving to Shedd's, loading up on whiskey, and drinking himself into a near-stupor, leaving just enough consciousness to get himself home. May had never been much of a drinker and even if he felt as if someone had scooped out his insides, leaving a big empty space that could never be filled, he wasn't about to endanger other lives by drunk driving at this stage of the game.

Besides, he didn't want to end up like Marty Salazar…

Why had he thought of that? Gracie was the one who'd been so interested in finding out about Salazar. He'd written it off as a tragedy in which her mother and his father had been involved bystanders.

That brought a wave of resentment against his father.

Damn it, Daddy, why did you have to get involved with Gracie's mother? Why did you two have to shack up...and why the hell did you have to suddenly want to unburden yourself? You kept quiet for twenty-five years. I'll bet even Mom didn't know, and now...

He wondered if his father had gone home and finished ruining everyone's life by confessing to his wife, too. Of how he'd screwed her best friend and he was certain the girl she'd met earlier that day, the girl her stepson stated he was going to marry, was his child, also, and her stepdaughter.

For the only time in his life, May hated his father.

Everything that had happened began flashing through his mind, like fast-forward on a movie...everything they had discovered...talking with Carter...the fights with Dix...

Then, out of nowhere, he remembered Kyle speaking to Sheriff Crockett... *He said he'd helped Mr. Ben with some problems before, like that business with Tuesday...*

He stopped the car so quickly it left a layer of rubber on the tarmac.

Could it be? May decided perhaps he needed to know more about *Tuesday, full of Grace.*

Maneuvering the car around, he got it headed back into town, aiming this time for the library.

Arriving at the library he had to wait until it opened, and that distracted him for a while. Lydia Lynch got him the films for the same issues Grace had looked at. He read them word-by-word. Remembering Carter's assertion that Marty didn't drink and assuming that was true, he searched for anything hinting at who else might've caused the accident, either deliberately or otherwise. No other cars on the road, no indication of any, no skid marks, either. It all seemed so cut and dried. If it had been planned, whoever did it was calculating.

If that doesn't fit Benjamin Troup to a T, I don't know what does.

After reading through all the articles, he found the brief wedding blurb:

Mr. and Mrs. Samuel Baker announce the marriage of their daughter Miriam Jean to Benjamin Troup McAllister, Junior, on Saturday, July 11. The ceremony was held at the groom's home, with only the immediate family in attendance, Reverend James Perkins officiated. Best man was the groom's brother, Carter Clements McAllister.

That particular sentence stopped May a moment.

Bet Benjamin Troup enjoyed rubbing salt into that particular wound, he thought, grimly. Angeline had been Miriam's maid of honor.

He also found the announcement of Gracie's birth, a single sentence.

Mr. and Mrs. Benjamin Troup McAllister, Junior announce the birth of a daughter, Grace Stephanie, 7 pounds, 3 ounces, on March 11.

May considered the date, doing some quick back-counting. They'd have been married eight months then. Seven pounds was big for a premature baby. Could Benjamin Troup have been so ignorant as not to figure it out by then?

Gracie's red hair. That was probably a wake-up call right there, if he wasn't already suspicious.

His father said Gracie was born nine months after

the last time he and Miriam had sex. He wondered if Bill could give him the exact day.

Probably, he thought. *He was so damned precise in everything else. If so, would it be exactly nine months? Would it be June 11?*

He shoved that thought aside, not wanting the anger he felt for Bill to be fanned back into life now that he'd momentarily got it under control. Thanking Miss Lynch, May left, returning to his car and the next leg of his new journey. He was going to see Alejandro Salazar. The last stone in the puzzle. Turn it over and finish Marty Salazar's story.

Whether it helps Gracie and me or not, I have to know.

As May had told Carter McAllister, he didn't know all that much about Alejandro Salazar. Carter said he'd come from Cuba via Miami, with wife and child in tow, had worked as a jeweler in McAllister, sponsored by Gus Keller, owner of Keller's Jewelry. By the time May came along, he'd been made a partner in the store and later, when Mr. Keller passed away, become full owner. That was how he always thought of Alejandro, a man who came out to greet customers even when he had clerks to do it for him. He'd helped May pick out the ring he gave Veronica, though she'd taken it back and chosen her own, a much more expensive one, later.

When May met the owner of Keller's, the man was a widower, no mention made of a son who'd died. He was in his sixties now, had suffered a stroke, and was currently in McAllister Christian Convalescent Home receiving therapy. That was where May was now headed.

****

The nurse at the information desk assured him there

was no problem in his seeing Alejandro.

"I'm certain he'll appreciate a visitor," she said. "He doesn't get many. His cousin's the only one who stops by, and that's usually only once a month."

"Will he be dismissed to go home soon?" May remembered hearing a cousin had come from Miami to take over running the store while Alejandro was hospitalized.

"I'm afraid he's got many months of rehab before he's going to be self-sufficient," she told him. "He's completely coherent, so you don't have to worry about communicating. Only his locomotor responses were affected. He's in a wheelchair right now, but the doctors are predicting a seventy-five percent recovery."

To May, seventy-five percent didn't sound like a whole lot, but he supposed if he'd been laid low by a stroke, it might be pretty good. Nodding to the nurse, he went down the hall to a door opening onto a little patio and, beyond that, a green lawn filled with shady trees.

A lone man in a wheelchair was on the patio, watching others being wheeled down paved paths or sitting on benches under the trees, with a few daring the summer sunshine to sit out in the open. It was a pleasant enough scene, peaceful in a way, with all the flowers bordering the paths and encircling the trees. Pleasant, if one were able to walk away from it whenever one wanted.

"Mr. Salazar?"

The man started slightly. Had he been dozing in the heat? May hoped he hadn't been parked there and left. The sun could get pretty hot plenty fast and wouldn't be a good place for a post-stroke patient. He repeated what he'd said.

"*Si?*" Hands went to the wheels, spinning the chair around. Whatever else might be wrong, Alejandro Salazar could definitely handle that chair.

May remembered he hadn't been a very tall man, probably just medium height. He'd looked down at Alejandro that day in the store. He definitely didn't look Cuban. Though hazel-eyed, he was relatively fair-skinned, and what hair he had left was a bright ginger-colored fuzz. *So much for the stereotypical dark-haired, dark-eyed* caballero.

"You were speaking to me?"

"Uh…yes." May pulled himself out of his thoughts. "I-I don't know if you remember me…"

"Of course. Mayfield." The old man nodded. "You buy the ring for the hard-to-please young lady."

May had to smile at his description of Veronica. Even now, though his pronunciation was perfect, Alejandro's English was still slightly stilted.

"That's right."

"She's not wanting to exchange it again?"

"I'm afraid the young lady and I have gone our separate ways," May answered, and saw him nod, as if he'd expected to hear that.

"*Mis condolencias.*"

"Thank you, but it was a long time ago." May was having second thoughts.

How to tell him why I'm really here? Maybe this isn't such a good idea.

Alejandro himself gave him an opening. "Why do you come here, Mayfield? Not to visit a sick old man, surely. No one really wants to do that." He looked out across the lawn again, sadly this time. "Except as a duty."

Was that what the cousin's visits had become? A duty?

"Actually, sir..." May smiled as a sandy eyebrow went up at that.

No one gives you courtesy any more, either?

"I was wondering if I could talk to you about Marty."

"*Mi hijo?*" That *did* surprise Alejandro. "It's been a long time since anyone has mentioned my boy." He looked toward the door. "It's getting hot. Let's go inside."

May held open the door while Alejandro rolled inside, then followed him to a room down the corridor. It was a small room with a window looking out onto the side of the building. On a dresser sat an eighteen-inch flat screen, a chair next to it. The bed was a hospital type, with a table and lamp.

As May sat in the chair, Alejandro spun the wheelchair around to face him. "Why do you want to know about Martes?"

"First of all, I guess I'd better ask if you've heard Benjamin Troup McAllister has died." That was as good a way as any to lead into what he really wanted to ask.

"That *híbrido?*" Alejandro's reaction was immediate, and vehement. "I knew of it and don't really care."

May knew enough Spanish to know he'd just called Benjamin Troup a bastard.

So, he holds the same opinion as everyone else.

He wondered how a man could bear living in a place where so many people disliked him. Did having money make a difference?

"Did you also hear what a dirty trick he played on

his daughter at the will-reading?"

"I'm in a nursing home, not another country." Alejandro quirked a smile. "The nurses here are great gossips. They all thought it indeed a *dirty trick*, as you say."

"I'm trying to help Gracie." With that, the story came out easier than he'd expected.

Alejandro listened quietly, making sympathetic sounds.

May told him everything, about speaking with Carter and his parents, leaving out his father's early morning bombshell, however, and ending with, "…and that's how we learned about Marty, and I wanted to talk to you about his accident."

For just a moment, there was silence, as if Alejandro were gathering his thoughts. He nodded.

"Martes was coming back from seeing his girl the night he…" He stopped, looking away.

May saw him swallow tightly and blink. Even after this long, just thinking about what had happened affected the old man.

"Was it Miriam Baker?"

That earned him a wary look.

"I know she and Marty dated a couple of times."

"More than a couple of times," Alejandro corrected. As May looked surprised, he went on, "For several months."

"But my father said…"

"Your father didn't know it all, Mayfield. They kept it secret. Her parents, you know." Alejandro looked angry. "Bigots. No matter that, in Cuba, I was a well-known artist. Here, I was *alien*, therefore illegal."

His next words were spoken with defiant pride.

"I became a citizen as soon as I could. My wife, also."

"I got the idea Miriam's parents were overly concerned with appearances," May said carefully.

"True. That's why I worried at first when Martes got interested in their daughter." Alejandro's eyes took on a faraway look. "Miriam was different, or so I thought. She and Marty had two dates, then no more. At least that's what her parents were led to believe."

"What do you mean?" May felt disappointment. If that was all…

"They meet in secret." Alejandro put a finger to his lips. "She tells them she goes to the library or to a club meeting. Instead, she meets Marty. Sometimes, she comes to our home. I know it was wrong. My Isabella, she says to me, 'Alejandro, you shouldn't encourage this. It will only lead to trouble,' but I say, 'If they love each other, 'Bella, they should be together.' So. I look the other way, and 'Bella, she does, too."

He rolled his chair to the bedside table. There was a pitcher and glass there. He poured water into the glass, drank some, then set it down and looked back at May.

"Sometimes they sat in the living room listening to music, or just talked. Other times, they walked in the garden. Often, they went to Marty's room and I didn't ask what they did there." He looked up at May. "Then one night, Marty comes to me and he says…"

He stopped, swallowing again. Once more, he drank from the glass, then sat studying it silently. May got the feeling he wished it held something stronger than water.

"He tells me Miriam's parents are saying they want her to marry Benjamin Troup, that it'll give them the respectability they wish…not that they *weren't* respectable, but they wanted *more*. Miriam doesn't want this, she loves *him*, and they are going to elope. That night."

May sat up straight at this. To say it was a shock wasn't an understatement. Even his father hadn't known that. They'd really kept it a secret. Had Carter somehow guessed?

"He told me because he wanted my blessing. Naturally, I gave it, told him he could bring his bride to our house, that she was welcome." Alejandro smiled. "I knew he'd never be allowed in theirs. He left that evening, telling me and his mama, *Next time you see me I'll be a married man*, and then..."

Alejandro lifted his head, his eyes meeting May's. A single tear fell from the corner of his left eye, trickling down his cheek.

"A few hours later, the doorbell rings, waking us, and they tell us they think my Martes is dead...a drunk driver...burned in his car..."

His head dropped, shoulders abruptly shaking. May could see tears spotting the thighs of his trousers.

"Mr. Salazar, I'm sorry."

Trite...and twenty-five years too late. Did it really make the loss any easier, those stupid words?

"In a little while, Miriam married that Benjamin Troup. I really thought she loved my boy." Alejandro raised his head and the confusion in his face stabbed into May's heart. Even now, the old man appeared confounded that Grace's mother could've been so fickle. "That girl...she ask 'Bella to teach her to cook his favorite dishes. Why'd she do that if she didn't care?"

May didn't have an answer. He shook his head, not speaking.

"Then they have that baby. She looked happy. Why not? She has a live husband, a *niña,* and we have nothing. My Martes is nothing but a verdict of 'death while driving under the influence.' and a headstone in the cemetery."

"Mr. Salazar, you said they were going to elope," May began.

Alejandro nodded.

"In that case, why was Marty on that road by himself? Why weren't he and Miriam together?"

"I don't know, Mayfield, and now, I don't care. Maybe her people found out, chased Martes away. Maybe he did buy that whiskey, to make him forget how she didn't have enough strength to stand up to them. All I know is my boy's gone and his death killed his mother a few years later and now I'm alone."

It hurt to hear the pain in the old man's voice.

"You never heard from Miriam after Marty's death?" He forced himself to go on. "She never got in touch with you or anything?"

"Never. No phone call, not even the…what do they call them…sympathy card. His other friends, your father, that little Angeline, even Carter McAllister, but from Miriam? Nothing." Alejandro sighed heavily. "Until…out of nowhere, that one letter."

"She wrote you a letter?" May straightened in his chair. "When?"

"The night she ran away. Everyone was talking. How Benjamin Troup's wife had left him, taking their daughter with her. I went into the back of the shop and laughed when I heard."

"May I ask what the letter said?"

Alejandro shrugged. "I didn't read it. I didn't care to

see that girl's words, five years too late. I wanted them when they were needed."

"I wish you hadn't thrown it away. It might tell something important."

"Who says I threw it away?"

"You still have it?"

"That box." Alejandro nodded toward the dresser.

On its top was a large wooden box. It was carved and decorated, one of those seen in furniture boutiques, made of sheesham wood, usually sold for women to keep jewelry in.

"Bring it to me."

May got up and went over to the dresser. He touched the lid of the box. It was smooth and cool, sanded and polished to a mellow golden brown. He brought it back to Alejandro.

The old man set the box on his knees. "This holds things I consider important. To keep me company in this place." He shrugged and smiled sadly. "Not that I consider that letter important, but it was a connection to my boy. I guess that's why I kept it."

Opening the box, he pushed through the contents with his forefinger. May could see some photographs, a couple of pieces of jewelry, the multicolored blues of a Social Security card, what looked like a woman's wedding ring, and some folded papers.

Alejandro tapped one. "Martes' birth certificate." He touched another. "Certificate of his death." He reached under that, drawing out a small envelope.

Alejandro held it out to May.

He took it, studying the handwriting. Neat, precise but graceful, done in black ballpoint. The stamp was twenty-five cents, first class, postmarked *Savannah*. The

letter had probably been mailed in McAllister, been sent to the postal distribution center in Savannah, then brought back for delivery. He turned it over. It was still sealed.

"May I?"

"Go ahead." Alejandro made a permissive gesture. "I don't care now."

May sat back down. Sliding a finger under the flap, he tore open the letter, unfolded it and read the words Miriam Baker McAllister had written the night she ran away from McAllister forever. When he finished, he got up and walked over to the old man, holding out the letter.

"I think you'd better read it, and do what it says."

Chapter 20

May leaned forward, resting his elbows against the table. He looked exhausted, as if he'd just gone through some strenuous and debilitating exercise. Perhaps he had. In that moment, I had no idea what he was thinking. He sat that way a minute, forehead resting against his hands. Then he sighed and raised his head.

"I drove back to McAllister and did what we should've done at the very beginning. Took the hair I pulled out of your brush to Tracy Crockett, prepared to beg him to run it through Forensics for me. I guess he took a shine to you, Grace. He agreed as soon as I told him what I wanted. Said he'd take care of any flak if someone protested. When I got the results, I was on the first flight I could get, to give them to you."

"The tests can wait," I said. "What did the letter say?"

"Read it for yourself."

May re-opened the folder, taking out the manila envelope. Pinching the clasp, he pulled up the flap and took out several folded sheets of stationery. They were yellowed and fragile-looking and I heard them crackle slightly as he held them out to me.

I took the sheets, opening them carefully. The top one had a design in the upper left corner, a single rosebud tied with a ribbon, the colors faded. There was a date at the top. *April 17, 2000.* I looked at the greeting.

Dear Mr. Salazar…

May got up and walked over to a nearby bookcase, getting very interested in the titles as I began reading.

Dear Mr. Salazar,

I know I'm the last person you want to hear from, especially after the unforgiveable way I acted after Marty's death. Please believe me when I say I had my reasons, and now, finally, I'm going to put them in writing.

When Marty met me that night, our plans to elope were interrupted by Benjamin Troup. I don't know if he got suspicious and followed me or what, but suddenly, he was there and there was a terrible scene. I told him exactly what I thought of him, how selfish and overbearing, and what a bully he was, and then Marty started in. He let Benjamin Troup know how we'd made a fool of him, meeting secretly while I let him think he had a chance with me. When he said we were eloping, I really thought Benjamin Troup was going to hit him. Then, he seemed to regain control, and without another word, stalked back to his car, and drove away.

Marty wanted us to leave right then, but I was so upset by that confrontation I asked him to wait until the next day. I didn't want what happened ruining our wedding night, and the way I felt just then, I knew it would. Marty agreed. He kissed me and drove away, and that's the last time I saw him alive.

Now comes the hardest part, Mr. Salazar. A week after Marty's death, I discovered I was pregnant. I know I should've told you. I imagine you'd have been much more receptive than my parents would've been, but I was so shocked, and still so upset over Marty's death, I wasn't thinking clearly. I knew if I told my parents, they'd hustle me off somewhere for an abortion, so the only thing I could think of was to keep my baby safe, and that meant finding it a father. I did a despicable thing. I started dating Bill Donovan and Benjamin Troup. They were both handy and glad to offer "consolation." I had sex with both of them, then decided to pick one, tell him of the "blessed event" and demand marriage. Benjamin Troup saved me the trouble by proposing. I accepted and didn't tell him about the baby. I swore to myself no one would ever know who Grace's father was, but at the last minute, I had to leave a clue. That's why I named her Grace Stephanie, so it was plain for anyone who bothered to think twice about it.

I suffered Benjamin Troup's jealousy and cruelty for the next five years, and lived in fear that one day he'd begin to mistreat Grace, also. The one and only time he struck her, I decided he'd never do it again. Carter was only too happy to help me get away. When I told Benjamin Troup I was leaving, he had to try one last time to hurt me. He confessed…no, he bragged, that he hadn't driven away that night but stopped at a filling station and called Taylor Dix. He knew the way Marty had to drive to go home, and sent Taylor ahead to wait for him at a certain spot. He circled around and came back to my house, then followed Marty when he drove away. Once they were on the County Road and came to where Taylor was waiting at that curve, Taylor forced Marty's car off the road. Marty got out and he and Benjamin Troup had a terrible fight, and Taylor killed Marty. Hit him with a bottle of whiskey he had in his car. I don't imagine I have to tell you the rest.

He laughed as he said it, but his boasting stopped when I told him Grace wasn't his child, that she was

Marty's and I only married him to give his name to another man's baby. That stopped him cold, and while he was recovering from that, I got Grace and left the house. Carter met us at the turnoff and drove us to Savannah. He was supposed to be out of town on business, so Benjamin Troup never suspected. I told him what Benjamin Troup had said, and he told me he already knew. His brother had told him right after the wedding but he'd let misguided loyalty keep him from saying anything.

I'm sorry for everything, Mr. Salazar. All I ever wanted was to marry Marty and have our baby and be happy. Instead, I got Marty killed and ruined my own life, but I promise your granddaughter's going to have a better one.

Please go to the police with this information and have them reopen Marty's case. Make Benjamin Troup pay. And please forgive me if you can.

Mimzi.

I let the sheets fall to the table.

I suppose I should've been celebrating. Now all the mysteries were solved…my father's identity, the secret Carter had known but never told, why my mother ran away…what did it matter? A man was dead for falling in love, another man was dead and couldn't be punished for the crime, and the woman who'd been the cause of it all was gone, also. Only I remained, and all I wanted was to forget everything…

Everything except the man now standing with his back to me, pretending to be engrossed in the titles of a bunch of law books on the shelf in front of him.

Hearing the papers strike the table, he turned and came back to where I sat. He picked up the envelope again and took something else out. A photograph. He dropped the last DNA report on the table in front of me, placing the picture on top of it.

"Gracie, meet your father."

I looked at the picture. Martes Salazar laughed up at me, his arm around an equally laughing young woman I barely recognized as my mother. He was thin-faced, with high cheek bones and a wide smile. I recognized that smile. I'd seen it enough in my own mirror, as well as his hazel eyes. His hair was gingery, the same color as mine. Their faces were together, cheek-to-cheek, and they both looked as if they didn't have a care in the world. Perhaps in that moment, they didn't. Perhaps, just then, they were simply in love, and prejudiced parents and a cruel bully of a suitor hadn't yet entered the picture.

As far as I was concerned, that moment, captured in time, was the way I would always picture him… them…in my mind.

"So now I know." I laid the picture down. "Everything."

He nodded.

"There's one thing I don't understand. How would my name tell anyone Marty Salazar was my father?"

"Think about it."

I did. Blank. Nothing presented itself. I shook my head.

"*Tuesday's child is full of grace…*" May quoted. "Marty was graceful, remember? He even joked about it. His name…Martes is Tuesday…Esteban is the Spanish version of Stephen, and Stephanie is the feminine equivalent of Stephen."

"Grace, daughter of Tuesday Stephen…" I muttered. "Not too plain, if you ask me. It'd take more than thinking *twice* to figure that out."

"I thought it fairly clever of your mother."

I guess it had been. Maybe *too* clever. I didn't answer.

"That's it, Gracie. What are you going to do? Or more importantly, what am I going to do?" May waved a hand at the door. "Walk out of here, or make plans to move to LA? There's nothing to stop us from being together. If you want."

I got to my feet, holding out my hand. He caught it, planting a kiss on my fingers. I was surprised when his body relaxed.

"Why did you go through all this rigamarole?" I asked. "Why didn't you just tell me?"

He shrugged. "I don't know. Maybe it was for the theatrics. It was certainly more dramatic than my simply saying, 'Grace, DNA proves Marty Salazar was your father and I have a letter saying Benjamin Troup killed him.' " His smile was a very slight one. "Besides, there was always a chance you wouldn't believe me if I'd done it that way."

"Oh, sure." I shook my head. "You weren't really worried, were you?"

"Sugah, I accepted a long time ago that with women you never can be absolutely certain what they're going to do. And with you...? Hell yes, I was worried."

"If you come to LA, it's going to be really different," I warned. "Culture shock and all that. Do you really want to leave McAllister?"

"Could you stand living there? Especially now?" he countered. He had a point.

"I guess we could always go back to visit. Your parents. My grandfather." I had to swallow before I could say that word.

"We could," he agreed, and added, "He really needs you, Gracie."

"You might have to work harder out here." I sounded as if I were trying to talk him out of it, but I wanted him to be certain he knew what he was facing. "I understand the school systems are pretty tough."

"Hey, I'm Saturday's child, remember?"

I got the Mayfield Donovan smile full force.

"I've worked hard before, and I can keep doing it…for a living…to make you happy."

"Can't ask for more than that, can I?" I decided.

He didn't answer, just caught me by the shoulders and pulled me onto my toes as he kissed me. I put my arms around May's neck and hugged him tightly, feeling myself lifted off the floor. Just as he'd done that night in front of the stairs. When he set me down, I looked back at the photograph on the table. They were still smiling, but now, I was smiling with them.

Tuesday's and Saturday's children were joining forces and heading for a great future.

A word about the author…

Toni V. Sweeney has lived 30 years in the South, a score in the Middle West, and a decade on the Pacific Coast, and now she's trying for her second 30 on the Great Plains.

Since the publication of her first novel in 1989, Toni has written 94 novels, with 90 of them published. This includes several series.

https://www.facebook.com/profile.php?
id=100048587829251

Thank you for purchasing
this publication of The Wild Rose Press, Inc.

For questions or more information
contact us at
info@thewildrosepress.com.

The Wild Rose Press, Inc.